A VERY MERRY MESS

A GOLDEN RETRIEVER BLACK CAT ROMANTIC COMEDY

CIDER COVE SWEET SOUTHERN ROMCOMS
BOOK 3

ELANA JOHNSON

feel-good fiction

ELANA JOHNSON

RYANNE

I HAVE NO IDEA WHAT TO DO WITH THE STARES. Everyone seems to be looking at us, and I can't decide if it's me in this designer gown, or Elliott in his sport coat that used to be his grandfather's, or the awful combination of us.

Almond, peanut, chili nut, peanut butter. I recite the nutty M&M flavors to try to maintain my sanity, but it doesn't seem to be working. Everyone just keeps staring and staring and staring.

"Don't they have their own problems?" I mutter to myself.

"What?" Elliott leans his head toward me, but I don't want to explain to him. I just shake my head, and he turns toward me as a couple squeezes by him in this crowded lobby. "Do you want something to drink?"

"Heavens, yes," I say.

He plucks a drink from the tray and hands it to me, no smile in sight. "Is being out with me so bad?"

"What?"

"You look like you've stepped in something foul." He lifts his champagne to his lips and takes a sip. He makes a face and lowers it, and I know he won't taste it again.

"I'm just..." Something. I don't know what. Concussed? I'd have to be to agree to come to this couples' movie night with him.

"Elliott," someone female says before I can come up with an explanation. The woman's face brightens, and she doesn't see me as she moves in to brush her lips along Ell's cheek. No one ever sees me, so I'm not sure why this tall blonde should. Or why it irritates me so much that she's now introducing her girlfriend to him.

Not that they're dating. They just came to this together, which is single-white-female code for, "I'm single, Elliott. Do you want to go out with me sometime?"

I take another sip—much bigger than Elliott's—of my drink and wait for her to walk away. "She was flirting hardcore with you."

"She was not." His smile drops, and I seriously don't know why he's so annoyed tonight. *He's* the one who asked *me* out.

"Was," I say, and not two seconds pass before another woman says, "Elliott Hutson? Holy gators and cattails, it *is* you!" Squealing happens, and this woman full-on hugs the man I can't drive from my mind no matter how many M&M flavors I recite, or how many bags of candy I eat.

I stand politely silent and invisible while Elliott chats up yet another woman, and then turns into me once more. He looks a little flushed, which only pushes all my buttons in the wrong way. "I want to go home."

He blinks at me, his expression going blank. "What?"

"In case you haven't noticed," I say. "And why should you? I'm invisible to everyone, including you. I always have been." My chest rolls left and right like a big ship on stormy seas. "I'm just standing here while you chat it up with all your potential girlfriends. Is that why you brought me? So you'd have an excuse to come and meet women?"

"Whoa, whoa," Elliott says, holding up both hands. "I'm not here to meet women."

I snort-scoff and look away. "Sure. That's how it totally seems." I drain the last of my champagne. If he doesn't want to take me home, I can call a ride. It's not that hard. "I'm leaving." I head for the door, and Elliott is right at my side.

"Ry," he says. "You don't want to see the movie?"

I push out of the theater, and the cooler air out here clears my head slightly. My face still feels too hot, and the alcohol still burns down my throat. Me and drinking is never a good idea, and I feel my tongue getting looser by the moment.

"I do," I say. "But it's just—it feels weird to be here with you."

"Why?"

"Because." I stop and stare right at him. "Can't you feel it too? It's just weird. I shouldn't have to explain it to you."

"Try."

I breathe in through my nose and out through my mouth, as if I'm in an active military unit and have learned to control my thoughts and emotions through breath. I have not.

"It's weird, Elliott, because everyone here is a couple. It's couples' movie night, with pink champagne." I wave my arm to make this a big deal. "And chocolate covered strawberries, and oh, we'll be passing out blankets because the theater gets a little cold." I sweep my arms left and right with each—romantic—thing.

I glare at him. "And yet, you've told me at least fourteen thousand times that this is not a date." I indicate my gorgeous dress. "But I'm all dressed up. Claudia curled my hair. I'm wearing eyeliner, Ell. Eye. Liner." I sigh when he still stands there, mute.

"And you look so...so amazing in that jacket. And it somehow goes with that silly t-shirt and those—" I look down to his pants. They're not really jeans, but they're not really khakis either. He has to wear black pants to work, and they're kind of like that, but a washed out blue.

"Pants," I finish lamely. "So it feels like a date, and it's weird, because we're *not* dating, but I don't want to have all this datey stuff so you can chit-chat with other women." I wipe my hand across my forehead, and oh, Claudia is going to be so mad at me. She spent a long time in hair and makeup with me, and I'm smearing it everywhere.

If I go home now, Lizzie and Tahlia will have a million questions. Everywhere I turn, I run into some major roadblock.

"Let's go walk around the Christmas Market," I say. "Maybe we can get into the Living Bethlehem on stand-by." I start walking toward the town square, and Ell comes with me.

He doesn't touch me, and he doesn't address anything I've just said. I wonder what it would be like to simply blow away. Would anyone notice? Would he?

I could duck between the theater and the diner, and I wonder how long it would take before Ell realizes I'm not sauntering along at his side.

My chest pinches, and I pull in a breath to try to stem the hurt now blitzing through me. I'm so tired of being invisible, especially to him. To my parents. To everyone.

Technically, I know I'm not. My roommates see and

love me. I want more, and maybe that makes me selfish. I'm not sure.

My phone zings, and I don't even bother to look at it. "That'll be my mother." She doesn't listen to me either.

"Yeah? Is she still asking about the Christmas party?"

"Several times each day," I say. "My sister is probably going to make a pregnancy announcement, and Momma says I need to be there." I sigh as my phone chimes again, and we pause on the cusp of the square so I can take it out and read her texts.

"Ry, it's December seventh. I must book airplane tickets in the next couple of days. I'm happy to pay for yours and a guest. Please let me know immediately what I should do." I look over to Elliott, and for the first time since he showed up on the porch at the Big House, he looks like himself.

Dazzling eyes, with that hint of mischievousness in them. Half-smile, slightly crooked. Adorable dimple. Straight, white teeth, and all the dashing and debonair of a true Hollywood heartthrob.

"Let me see." He holds out his hand, and I pass over my phone the way I have plenty of times before.

I look away and spot a hot chocolate station. Because of Claudia, I know more about this festival than the average attendee, and that hot chocolate is free. "I'm going to get some hot chocolate. Want some?"

"Sure."

I walk away, wishing I was dressed more like those who've come to the square tonight. Jeans, sweaters, even a scarf or two, probably just for festivities sake. I wait my turn, then fill two paper cups with hot chocolate. It's steaming and thick, and the first thing I have to smile about tonight.

I approach Ell and we do a trade—he takes the hot chocolate; I take back my phone. "What should I tell her?"

He calmly takes a sip of his hot chocolate. "I answered her for you."

My heartbeat thrashes against my ribcage. "What now?" He's never done that before. He reads my texts and tells me what to say. He doesn't actually type it out and send it.

"Yeah, yep," he says, and that makes me pause and blink. *Yeah, yep.* That's what Elliott says when he's nervous.

"Well, what did you say?" I lift my hot chocolate to my lips and blow gently. I like things hot that are supposed to be hot, but I like my taste buds to function too.

I start to take a sip, and oh, yeah, that's rich, full, and the perfect amount of chocolatey flavor.

"I told her you needed two tickets," he says casually. "One for you and one for me."

The hot chocolate in my mouth spews out—all over his father's jacket, that funny tee, and those sexy pants.

He stands there and takes it, not moving a single muscle. When I can get a breath, I pant and say, "What? Do you know what this means?"

Elliott finally blinks, and he reaches down to the hem of that shirt and lifts it to wipe his chin and neck. In doing so, he's completely flashing me his abs and chest, and raspberry birthday cake with fudge brownies, the man has muscles.

"Yes, Ry," he says. "It means your momma now thinks we're dating."

ELLIOTT

WATCHING MY BEST FRIEND SPUTTER IS ACTUALLY kind of funny. I hide my smile for now, because she won't appreciate it. I'm feeling lucky I just got sprayed with hot chocolate, because with something like this, Ryanne could skewer me with that sharp tongue of hers.

And there I go, thinking about her tongue again. Her mouth. Her eyes. The shape of her body. The way she laughs with me and the other employees at Paper Trail. The way she brings in a birthday treat for everyone at the office supply store we co-manage. The way her room-mates love her. The way she loves M&Ms. The way her momma pushes all the wrong buttons inside her.

"I can't—this is unbelive—how could you do this?" She finally rights her phone and looks at it. Oh, the text is there. In fact, Ry's momma has already replied how "delighted" she is to meet me, though, technically, we've met before.

"I told you weeks ago I'd be your boyfriend," I say smoothly. I have to put on this act or Ry will know why I've not started dating anyone else—it's because I want to date her.

I know, I was as shocked by that as anyone. Not because Ry isn't amazing. She is. It's not because she's ugly. She's one-hundred-percent not.

It's not because she's my best friend, and I'm terrified I'll lose her. She is, and I'm sure I will, so fine, maybe that's part of why I was shocked. I don't have many friends, and Ry is my very best one in the whole world.

But it's really because she's too good for me. It's because she wants long-term, and I just can't give her that. It's because she's a bad liar and won't be able to do the fake-dating thing.

"We can call this a date," I say. "Our first one."

"Are you out of your mind?" She shoves her phone under the strap of that stunning red dress, and oh, it's no fun to be jealous of an inanimate object. Ry looks left and right like we're doing something illegal. It sort of feels forbidden and dangerous, and I'll admit, that's part of the allure of the text I sent.

She folds her arms as her gaze comes back to me. "This is not our first date. First dates are supposed to be

magical. Amazing. You spent the first twenty minutes
flirting with other women."

"I did not." I glare at her. "I spoke to them like
human beings, but you know what? I don't want this to
be our first date either."

"Why not?" she demands.

"Because you spit hot chocolate all over me." I raise
my eyebrows and look down at myself, as if we both
don't already know where the sticky drink landed.

"You flashed me your *abdomen*." She whispers the
last word like it's dirty.

I grin at her. "Can we start over?"

"Start...over?"

I reach out and take her hot chocolate from her.
Then I take her hand in mine. "Yeah. I'll run home real
quick and change. We'll go to dinner somewhere far
away from here. Just me and you." I swallow, because I
know how smart Ry is. "On a date. Our first date, so we
can get things right for your family party in a couple of
weeks."

She looks down at our hands, but she doesn't pull
away. "Get things right."

"Right," I say. "Your family will want to know why
and when we started dating, how it's working out with
work, blah blah blah."

She pulls in a noisy breath through her nose, almost like
those cute little snorts she makes. "Work," she blurts out.

"Paper Trail. We can't date." She pulls her hand back, and I wish I had better ninja reflexes so I can keep it in mine. Unfortunately, I don't, and she even backs up a step as she does that left-right, left-right sweep for federal agents.

I chuckle, because Ry is always a little too serious. "Ry, honey, no one at Paper Trail cares if we date."

"Corporate does."

"I seriously doubt it."

"We're co-managers."

"So at least it's not someone in a position of power over the other."

She narrows her eyes at me. "You have an answer for everything, don't you?"

"No," I say.

She opens her mouth to argue again, then realizes what I've said, and closes it again. But given a few moments to think, she comes at me with, "Why do you want to do this?"

"Because." I sigh and look across the street to the market. "I hate hearing how sad and upset you are whenever you hear from your momma. This is an easy fix, Ry."

Liar! screams through my mind, but I ignore it. Yes, Ry is sad and upset when her mom and dad text her about who's she's dating—no one this year that I know of —and they've been pressuring her about coming home for Christmas for months.

But the real reason I want to do this is because I have

real feelings for my best friend. Real feelings that I have no idea what to do with, and this feels like a safe way to stick my toe out of the friend zone, something I've never done before.

She stares at me, and I'm having a hard time holding her gaze. Her eyebrows are thick and perfectly sculpted, and they frame her eyes in a sexy way I can't describe. She's a beautiful woman, and I've always thought so.

"I see you," I say next, and I hate myself the moment I do.

Because Ry crumbles right in front of me. Just simply falls apart, her perfectly made-up face plummeting as she starts to cry.

"Oh, no." I gather her into my arms, wondering why I have to say such stupid things. "I'm sorry, Ry. Don't cry." I keep her close to my chest, not caring at all about my t-shirt getting mascara stains on it. Now, this jacket... That's another story, but I know a good dry cleaner, and I'm not sacrificing this moment of holding Ry in my arms for a sport coat, even if this one has sentimental value.

"Let's go," I say quietly, and she doesn't argue with me about leaving the square. I help her into my SUV as she sniffles, and I head for my house. "I'm just going to change," I tell her when we get there. "Do you want to come in or wait here?"

"What are we going to do next?"

"What do you want to do next, Ry?" I ask.

She looks at me, and I manage to look back at her.

"I'll take you home so you can change, and we can just... be together."

She nods, and I'm not sure what that means. I have no idea where I'll take her after she shimmies out of that dress. Maybe she doesn't even want to change, or maybe after she does, she'll just want to crawl into bed and forget tonight ever happened. I honestly have no idea.

I also can't believe I brought her to my house. See, I don't exactly live alone, and while Ry knows my mom lives nearby, she doesn't know it's in the bedroom just down the hall.

Momma looks up as I slip in through the front door. "Elliott?" She's on her feet in less than a second, before I can wave her off, even.

"I'm fine," I say in a tired voice. I'm so sick of telling people I'm fine, or it's fine, or everything will be fine.

Sometimes things aren't fine, you know?

"I spilled some hot chocolate down me. I'm just gonna change and head back out."

My mother looks from me to the door. "Where's Ry?"

"Momma, leave her be!" I yell as I hurry out of the main part of the house and down the hall to my bedroom. "I'll be two minutes!"

Sometimes I trust my mother explicitly, but in this case, I change as fast as possible and head back down the hall while I'm still pulling my new tee over my head.

Because my mom might have gone outside and invited Ry in. Or at least shown herself.

Thankfully, she's sitting on the arm of the couch, her eyes on the TV. She does turn toward me when she hears me coming, and I give her a smile. "I'll be back later."

"Okay," she says. "You're okay?"

"Fine, Mom." I don't want to be rude to her—she's given up a lot to be here with me—but I don't want to talk about my co-manager and my feelings for her.

"Wear your night-driving glasses!" she yells after me, and irritation spikes through me. Of course I know to wear my driving glasses, especially at night. I let the door say what I want to as it closes loudly behind me, and I jog down the steps to the SUV.

Ry looks over to me as I get back in. "I do want to go home and get out of this dress."

My fantasies go wild, but I press my teeth together and keep everything inside. I've been doing that for a long, long time, and it gets easier every time. Except with Ry, I feel like I'm starting over at square one with everything.

So I almost let something slip like, *I'd like to help with that.*

But my one-liners that might work with other women will never, ever work with Ry. If I want to blow everything with her, then sure, I should let my mouth run wild. But for some reason, I don't want to do that.

At the same time, there's no way we can be together long-term. Thus, this fake-boyfriend-for-the-holidays fits the bill nicely. I suppress my inward sigh, because I'm too young to even be thinking "fits the bill nicely."

I take her back to her house—which she and her friends call "the Big House," where she looks at me fully for the first time since I got back in the car. "Do you want to stay here? Should we go somewhere else?"

"I'm following your lead, Ry."

She tilts her head to the side. "That's obviously not true. My mother has asked me about fifty-five questions since you texted her, and she's already got the tickets booked." She makes a face that displays disgust and irritation at the same time. "An four-ten flight, Ell. Do you know what that means?"

"Yes, I do," I say. It means traffic, and Ry hates driving in traffic.

"This is your fault."

"I'm sorry," I say. "You always just sound so frustrated by her, and I wanted to help."

"I think you wanted a free trip to New York City." She gives me that sexy smile that has kept me up at night for the past couple of months.

"Yeah, in the dead of winter," I say, returning her smile. "You caught me."

"You're such a soft Southern boy."

"I'm thirty-three years old," I say. "I'm not a *boy*."

Ry grins at me, and there's the best friend I know and love.

"Go change," I say. "And I'll take you to that gourmet street taco truck that is a total contradiction."

"They have pork belly, which is total gourmet, in a taco. It's the best thing you'll put in your mouth."

I laugh, because she says the same thing about the veggie taco—and I'm not even sure something can be labeled a taco if there's no meat. "All right, all right," I say. "Do you want to go in that gorgeous dress, or...?"

"No, I already said I wanted to change."

"But you're just sitting here." I lean my head back and gaze at her. She really is beautiful, and the whole office at Paper Trail smells like warm cinnamon toast and fruit champagne, which is the body spray Ryanne loves so much.

It's called Fairy Woods. I know, because I ventured out of my usual buying routine and went to the mall to get her some for her birthday last year. To me, she's a fairy tale, a princess in a tower I'll never have.

I want to be with someone long-term, but I won't doom them to my fate. So I've put on the player hat, and I'm never serious about anyone. I date a lot, because who wants to stay home with their momma when they're thirty-three years old?

Sometimes, I feel completely trapped in my life, and Ry has always been an escape for me. Maybe I acted a little rash tonight by texting her mother. Maybe this will be the worst Christmas in the world. *A very merry mess,* I think.

But then my eyes drop to her mouth, where her lips shine with something pink and tasty-looking, and my thoughts flip. Maybe, just maybe, this will be the best Christmas ever, and I'll finally get to kiss my gorgeous, kind, and hard-working best friend.

Maybe I'll even get to do it tonight. For practice purposes, of course.

"I'll be right back," she says, and Ry slips from the SUV. I watch her go, my plans for a good-night kiss swirling and taking form as she walks away from me in that sexy dress.

"You're in trouble, Ell," I whisper to myself. "Remember who you are. Remember what your life is." There's more for me to tell myself, but I don't say it out loud.

Remember, you don't want to hurt Ry.

So maybe there won't be any kissing tonight after all.

RYANNE

"I'm only here to change," I say as I start my march through the living room. Doesn't matter. Tahlia is on her feet in less time than it takes for me to inhale again.

"What happened?"

So many things, but none of them I want to expound on. "Nothing," I say. "The movie theater thing was too... romancey for me and Ell." I give her a look I've filled with spikes. But Tahlia's seen it so many times, she doesn't even flinch.

"Romancey?"

"Stupid," I say as I reach the steps and turn to go up them. As I climb, I lift the hem of my dress, so I don't trip. "I'm not dating Elliott, and it felt weird. I'm going to change, and we're going to go get tacos."

Because *that's* what best friends do. When they

don't have a date on a very romantic evening, they get together, and they go eat greasy food from a truck. And while I wish I could hang all over Elliott, giggle with him, and sip my pink champagne with him, that's not my reality.

I climb the steps in my heels to the second floor, and then I kick them off on the landing. Stooping to pick them up, I sigh out all my breath. Dealing with my parents during the holidays isn't fun on a good day, and having Ell there with me will make me twice as tense.

"Especially because now you have to act like you like him."

That's the problem—I *do* like him, but I've spent so long pretending like I don't, boxing up those feelings, hiding them from him, from everyone, that letting them show feels like it'll choke me.

I manage to get out of the red sequin dress, but I'm sweating by the time I toss it onto my bed. My stomach roars for something to eat, and my legs wobble a little bit from the single drink I consumed at the theater. I lean my hand on the nightstand and hold there for a moment, my eyes pressed closed.

Maybe Elliott will just come inside, and I can order food to the Big House. I don't even care if we eat it with Tahlia.

I open my eyes, acknowledging that I've just lied to myself. I need to start being more honest. Because I don't want to share Elliott with Tahlia. We need to talk about our fake romance anyway, and I can't do that in front of my roommate.

I pull on a pair of wide-leg jeans and a black sweater with tiered, puffy sleeves. With my fancy hair and makeup, I'm totally ready for a date with my fake boyfriend, and I slide my feet into a pair of pink crocs that Elliott has teased me about before.

I don't care. I think crocs are the bestest footwear in the world, and I swipe a handful of almond M&Ms from the candy bowl on my dresser before I head back downstairs.

"Where's Lizzie?" I ask when I once again find only Tahlia in the living room. She's put something on the TV, but she seems more involved in her phone than the movie.

"She got a last-minute date," she said, looking up at me. "Aaron Stansfield, believe it or not."

My eyes widen. "What?" I asked, my voice mostly made of air. "*Emma's* Aaron?"

This is going to make for some juicy gossip inside the Big House, especially since Aaron now lives next door to us, in the house where Liam used to live, before he and Hillary moved to LA.

But he works next door to Emma, as the flower shop she just bought is directly adjacent to the hardware store Aaron is taking over from his father in less than a month.

And Emma's had a crush on Aaron for *ages*, and I

wonder how the whole thing with Lizzie and Aaron went down.

"I can't wait to hear more about this," I say. "But I'm starving, and Elliott's outside."

"I'm sure there will be a whole meeting," Tahlia says. "Go have fun."

I don't know about that, but I give her a smile and as I step out of the Big House, I tell myself, "Don't be so grumpy, Ryanne. Try to have fun—and an intelligent, grown-up conversation."

Elliott jumps out of the car when I'm halfway there, and he's changed his glasses. Of course, this pair is as sexy as the last one, because everything Elliott does seems to be plated in gold and made just to make him look even better than he already does.

"You look great," he says, his eyes falling to my crocs. He makes no comment on them, and that confuses me a little bit. "I love this sweater."

He reaches out and touches one billowy sleeve, his eyes coming back to mine with loads of light in them. "Do you still want tacos?"

"What else did you find while I changed?"

He drops his hand, easily slipping his fingers between mine. I pull in a breath as sparkles and glitter fizz in my blood. I can't move my feet, and Elliott makes no attempt to take me around to the passenger seat of his car. His gaze has dropped to where our hands touch, and I have no idea what he's thinking or feeling.

"Edna's is holding a table for us," he murmurs. "You love their fried chicken." He looks at me now, all of his emotions shuttered away behind a mask I can't see through.

So not what we've done as best friends. And he didn't comment on my shoes, and I hate that things are changing already.

I pull my hand away gently. "If you're going to be my boyfriend, you have to promise me one thing."

Maybe more than one, and I hold up my hand as it continues to tingle and shout at me to hold Elliott's again. "For tonight. I might have more rules in the future."

Ell smiles at me in that sly, teasing way he has. "All right," he drawls out in his Southern boy style. "What's the promise for tonight?"

"I don't want this to ruin us," I say as boldly as I can with all these pops and crackles in my bloodstream. "My best friend would've poked fun at my crocs, and he would've shown me what he was thinking when he held my hand, and he would've just gone along to eat the pork belly tacos."

He blinks almost lazily and takes my hand again. He immediately turns away from me, though, once again hiding how he feels. "The shoes are hideous, Ry," he says as he walks me around to the passenger door. "They're barely shoes at all."

"Thank you," I say, holding my head high.

"And I told you I wanted this night to start over. Be a real date." He throws me a look out of the corner of his eye. "So yeah, I'm going to hide some things from you in the beginning. It's what people do when they're starting a new relationship."

I pause, my diva-glare amping up in ferocity. "You don't need to mansplain to me about how relationships work," I say. "And you've just illustrated my point. *We* don't have to act that way, because we're not in a *real* romantic relationship."

He reaches to open my door, dropping my hand in the process. "If you say so."

I get in the car before I've processed what he's said, and he slams the door just as I say, "What does that mean?"

He glares at me through the glass, and then goes around the back of the car, so I can't see him.

"If I say so?" I repeat, my mind in riddle mode now. My heartbeat pounds as I wait for him to get behind the wheel again, and it takes him so long to make the few-second trip around the vehicle.

"What were you doing back there?" I ask.

"Praying for patience," he says dryly as he clips his seatbelt into place. His car makes the most annoying beeping sound in the world if you don't buckle up, so I hurry to pull my belt into place too.

"I just want us to still be friends," I mutter.

He backs out of the driveway and starts down the

road. After a few minutes and a turn or two, he says, "If we weren't best friends, do you think you'd ever go out with me?" He grips the steering wheel like he needs all ten fingers strangling it to keep breathing. "You know, if I ran into you at the coffee shop or even just shopping in the aisles at Paper Trail."

Elliott cuts me a look out of the corner of his eye, and I've seen this tactic before. Usually when he needs me to rescue him from a conversation with another co-worker or a customer. He swallows too, his throat moving like he's just sucked in a boulder and can't quite get it to go down.

"Of course," I say as diplomatically as possible. My voice sounds cool and detached to my own ears, so there's no way he'll know I've crushed on him multiple times over our several-year friendship. "You're handsome," I add. "And employed. What's not to like?"

He makes a dry coughing sound that takes me a realize is a scoff, and he keeps his eyes straight out the windshield. "Those are your criteria for a boyfriend?"

"Sure," I say. "I think you'll find them standard for most women."

"Hot and employed," he said.

"I didn't say *hot*," I argue with him. "But women would like to be attracted to their boyfriends, I'm sure."

He pulls to a stop at a four-way intersection and looks over to me finally. "There you are," I say with a smile.

"You're attracted to me?"

It's my turn to try to get down a big boulder. I can't do it, and in fact, I clear my throat and cough like I've just contracted the next infectious disease that will start a world pandemic.

Sitting in the road makes me nervous, and I glance into my rearview mirror like there will be a whole line-up of cars behind us. Not one.

"We've always been honest with each other," he says next, and I look over to him. The radio plays quietly in the background, nowhere near loud enough to distract me.

Elliott reaches over and tucks a curled tendril of hair behind my ear. To my horror, I lean into his touch as I duck my head, and that's a move a woman only does when she's trying to flirt with a man.

"I think you're stunningly beautiful," he says, not a stitch of teasing in his voice at all.

Surprise catches me right in the gut, but I still manage to lift my head up and look into those beautiful eyes. "You do?"

He nods, drops his hand, and glances up to the rearview mirror. I already said he was handsome, and he obviously knows a lot of women are attracted to him. He has to know I am too, whether I say it out loud in words or not.

He eases through the intersection and says, "I don't want to lose you as my friend either."

"Okay," I say.

"You mean the world to me, Ry," he says, his voice strained and rough. Or, if he were my real boyfriend, maybe I'd classify his voice as husky and hot.

Everything inside me settles, the way it does when Elliott can finally get to my center and help me calm down. "You mean everything to me too, Ell," I whisper. "That's why I don't want this fake-thing to ruin us."

"It won't," he says with enough conviction that I believe him. "It's just a little hand-holding and kissing."

He says it seriously, but I still think he's teasing. "Those things mean something to me, Ell," I say, my voice taking on the whippish quality it can sometimes get when I'm being grouchy over something. "I know they don't to you, but— "

"Of course they mean something to me too," he says, his tone just as harsh as mine.

I gape at him. "What are you talking about? You've been out with seven women this year alone, and you break-up with anyone who even *dares* to suggest making the relationship one tiny titch past casual."

He has to be kidding. Hand-holding and kissing *don't* mean anything to Elliott. Not the way they do for me, or he wouldn't have spent the past few years moving through girlfriends like he's trying to find the flavor of bubblegum he likes best.

"I don't think *titch* is a word," he says, his grip on the steering wheel positively feral now.

"It so is," I retort. "And this might actually be perfect. You don't want anything that's not casual, and I just need a boyfriend for the holidays."

What am I so worried about?

He pulls into the parking lot at Edna's, and I reach for the door handle to get out as he asks, "When did we start dating?"

I turn toward him, once again confused. "What?"

"For your family," he says. "I mean, we're serious enough for me to go home with you for the holidays. So, that's...what?" He pauses, thoughtful for a few moments. "For you, I'd say we probably should've started dating this past summer."

He smiles at me and puts one hand on my knee. "Stay there. I'll get the door, and we'll establish a time-line while we eat." Then he gets out and crosses in front of the car this time.

How he's so calm about all of this makes no sense to me, but at least he hasn't gone quiet and still, that maddening mask in place like he had back at the Big House.

You mean the world to me, Ry.

I think you're stunningly beautiful.

What do those things mean for our friendship—and does he really tell all the women he goes out with the same things?

"He must," I mutter just as he opens my door. No matter what, I can't start to think things can be different between me and Elliott. I'm no one—and certainly not anyone strong enough or beautiful enough to make a player like Elliott change his ways.

This is just something fun for him to do for the next month—and he *will* get a free trip to New York out of it. And the holidays away from Charleston, where his family descends every year and complicates his life, reminds him of the absence of his father, and all kinds of things Ell would rather ignore.

I can't ever forget that, even as Elliott takes my hand again and my hormones shout at me to try to kiss him before he drops me off tonight—this is just something fun for him.

He doesn't have real feelings for me.

This is just something fun for him...

ELLIOTT

I don't know what I want from Ryanne. Rather, I do, but she's never going to give it to me, not when the picture of me she has in her head is so different than who I actually am.

But I don't know how to tell her about everything I have going on in my life, and I distract myself by changing my glasses from the night-driving ones to my regular pair.

"I've never seen that pair," she says, and she has some high walls going up between us. I thought I'd knocked down a few layers of bricks there for a minute, but nope. They're all right back up—and getting higher.

"I need them for night driving," I say, flirting with danger now.

Ry looks at me, and now would be a great time to spill my guts to her. Really lay out why I haven't dated seriously in years, and why this has to be temporary between us, even if I want it to be more.

I swallow everything, because I've already done and said too much. Calling her beautiful? Touching her hair?

My mind is clearly going—along with my eyesight.

"I didn't know people had different glasses for day and night," she says.

I open the door to Edna's, ready to be distracted by the menu, though I already know I'm getting the chicken pot pie. "I do," I say.

"Your prescription must be really bad," she says, and I want to bark at her to let this go.

"It is," I say, and I edge by her to the hostess station. "Hey, Carlie." I grin at the woman there. "I have a reservation for two."

"Elliott." She laughs and comes around the podium. "How are you, sugar?" She's at least a decade older than me, and I hug her back like we're best friends.

No one knows me the way Ry does, and I've kept things even from her. Pure guilt guts me, and I step away from Carlie. "Just fine, ma'am," I say, so Ry won't think I'm flirting with someone when I'm so not.

In fact, I reach back and take her hand and tug her closer, so she'll stop hovering behind me. "This is Ryanne. Have you met her?" I smile for all I'm worth and then look at Carlie. "Edna's is one of her favorite places."

"I usually just order out," Ry says, and she's still

somewhat stiff beside me. I'll have to tell her she needs practice to convince anyone she likes me—and that'll only allow me to see her plenty before we have to go to New York and put on a show for her family.

"Well, welcome in, my dears." Carlie plucks two menus from her stand and adds, "This way."

By the time we're in our booth, I feel winded, like I've run a mile by walking through the dining room with Ry's hand in mine.

She slides in first, and I do something I've done with other women I've liked—I sit on the same side as her, crowding her closer to the wall.

She says nothing as Carlie hands out our menus. The moment she's out of earshot, Ryanne mutters, "You're sitting on this side?"

"Yes," I fire back in an equally powerful whisper. "Then we can talk without anyone overhearing." And I can sit closer to her. Inhale that warm scent of her body spray, and fantasize that this is real.

Yes, I'm delusional—and on a roller coaster of hot-cold-hot-cold. Tell her everything, insist on honesty, touch her the way only a boyfriend does—then, close down. Shut off. Stuff everything away.

I sigh, because I'm honestly exhausted.

"I know that sigh," she says.

"You do not," I say.

"You're wishing we'd stayed home and ordered in."

"That's not what people do on their first dates." I set

down the menu, tired of pretending when I don't need to. "So what do you think? July? August?"

"You didn't break-up with Meri until September," she says.

"Her name was Millie," I say, though it doesn't matter. "And what? I have to give my whole dating history while we're New York?"

"Well, you can't go from dating *Millie* on Friday to me on Saturday," she says. "And I would never go out with someone while they have a girlfriend." She lifts her glass of water and takes a sip. "October?"

"That's not a very long time." I copy her and take a drink of water. The ice clinks against my teeth, which I hate, and I'll have to ask for a straw before I take another sip.

"We work together," she says matter-of-factly. "I've known you for years. It won't be that hard to believe that our, uh, relationship has advanced faster than it would've otherwise."

She turns toward me and pins me with one of her diva-death looks. "And I don't appreciate the implication that it takes me a long time to make a connection with someone."

"That is not what I said."

"It's normal for people to date for months or even *years* before they introduce their partner to their family."

"I know that."

Her eyebrows go up, clearly challenging me.

"I just...want this to go really well for you, Ryanne."
I drop my head, wishing the waitress would show up
already. I even look for her, but there's no one within
twenty feet of us.

"And I'm willing to do whatever it takes for it to go
really well for you." I look at her then, and she doesn't
skirt her gaze away either. Fire could fall from heaven
and neither of us would notice. So much chemistry boils
between us, and I want to bathe in it, let the hot bubbles
pour over me, drown me—because at least I'll be
with Ry.

———

"ALL RIGHT," I say with another sigh a couple of hours
later. I've just arrived back to the Big House, and lights
burn from every window on the bottom floor. The top
two levels are completely dark, and I look up to where
Ry's room sits.

She hasn't moved, and once I'd blinked my way out
of our staring contest at the restaurant, I'd said, "Let's
just talk about something else for the rest of the night.
We have time to work through this before we actually
have to go to New York."

Ryanne had agreed, and we'd managed to have a
pretty decent dinner date, if I do say so myself. If I'd
gone out with anyone else tonight, I'd ask them out
again.

So I take a breath and ask, "What are you doing tomorrow night?"

She swings her gaze to me lazily, almost like she's just now clued in that we're in the car together, that we've been out for a few hours now. Together.

"I don't know," she says.

"How about we go around to all the houses who have their Christmas lights set up with that timed music?" I raise my eyebrows, wishing I didn't have to wear my night glasses. But I'd tried getting out of the parking lot without them, and nope. I'd have killed us on the way here.

In fact, I can barely see Ry nod as she does it. When I get tired, my vision worsens, and it's definitely time for me to get home.

"You know," I say, despite the nod. "The ones with the radio stations we can tune into, and see the snowmen wave along with *Little Drummer Boy*?"

"Yes," Ry says. "I know what a Christmas light show is."

"I'm at the store until eight," I say, ignoring her jab. "But we can't go until dark anyway, and then I can stop by and do the closing routine."

"I can help too," Ry says, and she bends to pick up her purse.

"I'll come walk you to the door," I say, my voice turning into a ghost of itself. We did not set any rules for our false relationship. I've kissed women on the first date before, but if this really had been mine and Ry's first date, I wouldn't kiss her.

Whether I said it or not, Ry *does* have a hard time making connections. Okay, that's not true. She just takes longer, and she only invites a select few into her inner circle.

I open her door and say, "They're releasing more of the rover communications on Mars tomorrow."

Ry rises from the car like the queen she is, placing her hand in mine. It might as well be gloved, and I should be kneeling in her presence.

"That's amazing," she says with a smile, and the fact that she doesn't tease me about my obsession with the rovers on Mars speaks to how well we know each other.

I don't tease about her M&Ms—but I do about her crocs—and she doesn't make light of how fun I think the Mars rovers are. Or my insane desire for bacon at every meal.

This fact stands in stark contrast to how I haven't told Ry about my health problems, or the real reason I don't date seriously.

Standing there in the driveway of the Big House, I can admit—only to myself—that I want to date Ry for real.

Not fake.

"You don't have to walk me up," Ry says, and she tips up onto her toes before I can truly protest and brushes her lips along my cheek.

"I'm sorry I was so grumpy at the theater. Thank you for booking us at Edna's."

She settles back onto her croc'ed feet and looks at me.

"Did you get your leftovers?"

She shakes her head. "I won't eat leftover fried chicken."

I grin at her. "So spaghetti is okay, but fried chicken is not."

She smiles back, and it's so glorious and so beautiful. I want to make her smile like this every day for the rest of my life.

With that thought comes the demoralizing and debilitating one that reminds me, *Soon enough, you won't be able to see her smile like this.*

My resolve to keep my fate for myself and myself alone hardens, and I lean into her and wrap my arms around her. She melts into my chest, and even when I'm blind, I'll be able to feel her heart beating against my ribs.

Maybe that could be enough.

Yeah, and then what, Elliott? She'll have to take care of you completely.

No, I won't do that to someone. I simply can't.

"I would like to practice the kissing before we go to New York," I whisper.

She stiffens against me and steps away. "Maybe tomorrow night." And with that, Ry slips past me and goes around the front of the car before I even know what's happened.

I follow her, pausing at the front corner of my car and watching her walk up the sidewalk to the Big House. She opens the door before she turns back, and the inside light halos her as she lifts her hand to me in a goodnight wave.

I return the gesture, smiling, and then I get behind the wheel again. Someone else pulls into the driveway beside me as I start to back out, and I glance over to Aaron Stansfield. I can't quite see who's in his passenger seat, but I can find out with a single text to Ryanne.

But I never text and drive, because it takes so much energy just to see the road, and I focus on getting myself home without hurting anyone.

To my great relief, my momma isn't awake, and I go through my nightly routine of locking down the house before whistling for Peppermint, my gray and white cat, and then heading down the hall to my bedroom.

I hold the door for my feline, and I toss my glasses on the nightstand as I peel my clothes off. With just me, Peppermint, and my boxers, I finally get in bed, utterly exhausted.

I expect to fall asleep instantly, but instead, I close my eyes, and every fantasy I've ever had about my best friend roars to life.

My phone buzzes, and I'm sure it's her. No one else

ever texts me this late at night, but my eyes hurt too much to look at my phone in the dark.

Peppermint meows and finds a place to curl into my legs, and I simply live inside the dream of what it would be like to kiss Ryanne for real.

"Tomorrow," I tell myself. The new rover communications will be out, and Ry and I will be on our second date, and I'll tell her about my vision, and how I really feel, and I'm definitely going to enjoying kissing her.

Tomorrow.

RYANNE

I'VE LET DOWN MY HAIR AND JUST OPENED THE packet of makeup remover wipes when Lizzie appears in the doorway. I meet her eyes in the mirror, at a loss for what to say when I see the stars in hers.

"You're home," she says needlessly.

"Yes," I say. "How was the movie?" I turn to face her and start wiping off my eye makeup.

"You didn't go?" Lizzie's glow fades slightly. "I thought you and Elliott were going to Claudia and Beckett's couples night."

"We did," I say airily. "For a little bit. Wasn't our vibe." I motion for her to come into the bathroom further. "You and Aaron Stansfield?"

Lizzie steps into the bathroom and reaches up to remove the clips in her hair. It's not curled and sprayed to the nines like mine, because she obviously got asked out at the last minute.

"No," she says with a sigh. She runs her hands through her hair. "He's cute and all, but..."

"You're not fourteen," I say. "And *cute* doesn't cut it anymore."

"Aaron's hot," Lizzie says in the same higher-pitched voice that I just used. "For someone else."

I grin at her and toss my used wipe into the sink. I take out another one and say, "Yeah, for someone like Emma."

"I texted her," Lizzie says quickly. "She said it was okay, and we actually ran into them at the theater."

"Oh, okay," I say. I wait for her to go on, but she finishes with her hair and reaches for a wipe too. "And?"

"And." Lizzie sighs. "You know what? It was weird. Emma says she doesn't like him, but they've got some-thing fizzing between them."

"Maybe it's him," I say.

"Maybe. But she was holding Taylor's hand until the moment she saw us. Then she dropped it and put more distance between them."

"Hmm," I say. "Seems suspicious."

"Right?" Lizzie meets my eyes again. "I just wanted to go out. There's nothing between me and Aaron."

I nod, because I so get it. It's no fun to see your friends getting dolled up and going out on hot dates when you're not. Now that Claudia seems blissfully happy with Beckett, they'll probably get engaged and married soon enough.

My worrisome mind goes to who will live on the third floor of the Big House. Tahlia can't afford this place without roommates, and with Hillary gone already, and Claudia and Beckett...

I push the thoughts away, because I'm not leaving the Big House. I might even bring it up with Tahlia— how much the four of us need to pay in order to keep it just the four of us here.

Besides, it's not like Claude is married yet, and she likes big parties with plenty of pomp and ceremony. So even after she gets engaged, it could be several months before she actually moves out.

"Maybe you should try Matchmakers," I say.

"You and me both."

"I..." I'm going to have to tell everyone about me and Elliott soon enough. I'd rather start with Tahlia, but she'd been asleep on the couch when I'd come in.

"Elliott and I are..." I can't say *dating* in that space. We're *not* dating, though he absolutely did ask me out for another date tomorrow night.

"He's coming to New York with me for the holidays," I say in all one breath. I feel like I can't get enough air in the next moment, and I try to take a slow breath that actually sounds like a gasp.

Or maybe that's Lizzie, who's eyes go round as the

big South Carolina moon. "What?" also gasps out of her mouth.

"It's nothing," I say quickly, though there is absolutely something between me and Elliott. I just don't know what yet. "He's just coming with me, so I don't have to endure my sisters' perfect lives *and* Christmas on my own."

"Oh, honey, I said I'd go with you." Lizzie hugs my shoulders, and she has gone with me for other familial things in the past.

"I know," I say. "It's just...this sort of kills two birds with one stone."

"How do you mean?"

"I mean, now my momma will stop bugging me about who I'm dating." I finish up with my makeup removal and face Lizzie. "Come on. Let's get you out of your dress." I smile at her and go with her into her room.

We don't say much as I help her with the zipper and she steps out of her gown and into a pair of pajamas. Then she collapses onto her bed and scoots over to make room for me.

I climb in next to her, and we both sigh together. At our synchronized sighing, I start to laugh, glad when her giggles join mine.

"I just want to meet someone amazing," Lizzie says into the golden light from her lamp. "Someone who thinks I'm amazing exactly how I am, and who can't wait to see me every day after work, and who asks me out months in advance for an event like tonight, not someone who calls as it's starting."

I reach over and take her hand in mine. "You're going to find him," I promise her. I take a big breath and then roll out of her bed. "I have just what we need."

"I ate so much at the theater," Lizzie calls out to me as I head for the door. "I don't want any M&Ms."

"You'll want these," I yell back to her, and I hurry into my room and open the bottom drawer of my dresser, where I hide my most coveted candy.

Sure enough, the last remaining bag of pumpkin M&Ms sits there, and I grab it, ready to take a leaf out of Elliott's book—and not talk about my situation with him tonight.

I shiver as I get back in bed with Lizzie, but that's because she's switched on her fan, and it's blowing right on my bare skin—not because I've just thought about kissing Elliott tomorrow as we watch Christmas light shows from his car.

———

ELLIOTT IS WEARING YET another pair of glasses when I come face-to-face with him at work. This pair has a bright blue frame at the top, that fades to clear at the bottom, and they're more square than any other pair I've seen him wear.

I find him sexy and confident in the way he refuses

to wear contacts, and instead perches those glasses on his nose like they're the most fashionable accessory he can find.

His fingers brush mine as he reaches for a ream of sky blue paper at the same time as me. "We're still good for tonight?" he asks.

He's just gotten to work, and I've been here for four hours already. Our staggered schedules ensures that there's a manager in the building from the time we open —ten a.m.—to the time we close—eight p.m.

Elliott almost always closes, and I almost always open. That's our routine, and it puts us with the same people to manage, the same problems—daytime customers are not the same as the harried people stopping by the office supply store on their way home from work—and we have a good four or five hours in the afternoon where we share the office in the back.

"Yes," I say, the word coming out a bit tersely. I can admit that, and I swallow like that will somehow take the bite out of my words.

Elliott only smiles as he puts the paper on the shelf. "Great," he says. "I've found the perfect thing for dinner."

"You never said we were going to dinner."

"We're not," he says. "It's car food."

I don't see how car food can be anything close to perfect, but I keep that grumpy-cat statement to myself. "Okay," I say. "But Tahlia has called a pizza party confession party, so I won't be starving or anything."

"Save a little room, at least," he says. "This really is right up your alley." He gifts me a winning smile and then waves as he walks down the aisle. "I'll see you later, Ry."

Nothing about him seems off, but I stare longingly after him—and that's definitely odd.

"No, it's not," I mutter to myself as I finally tear my eyes from his retreating form and focus on my job again. I've been pining after Elliott for a while now, and those feelings have only been compounded by the text he sent my mother only last night.

Has it really only been one night? Feels like a lifetime.

I'll be there, Mom, he'd said. *And I'm bringing Elliott Hutson with me. Please don't make a big deal about it, okay?*

But he'd known what my mom would think of that, and sure enough, she's messaged me at least a dozen times about what "my boyfriend" likes to eat for breakfast and that she'll have the entire guest shed ready for him, complete with plenty of firewood for the wood-burning stove that keeps the place toasty warm in the winter.

I haven't dropped that little gem on him yet, and I reach into the big pocket of my apron and pull out a couple of caramel cold brew M&Ms and pop them into my mouth. I love that they don't melt in my pocket or with my touch, because I can carry them with me everywhere as I work around the store.

"Ry," someone says, and I turn toward JenniLynn. She's one of our runners, and she's holding two printer cartridges. "I need your help for a second, please."

"Yep." I leave the cart with the blue paper on it and go with her, ever the exciting life of an office supply store manager.

No wonder I can't get anyone to ask me out. My life —and by extension, my very existence—is so mundane.

I suffer through the rest of my work day, the confession session also putting me in a bad mood. By some miracle from above, Tahlia texts just as I'm pulling up to the Big House that she's stuck in a meeting about the arts funding at her school, and we'll have to postpone.

"Thank you," I breathe to no one in particular, and I head inside through the kitchen entrance because it's closer to the stairs.

By eight p.m., though, everyone will be home, and if they're not being diva-cats like me, they'll be in the living room. Right there, waiting for Elliott to pick me up.

I think about texting him that I'll meet him down the lane, then veto the idea. He'll argue with me about it anyway, and I'd rather not start off our second date with another spat.

Instead, I work on the online form I need to fill out for my vacation over the holidays, and I get that submitted. I take a shower and blow dry my hair out straight, then step into a pair of jeans that are probably a size too small for me—at least if I want to breathe.

But Lizzie says they look amazing on me, and I'm going to trust her on this. In fact, I head next door to her bedroom and knock.

When she doesn't answer, I text her about borrowing one of her modeling sweaters.

I'm coming up, she says. *Go in and see what you like.*

I enter her bedroom to pure chaos. How she's a chemist and lives like this, I don't understand. But she says the best creatives and logical solutions come from a messy mind, and I'm certainly not going to argue with her.

I simply put the bag of caramels I got for her at the store on her desk and then move to her closet.

"Who are you going out with tonight?" she asks as she enters her bedroom.

"Ell," I say absently, moving the hanger with the brightly striped sweater to the side.

"Elliott?" She doesn't have to sound so surprised, but I refrain from rolling my eyes at her. "Again?" She joins me, her eyes searching for something I'm positive she'll find.

"He asked," I say. "Wants to be prepared for our trip to New York." It's not exactly a lie—in fact, it's nothing but the truth.

"What are you doing?" She joins in the hunt for the perfect sweater to go with my poured-on jeans.

"We'll just be sitting in the car," I say. "He's taking me around to the Christmas light shows. Says he's found the perfect dinner, and we'll eat it in the car too."

"How romantic," Lizzie says, and she means it. Neither of us are terribly outdoorsy, and sipping hot chocolate with a candy cane as a stirring straw is her idea of a perfectly romantic date. Truth be told, I'm really looking forward to it too.

"So something sexy," she said. "That you can wow him with when he opens the door and that falls just right when you sit." She extracts one sweater the color of deep, ripe plums and another that's a gradient of blue. "Either of these will work."

She holds them out, one to each side, and raises her eyebrows at me.

"Am I a plunge-neckline kind of woman?" I ask, eyeing the eggplanty sweater.

Lizzie's gaze falls down my torso. "In that bra? Yes."

"I like darker colors over lighter," I say. "We're eating in the car." I reach out and finger the fabric of the purple sweater. It's really the color of eggplant skin, and it'll brighten my eyes and hide my winter paleness. "Let's try it."

Lizzie grins as she takes the sweater off the hanger and hands it to me. I know the moment I put it on that I'll be wearing it. It's short-sleeved, so Elliott can still blow the heater, and it really does look amazing with my jeans—and the full-support bra I've put on.

"Gorgeous," she says just as the doorbell rings. Panic parades across her face, and she tosses the gradient sweater away. "He's here. Dang it. I wanted to be downstairs."

"Lizzie," I say, but she's already flown out of the room. Great. Now I'll have to make an entrance, and my heartbeat pounds. Maybe I want to make an entrance.

I smooth my hands over my stomach and the sweater, and everything inside me flutters.

That's how I know I'm in trouble, and I start coaching myself again that Elliott just wants to get all our ducks in a row for the trip in a couple of weeks.

I couldn't talk about it last night, but I can tonight. We will. Everything will be fine.

"I'm fine," I whisper to myself. "It's fine. Everything is fine."

ELLIOTT

IT'S NOT EXACTLY WARM STANDING ON THE FRONT porch of the Big House, a place I've been many times before. Tonight, it's totally different, because I don't just walk in and announce myself, and it takes far too long for someone to come to the door.

With plenty of self-consciousness streaming through me, I tuck my hands into my pockets and wait. That's what boyfriends do. They don't just walk into their girl-friends' houses.

"...to wait," one of Ry's roommates says as the door to the Big House opens. Lizzie, a pretty blonde brushes her bangs out of her eyes and looks a little flushed as she looks at me.

Claudia, a brunette bombshell gazes at me in today's full makeup, her eyes appraising. She's starting her new job for the city of Cider Cove in only a few weeks, when the New Year arrives. I hope Ryanne and I are still talking and sharing every part of our lives with each other when that happens.

Our trip to New York will be over by then, and while my mother raised me to be prayerful and religion played a deep part of my Southern boy upbringing, God hasn't healed me of my impairment, so I've kind of stopped talking to him.

Until this morning, when I swear I've been praying for everything to go well between me and Ry every other minute. Even now, grinning at all of her current roommates, I think, *Please* before I say, "Hey, ladies."

Tahlia smiles at me and pulls the door back even more. "Come in, Elliott."

The last roommate—Emma—matches Claudia's look of skepticism, no smile in sight. "Yes," she says, though it sounds like she's inviting me inside to meet my demise. "Come in, Elliott."

I have no idea what Ry told her roommates, but she did have a confession party or something tonight, and I scan all the women again.

There's no scent of pizza, no garlicky goodness hanging in the air, and I feel like I've been blasted off to Mars, the way the rovers have been.

I am enjoying my time on Mars, runs through my mind in the cute robot rover voice, and I tell myself to absolutely not say it in front of Ry's roommates. Yes, the *Perseverance* rover said it—a new round of communications were released today—and I definitely feel like I'm exploring a foreign planet, hoping for a place I can thrive. But I don't need to speak literal robot-language.

I reach up and push my glasses further up onto my nose, the frames tonight the lightest pair I own. They're almost rimless, with the lenses practically disappearing on my face. Silver goes across the corners of them, and back to my ears, and they're driving glasses, suitable for evening, as well as far-sight assistance.

It's December, and I'm not overly into the holidays, so I've chosen a pair of navy blue shorts and a button down shirt in pale blue. It somehow feels all wrong as the four women continue to stare at me.

"Is, uh, Ry here?" I glance toward the living room, but I don't see her.

"She was right behind me," Lizzie says.

"I bet she's getting something to drink," Claudia says. "She gets a little dry-mouth before a date."

"Claudia," Tahlia says, nudging the taller woman. "Go check in the kitchen."

Claudia wears a hint of a flush as she goes to do that, leaving the three blondes to blink at me.

A bit of a commotion comes from the kitchen, and we all look that way. "How's the store?" Tahlia asks, but Ry has just come through the doorway and into the living room, a glass of orange juice in her hand.

She's glaring at Claudia, her face turned toward her as they argue a bit back and forth.

I can't breathe, because Ry's wearing a pair of jeans that make her look absolutely incredible. It's like the waistband of them has tightened around my lungs, and I suck in a breath in a horribly loud way.

I step toward her, my only goal to touch that soft denim, feel what that sweater will do as I bump my fingers over the knitted cables of yarn.

I'm so going to miss my ability to see, but if I can burn this image of Ry into my memory, I'll happily die blind.

I'm very touchy-feely, as it helps me form a sight memory that I'm hoping to call on later. My therapist told me to do that, and I've taken her seriously.

"Hey," I say, and Ry finally faces me. In the next moment, she stumbles, and I lunge toward her to catch her before she spills to the floor.

Unfortunately, something is going to spill—either her, me, both of us, or that orange juice.

She seems to make the decision that it has to be the OJ, because she splashes it into my chest, the glass flying out of her hand, and landing with a terrible breaking sound as it hits the floor.

My momentum propels me forward, and I wrap her in my arms, pressing my OJ'ed chest to hers as I say, "Okay, I got you."

Everything slows down then, as neither of us are going to skin our knees on the rug bunched at Ryanne's feet.

My heart pounds behind my ribs, like it's been caged there and feels like it's been held hostage. My face is only inches from hers, and it takes every ounce of pride and self-control I possess not to kiss her right there.

Roommates blares through my head like the alarms on the Mars rovers, and I step back. In that moment, the scent of oranges overwhelms me, and the entire front of my body feels too cold now that I've realized it's wet.

I hold my hands out to the side and look down at myself.

"I'm so sorry," Ry gushes, moving forward again, brushing at the fabric of my shirt. A literal drop of OJ goes flying, but I lose it somewhere outside the range of my vision.

"Ry," I say.

"Ry," Claudia says.

She keeps brushing at my clothes—my *abdomen*—like she can erase the sticky juice that's seeped into the cloth.

"Ry," I try again.

"It's fine," she says, and I recognize her babbling tone. "It's just juice, and it's—"

"Ryanne," I bark, and Claudia physically grabs her hands and pulls them away from my body.

She finally slows, her face turning a glorious shade of pink, and I grin at her. "What were you trying to do?"

Ryanne looks helplessly at Claudia as her other roommates gather around us.

"We're just going to be sitting in my car," I say. "It's just orange juice."

Salty Ry returns, and she cocks one gorgeous hip and folds her arms. "You're not spending the next couple of hours wearing sticky orange juice."

"So we'll just go back to my place, and I'll change. Again."

"Again?" Claudia and Tahlia ask at the same time.

Ry drops her chin to her chest, a slow sigh seeping from between her lips. When she looks up at me, her expression is all vulnerability with a rim of hope in those pretty eyes. "Can we start over?"

"Is this date one or two?" I ask, and I'm really shooting myself in the foot by having this conversation in front of everyone.

Ryanne's eyes sparkle now, and I want to dive into them and fly through space, bumping from twinkle to twinkle inside those mysterious, midnight-dark depths. Star to star, until she lets me orbit her and stay with her and cherish her.

"It's our first," she said. "You said you didn't want last night..." She trails off and glances over to Lizzie. Then Emma.

"Last night what?" Claudia asks.

"I think the Christmas light shows will be running in a half-hour as easily as they are now," I say. "I'll run home and change and come pick you up again."

"Ell," she says. "You don't have to do that. I'll just come with you."

I hold up one hand and give her my best co-manager glare. That usually gets her to calm enough to quiet. This time, she either misses it or ignores me, because she turns to Claudia.

"I just need my purse."

I move into Ry and curl my fingers around the back of her neck. "Ry," I say quietly. "I'll be back in a half-hour."

The whole house has come to a standstill. No one seems to be moving, not even me. My lungs continue to breathe, and that gives my brain something to grab onto.

"Thirty minutes," I say, and then I drop my hand and back up a step. I very nearly trample Emma as I turn, and I thankfully dodge well enough to avoid her. "Sorry," I murmur.

Then I get out of there before I kiss my best friend and fake girlfriend in front of all of her roommates.

Thirty-four minutes later, I re-arrive at the Big House only to find Ryanne sitting on the front steps with Lizzie, who takes one look at me through the windshield, gets up, and heads inside.

I get out of the car and walk toward Ry, who's also traded out her sweater for a pretty black blouse with colorful ribbons snaking across it. "Hey," I say as I approach.

"Hey." She looks up at me, all the stars still there.

I settle next to her and look out into the night. No one lives across the street from the Big House, so it's darker there, leaving plenty of silence to consume us both.

"Okay, well, I can't stand this," I say. "I'm just going to start."

Ry leans forward and turns toward me, resting her head in her hands as if she can't hold it up herself.

"You're my best friend in the whole world," I say to the darkness across the street, the universe. It's always been big enough to hold all my thoughts, all my words, all my feelings and confessions.

"But I've been feeling things for you that go beyond friendship, and my offers to be your fake boyfriend haven't been entirely altruistic."

She says nothing, which is Ry's default when she's got a lot on her mind. She needs time to sort through things, and I'm ruining our second first date by sitting here talking instead of just escorting her to the passenger seat and taking her to get pulled pork deliciousness before we go watch Frosty the Snowman and Rudolph the Red-nosed Reindeer while Christmas tunes blast through my car.

"I think you're absolutely stunning, you're my favorite person to talk to, and you're so smart. If I didn't..." I suck in a breath, because while I have plenty streaming out of my mouth, I don't know how to say everything.

"I don't want to pretend to be anything with you," I say next, and this should open enough doors to buy me some time to find a way to confess the other things.

"I want to be your real boyfriend. I don't want any hand-holding or kissing between us to be for practice purposes." I reach over and take her hand in mine. "I know you want something serious, not something casual, and I guess this is me saying—trying to say—telling you that, in the words of *Curiosity*, I'm willing to try."

I finally tear my eyes away from the darkness, glad they can still see the lights from the Big House spilling onto Ry's completely shocked face.

"For you, Ryanne, I'm willing to try." I search her face, trying to find some inkling that she's heard me. Really heard me.

She gives nothing away, in true Ryanne fashion.

So I lean closer, take her face in the palm of my hand, and do what I've been dying to do for months now.

I match my mouth to hers and kiss her. When she doesn't immediately push me away, slap me, or verbally protest, a growl starts somewhere in my stomach and surges upward.

Kissing her in real life is better than anything my imagination has come up with. She's pure female—soft and supple and sweet—and her lips become oxygen to me.

I'll never, ever, ever get enough.

RYANNE

I don't know how Elliott does the things he does with his mouth. From the words he's said tonight, to the way he kisses me like I'm his One-and-Only, the man is extremely talented with his mouth.

"Are you going to respond to what I've said?" he whispers as he pulls back an inch or two, then lowers his lips to my jawline. Then my neck. Up toward my ear.

He's stolen every thought and every word straight from my throat—and that takes a lot of talent too.

Elliott straightens again, and the loss of his touch leaves me cold and somewhat petrified. My blood vessels are just going to be preserved in this state forever, with the passion he's kissed me with living inside them.

"I'm going to need you to say something." He takes my hand in his, aligning our fingers just-so, then sighs.

"Let's go get dinner and watch the lights. I promise I won't say another word until you've had time to think."

Just the fact that he knows I need processing time speaks to the first thing he said: He's my best friend in the whole world too.

The fact that I kissed him back as enthusiastically as I did must've told him something about how I feel about him too.

He'll need to hear it in words, though. Sometimes Elliott can't see what's right in front of him. I know, because I've told him about several women who were so much more into him than he was them, and he simply didn't see it.

"Do you still want to go?" he asks.

I nod and let him pull me to my feet. "I'm really sorry about the orange juice." I reach out and slide my palm down his chest and abdomen again, feeling the silky quality of this second shirt beneath my touch. Maybe a muscle or two as well, but mostly the smooth fabric of his polo.

"If our next date starts with some sort of liquid getting thrown all over me..." He grins, and I manage to return it. He leans closer, an unusual intensity in his dark, dazzling eyes. "It still won't be enough to drive me away."

I sigh, because what woman doesn't want to hear an incredibly handsome man tell her she can do no wrong?

"Let's go," I say, and I start down the sidewalk, hand-in-hand with Elliott. When we reach his car, my pulse is a lightning storm, and words will have to come out before I can get in.

"I kissed you back," I blurt out as he reaches for the door handle.

His gaze meets mine, and I swear, it's like two trains going in opposite directions, colliding until the individual pieces of them melt into a whole new unit.

"Surely you realize I kissed you back."

"It seems you did, yes," he says.

"This is not the first crush I've had on you," I say, and that gets his eyes to widen slightly. He blinks an extra time or two, but my cells have started to settle now that I've confessed a few things.

He opens the door. "Can we agree to get rid of the fake label?"

I nod, the word *yes* lodged somewhere too deep for me to unearth it right now. I step past him, finally escaping his gaze, and start to slide into the car.

Something waits on the seat for me, and I quickly swipe it up as I slide in. Elliott closes the door at the same time I ask, "You got me mini crispies?"

I look up through the window, but Elliott has already gone toward the back of the car, and I realize it's a tactic he uses when he doesn't want me to see him.

It's ten seconds where he can compose himself in private, ten seconds where he gets a reset, ten seconds he gives to me to do the same.

When he opens the driver's side door and sits behind the wheel, I immediately reach for his hand. "So it won't be fake when we go see my family for Christmas."

"No," he confirms.

"But we still need to get a few things straight about when we started dating." I look out my side window as he starts the car. He needs both hands to back out, so he drops mine to focus on that task.

"I think my momma will lose her mind if I tell her our first date was the day *after* I texted and told her you were coming."

He chuckles, the sound amazing and one of the most authentic things I've heard out of his mouth.

"Plus, you said you wanted to start over, so I'm not sure our first date is even today," he says.

"Oh, it has to be," I say. "We can't have kissed *before* our first date."

He shakes his head, clearly amused. "I suppose not."

Elliott sticks to his promise about giving me room to think tonight, and he doesn't' say much as he drives along the suburban streets toward downtown Cider Cove. It's the Christmas Festival for a few more weeks, and the food trucks have shown up.

"I thought you said we wouldn't have to get out of the car."

"I'll go for you, kitty-cat," he says, using a nickname that used to drive me mad, because he's used it to indicate how detached I am, while expecting to be cared for in a very specific way. Like a diva kitty cat.

Now, though, it feels like a term of endearment.

"Which one are you going to?"

He nods down the row of them, but it's impossible to see them all. "Let me surprise you."

"You know I hate surprises." So like an aloof, solitary feline, so maybe the name fits.

"Maybe they aren't for you," he shoots back. "Maybe you can simply let someone else do something for you that will make *them* feel like a rockstar."

"All right, *rockstar*," I say, really sliding out the last word. "Go get your surprise."

Elliott gives me a hot look, filled with searing things, but he says nothing more. He simply eases out of the car with all the charm, power, and grace with which he usually moves, and then he crosses the street to the row of food trucks.

He strides down them until I lose sight of him among the crowd and distance, and I reach down and pull the lever that will lower the seat.

I squeal as I fall down, my laughter bubbling up in the next moment.

Because Elliott kissed me.

This is not just for-fun for him. He wants this to be real.

"Whatever *this* is," I whisper to myself. I know what I want it to be, and I sober as I think of his pledge. He's going to try to have a serious relationship, and that means there's a reason—maybe more than one—why he hasn't in the past.

Maybe not the right woman, but surely I'm not her. No, there's definitely something else Ell isn't telling me, and I sit myself up and reach for my phone. He's only said that one thing about the robots on Mars, and I want to speak his language when he gets back with my surprise.

It only takes a few taps and a single search—and a mini-handful of mini crispy M&Ms—to find the newly released communications from the Mars *rovers*—not robots.

They're programmed to say cute things to each other, and to Earth, and I find myself smiling as I read through their travelogue.

"What are you smiling about?" Elliott asks as he lets in a blast of colder air. Then he's in the car, closing the door, and holding two plain white Styrofoam containers.

"Curiosity had a birthday," I say.

Pure joy lights up his face, and it makes me so happy too. "She did," he says. "Only a couple of days after my daddy's. Did you find the feed of her singing to herself? Or was it Perseverance doing the duet with himself?"

"There's a Mars rover duet of *Happy Birthday*?" I practically dive back into my phone, but Elliott plucks it away from me.

"Later," he says. "I didn't see or smell any pizza at

the Big House, and that means you guys didn't have your dinner."

"No," I say, a blip of irritation shooting through me at the loss of my device. "Something came up at school for Tahlia. We're going to do it tomorrow." I look down at the food containers. "Then Hillary can video in with us. Give her own update."

"What are you going to update everyone about?" he asks.

"Nothing to say," I tell him, lifting my eyes to his. "You're the one who came crashing into the house today like a wild bull, saying all kinds of things."

"Everything I said happened after I got back wearing a new shirt."

I half-laugh, half-scoff. "Right," I say. "You said plenty in front of my roommates."

"Is this one of those things where women can see more than men?"

"Yes," I say simply, smiling at him. "Surprise me already. I'm starving."

He glances to the tube of mini M&Ms. "The seal on that is broken, so you're fine."

"It's candy," I say. "Not real food."

Ell gives me his delicious smile and pops the top on the uppermost container. "I give you...Hawaiian haystacks with Kalua pork!" He says it like he's the ringleader at the greatest circus on earth, and he's just announced the most bizarre trick of the evening.

I do want to cheer. Or lunge across the space and kiss him. But I've already spilled too much on him today, and I do love the Kalua pulled pork Hawaiian haystacks from Give It a Poke.

"They're here?" I ask, automatically looking out the window to find their food truck. "How long are they here?"

"Just tonight," he says. "According to their social media."

"Just tonight," I repeat. Warmth fills me from head to toe as Elliott tucks a fork into the most delicious version of Hawaiian haystacks known to mankind and offers me the container.

"You're my favorite person," I tell him as I take it.

"You always know how to give me the reaction I want." He laughs and opens his own container. I can guess what he'll have ordered from my favorite food truck.

"Sushi," I say at the same time he says, "Ah, I love sushi."

I shake my head and pick up my flimsy plastic fork. "I don't know how you eat raw fish from a food truck."

"It's good," he says.

"It's unsanitary."

"It's fish," he says. "No different than getting it from the restaurant next door."

"Don't call me upset when you're puking tonight," I say.

"We're not even open tomorrow," he says. "So it doesn't matter." Then he uses a legit pair of chopsticks to lift a sushi roll out of his container. It is beautiful, sushi, though I don't particularly like it.

But my Kalua pork, shredded over white sticky rice, with edamame, pineapple, and a Hawaiian spiced red-eye gravy? Yes, please all the day long.

And Elliott even got the crunchy lo mein noodles— my favorite. I glance over to him, and I haven't spoken incorrectly.

He *is* my favorite person in the world, and I should be giddy with the way tonight has gone. I am, for sure, but my heartbeat also twitches in fear. I take a bite of my favorite food and look over to him.

"What?" he asks.

I let the party continue in my mouth, really hamming it up with a moan and a roll of my head. Ell smiles and laughs, and he's the most handsome man in the world.

When I swallow the best bite of my life, I look over to him again. "What happens if you try to take things seriously between us, but you just can't do it?"

The smile disappears right off his face. Just slides away, and I kick myself for ruining this first-date-for-the-second-time for the second time that night.

ELLIOTT

By some miracle, Ry lets me drive to the first house in silence. Probably because I've just given her the Kalua Hawaiian haystacks she loves with her whole heart, all of her taste buds, and every fiber of her soul.

Her words, not mine.

But her question plagues me—and it has internally for a while now.

I pull up to the first house on the list provided by Cider Cove for light shows, and I kill the lights, put the car in park, and reach to set the radio to the right channel.

Carol of the Bells streams through the car, and Ry says, "I love this song."

I give her a closed-mouth smile and move my seat back to give myself room to eat my own dinner. *Just Give It a Poke* does all kinds of food, and I love sushi so much.

Maybe with one of my favorites at the end of my chopsticks, I can talk to Ryanne. Really talk to her.

"I've thought about you more than anyone or anything else since I broke up with Millie," I say. "Our friendship is the main reason I haven't asked you out or said anything about how I feel."

Ry doesn't answer right away, and I decide I'm not going to have another one-sided confessional. I stuff a California roll into my mouth, determined to wait until she says something before I go on.

A few chews in, and she looks over to me. "It would kill me if we weren't friends."

I nod, because I feel the same.

"And you can't quit either," she says. "I would die at Paper Trail without you."

Not true, but I still have too much fish and rice in my mouth to argue. I'm not looking for another job anyway.

"I guess this is just me worrying." She sighs, and I look over to her. Everything about her is soft, and lush, and wonderful.

I quickly finish and swallow. "It's okay to worry about this. I have been too."

She looks out the passenger window at the light show on the lawn. "They've got cute polar bears here."

I chopstick up another bite of sushi. "I'm going to do my very best, Ry. No matter what, you can rest assured that I will never, ever do anything to hurt you on purpose."

I can't promise her more than that. Relationships are messy at the best of times, and Ry and I are trying to obliterate previously established lines between us. Make new rules. Be friends *and* lovers.

Again, I'm using vocabulary someone my age so shouldn't, and I'm glad I know how to keep my thoughts from exploding out of my mouth.

"Okay, Ell." She reaches over and squeezes my forearm. "I promise the same thing."

"What's that?" I pop the sushi into my mouth, hoping she'll spell out what I just promised her.

"I would never do anything to hurt you on purpose. So if you get hurt, you have to tell me. Then we can talk about it, and I'll tell you if you're doing something that's hurting me."

I nod again, because that sounds like a good deal. That done, we settle into watching red, green, blue, white, and gold lights, and I drive her to four more places before I look at her fully again.

"Home now?"

She gives me a sweet, soft smile that makes my heart pitter-patter in a way only my granny would say, and nods. "Home now, please."

I take her back to the Big House, the evening dark and quiet between us. The house has a triple-wide paved driveway, with more parking on gravel beside that. The front lawn has been cut back to accommodate for the extra parking, and it's all marked by decorative rocks.

Other cars, including Ry's, are parked in the driveway now, and I inch down to take the last one in the graveled area.

"Watch out," Ry says just before I hit one of the rocks with the front bumper of my SUV. She yelps and throws her hand up to hold onto the bar.

I swear and blink, trying to get my eyes to focus. They don't. I'm so tired, and my first instinct is to panic. If I can't see, how will I get home safely?

I've agreed to call my mother if I can't drive, but so much foolishness streams through me that I'm not sure I can do it. I mean, I'm thirty-three. What thirty-three-year-old needs their mommy to come pick them up after a date?

"Did you not see that?" Ry gasps. "Is this car drivable?"

Before I can stop her, she's out of the vehicle and rounding the hood. My pulse fires through my body like someone has depressed a button to set off rapid-fire machine gun shots. It pings and blitzes through my body, and I unbuckle as Ry meets my eyes through the windshield.

She looks scared and worried at the same time, and she says, "I don't know if you can drive the home, Ell."

"I can call my mom," I say. "She'll come get me."

Ry's expression settles, and she looks down at the bumper and wheel well again. I join her, and yep, things look a little skiwampus.

"Your mom?"

"She lives close enough," I hedge, already pulling out my phone.

Ry covers the screen with her hand. "I can take you home."

Our eyes meet, and since she's so close, I can see everything clearly. Those pretty, curled eyelashes. The depths of her starry eyes. How she feels.

"Okay," I murmur. "I'll call someone in the morning to help with the car." I tear my gaze from hers. "Will it be okay parked here?"

She grinds her voice through her throat before she says, "Yes."

I sigh, part annoyed but part relieved I don't have to drive home.

"I'll go get my keys," Ry says, and she turns toward the Big House and strides across the lawn.

I move down the row of cars to hers and wait, and when she pulls up to my house, I know my momma isn't awake. Of course, Ry doesn't know she lives with me, so it's a good thing my house looks like no one else lives there.

"Thanks, Ry." I smile at her. "You wanna walk me to the door and kiss me good-night?"

She looks like she might just as soon eat squirrel stew, but she nods. I get out on the passenger side and meet her at the front corner of her sedan. I take her hand and squeeze it. "Feeling nervous?"

"Yeah," she says. "Yep."

I laugh, because that's what I say when I'm nervous. "Now you know how men feel when they walk you to the door."

"It's terrifying," she says.

"We've kissed before," I say.

"Not here." Ry goes up my front steps ahead of me, and I stick close to her side. Once I'm on the porch with her, I pull her into my arms and touch my forehead to hers, praying with everything I have that my momma took her melatonin that night. Sometimes the alarm system buzzes her awake, though I've told her a thousand times to turn off the camera notifications at night.

"Thank you for talking with me tonight," I say, and then I touch my lips to hers. I've kissed plenty of women, but none of those kisses are anything like kissing Ryanne.

She has full lips, and she's no amateur when it comes to making me feel important and valued—and now wanted.

"See you tomorrow," I say.

"Will you?" She tucks herself into my arms and presses her cheek to my chest.

"I mean, I want to."

"The store is closed," she says. "Normally, I wouldn't see you until Wednesday after a Saturday." She tilts her head back and smiles up to me. "And I never heard you ask me out on another date."

"Maybe you should ask me."

"Absolutely not." She tries to step out of my arms, but I tighten my grip on her.

"I'm kidding," I say. "But I would like to see you tomorrow." It's Sunday, so Ry will sleep late. She calls her mom in the evenings—every Sunday evening—but anytime from ten in the morning until six at night should be available.

"Lunch?" I ask. "Matinee? Christmas market? Living Bethlehem?"

"Yes," she says, not specifying which things she'd like to do.

I grin at her and ask, "Eleven?"

"I can be presentable by eleven."

"You're always presentable, Ry." I kiss her again, because I can. It is a little odd to be doing this on my own doorstep, but I kinda-really like it too.

"You should go," I say as I dip my mouth to the tender skin along her neck.

She pulls in a breath and holds onto my shoulders. "I should, yes."

Normally, I'm the one to leave, but tonight, Ry's going to have to do it. She doesn't, and I keep kissing her, wondering if my momma will check the overnight footage and see me making out with my best friend.

That thought gets me to pull back, and I breathe in deep and exhale out, "Okay. Eleven tomorrow."

Ry looks at me, but her eyes seem unfocused, and

boy do I know how that feels. I squeeze her hand and step back, finally putting distance between us. "See you tomorrow."

I reach to open the door while she stands there, and I say, "You have to go back to your car now, Ry." I grin at her, knowing she's in her head right now, imagining and reliving kissing me. "Can you get yourself home?"

That snaps her back to herself, and she gives me a semi-glare. Her kitty-cat diva glare. "Yes," she says as she lifts her chin. "I can get myself home." She mutters something as she goes down my front steps, and I ease into the house with a sigh.

I've never been dropped off by a woman before, and I have to admit—I like it. "You like Ry," I mutter as I lock the door behind me and go through my nightly procedure of securing the house and turning off lights. "You like Ry too much."

And I know I do, even though she kisses me back like she likes me a whole lot too.

Be careful, Ell, I tell myself, and for the first time since I got my degenerative vision diagnosis, I'm reminding myself that I need to be careful with my heart, and not merely careful that I won't trip over something.

Because falling in love is as scary as not being able to see.

———

"THERE YOU ARE," Momma says the next morning. She's made coffee, scrambled eggs, and lifts a few pieces of bacon from the frying pan as I sweep into the kitchen beside her.

That only means one thing. "Brandon's coming?" I ask.

"Should be here any second." She beams up at me. "What time did you get in last night?"

"Not too late," I hedge as I pull down a mug for my morning coffee. Before Momma can do what all good Southern mommas do—pepper me with questions—my brother walks in the garage door with, "Good morning! I have doughnuts!"

Brandon yells everything he says, and I swear he has a hearing impairment. He doesn't; he's just loud.

"Indoor voices," I say to him as my cat streaks down the hall to my bedroom.

He slams the box of doughnuts on the counter like he's trying to flatten them, and smiles at me. "You're here."

"Where else would I be?"

"I dunno, but your car isn't out front, so I thought you were somewhere else."

"Why isn't your car out front?" Momma asks, and I press my eyes closed as I stir in a spoonful of sugar for my coffee.

"Uh, I—"

"How did you get home?" she asks next, and I look

over to Brandon. He wears a look of sympathy and lifts one shoulder as if to say, *Sorry, bro. I didn't know she didn't know.*

And how would he?

"Were you drinking?" she asks, and I roll my eyes now. I lean against the countertop and raise my coffee mug to my lips. I'm not wearing glasses, because sometimes it's nice to just be...yeah, just be.

No, I can't see well, but good enough to pour coffee and put a few pieces of bacon on a maple long john and sit with my family for a minute.

But Momma's gone into question mode, and she fires off, "Was it too late for you?" She cocks her hip and puts the hand holding the tongs on it, the utensil sticking out to the side. "You couldn't see, could you?"

"Momma."

"You promised me you'd call if you needed a ride."

"I'm home, aren't I?" I take another sip of my coffee.

"Elliott, you—"

"Momma," Brandon shouts. "You ask so many questions at once and don't even wait for an answer."

I gesture my mug toward him as my eyebrows go up, silently agreeing with him.

"You're just spiraling out of control," Brandon says. "Since when does Elliott drink?" He shakes his head and edges in next to me to pour his own cup of coffee. "Mylanta. No wonder Shirley skipped out on this today."

She pivots to him, and the fact that he's thrown himself to Momma Shark isn't lost on me. "Shirley was going to come?"

"I told her we might have breakfast this morning, and that you guys are fun." He stirs in some sugar and reaches for the cream. "That she'd like you and you'd like her."

"Of course I'm going to like her," Momma says indignantly.

I grin at my brother, who grins back.

"It must be getting serious for you to suggest she come meet us." Momma tosses the tongs into the sink and starts to wash up. When she's nervous she can't keep her hands still, and I fully expect the kitchen to be spotless before she sits down to breakfast with me and Brandon.

"We've been dating for eight months," Brandon says. "It's been serious for a while."

"And I haven't met her yet?" Momma swats at Brandon's shoulder as he turns to face her. "I want to meet her."

"And I want you to not fire questions at her so fast that she can't even answer one."

"And I want to have breakfast in my own house without...this." But I grin at the pair of them as they look at me, both of them wearing different expressions, ranging from shock—Momma—to disbelief—Brandon.

I laugh and set aside my coffee so I won't dump it

down their backs. Then I move in to hug them simultaneously, and we sigh together as a family as they embrace me back.

I step back, my feelings so swirly lately, like big, billowing clouds that bubble and bulge and boil though the sky.

"Can we eat now?" I ask. "With quiet voices and one question at a time?"

"Yes," Momma says crisply. "And I want to know how you got home last night."

"Ry drove me," I say, clearing my throat and ducking away from them to get my coffee. "It would be great if you didn't check the security cameras, okay, Momma?"

Simply me saying that has thrown gasoline on an already raging fire, and Momma gasps. "Are you dating Ryanne? Did she kiss you? Oh, this is so exciting. Why did she have to drive you here, though? That's the *real* question."

She puts the plate of bacon on the table while Brandon brings over the doughnuts. I sit down, saying nothing, as Brandon starts to laugh. Momma doesn't even seem to notice—and how can she? Brandon's chortles are *so* loud, I can barely hear myself think.

"Will we have to go get your car somewhere?" Momma asks as she sits down, and I can't decide if I'd rather talk about my new relationship with Ry or admit that I hit a giant rock with my car because I couldn't see it.

Neither sound all that fun, and I accept the maple-frosted doughnut as Brandon hands it to me.

"Yeah, yep," I say. "I'll call a tow truck, though. I think the car needs to be taken to a mechanic shop."

"Elliott Alexander," Momma says, and she's the one shouting now. "Did you get in an accident last night? Why didn't you call the police? Where is your car?"

I meet Brandon's eyes, and we burst out laughing together. Our poor mother. She really needs some girls to gab with, as Brandon and I don't usually have it in us. I reach across the table and cover her hand with mine. "Momma," I say. "Breathe. I'm a grown man, and I can take care of my business."

Now, if I can just figure out how to make sure I don't hurt Ryanne, I might be able to simply go back to worrying about my eyesight instead of losing everything in my life that I hold dear.

Oh, and the eighty-year-old vocabulary strikes again.

RYANNE

"It hasn't been too weird," I say to Hillary, who's video-called me from her apartment in LA. "What do you think of this dress? Am I trying too hard?"

"What are you doing?" she asks. "It's adorable. I love the puffy sleeve."

The dress is black, with a square neck and falls in tiered waves in a boxy style over my ample chest and hips. I love it because it feels like wearing nothing, and while it's simple, it has some embellishments—like the puffy sleeve—that make it seem like more than it is.

"I don't really know what we're doing," I say. "He mentioned a lot of things. I just said yes."

"Mm, yes, you did." Hillary smiles when I look at her. "Oh, don't wear that face."

"What face?"

"The one that says you're worried about this."

I sink onto my bed. "I *am* worried about this."

"It's Elliott."

I give her my eagle-eyes. "Exactly. It's Elliott."

"Did he say why he's never wanted to be serious with anyone? Until now," she adds quickly.

Everyone is always very quick to add that, including me. I shake my head. "I didn't ask him." I study my hands, and I sport some pretty, newly-painted-pine-tree-green fingernails, with the fourth one a bright white. My nod to the Christmas season without going overboard.

"I should ask him, right?"

"I mean, maybe?" Hillary seems to be guessing as much as I am.

"Did you feel so...uncertain about Liam?"

"Yes," she whispers. "Remember how I sent him a text meant for that other guy? I actually think he was the one who was super uncertain about me."

"I was not," Liam calls from somewhere off-screen. He enters the frame as Hillary looks to her left. "I mean, not after you explained." He leans down and presses a kiss to Hillary's forehead, all while using a towel to dry his obviously wet hair.

"What are you two doing today?" I ask, my eyebrows sky-high.

"Liam's apartment is being fumigated," she says. "So we're going for a bike ride today."

I lean closer to my phone as Liam exits the frame. "He's living with you?" I hiss.

"No," Hillary hisses back playfully, her dark eyes sparkling. "He helped Mister Jacobs next door with his garbage disposal and got all wet. So he rinsed off here—in the kitchen sink—and is just drying up."

"No diamonds?"

She holds up her naked left hand in response.

"The documentary is almost done?"

"We're on schedule for our March-one deadline," she says.

"So maybe you'll get married in April and move back to Cider Cove." I lift my eyebrows, glad when Hillary smiles in return.

I miss her, and while I know things will change when she and Liam get married, at least she'll be next door instead of across the country.

"What's the hot-goss with Claudia?" Hillary asks. "She won't tell me anything."

"She's crazy-busy," I say. "Moving offices in a couple of weeks. Beckett is looking for another house a little closer to Beaufort, and neither of them will say anything about a proposal or a possible wedding date or where they'll live when they get married." I sigh, because while I'm happy for Claudia, I want to know all of the above.

It takes some time for me to adjust to change, and I just want things in the Big House to stay how they are. Of course they can't, and we've enjoyed a few good years here with just the six of us.

"What are you doing with your hair?" Hillary asks, and I reach up to touch it.

"I'm just going to go with my standard—a ponytail I'll curl into one big ringlet."

She smiles at me and touches two fingers to her lips and then the screen, covering herself for a moment. "Love you, Ry. I want a full debrief tonight."

"You and everyone else," I grumble, though I've always wanted all of their dating news too. I've never really had a boyfriend to talk about, and while my roommates know about my insane crush on Elliott, I've never really delved deeper or confessed more to them.

The call ends and I finish getting ready. I skip downstairs and snag one of Tahlia's banana nut muffins from the cooling rack in the kitchen. She's put up a cheery Christmas tree window cling on the microwave and written "Family meeting 7:30 PM" on it in black erasable marker.

I should be done with my phone call with my mom, safely in my stretchy pants, with a bag of cookie dough M&Ms, and ready to give an update by then.

Someone knocks on the front door, and I turn that way. It's not eleven yet, which means it can't be Elliott— unless I missed a text from him. I check my phone on the way out of the kitchen, and I didn't.

No one else seems to be home, or at least downstairs, so I open the door to find a man wearing gray-blue clothing from head to toe, and it only takes me two seconds to realize he's a tow truck driver.

"I'm taking that SUV there." He gestures somewhere lazily behind him. "I was told someone here could sign for it."

"That's me," I say, and I take the tablet he hands me and use my finger to sign for the removal of Elliott's car.

"You'll get an email when I drop it off at Clydesdales." He nods at me and leaves the porch. I stand in the doorway and watch him load up Elliott's car, which definitely looks like the front wheel needs to be reset.

I snap a quick pic and send it to him. *They just took your car, and I just realized you might be waiting for me to pick you up this morning.*

He calls, and I swipe it on with a giddy smile on my face. "Hey."

"Heavens, no," he says, and I giggle at his disgusted tone. "I'm ten minutes away."

"What are you driving?"

He clears his throat, and I move to sit in Emma's rocking chair. "My mom's car."

"How did you get to your mom's?"

"Does that really matter?"

He's grouchy this morning, and somehow that makes me smile. "Yes," I say. "It matters to me. I could've come to get you. I'd have let you drive my car."

"I already had to sign away my firstborn so my mom would let me take hers," he says, his tone grumbly and husky and delicious all at the same time. "Which is better for me, because I'm not going to have a firstborn for a while, and she'll forget by then."

I laugh and toe myself back and forth. "So you want kids?" This is a new development, because Elliott has never wanted anything serious—and kids are Serious with a capital S.

"I mean..." He lets the words hang there, and I'm not sure what to make of them. "If they could have your starry-starry eyes, I'd take a couple of kids," he finally says.

The air gets whooshed right out of my lungs. Things between us shift violently, and I wish he was here so I can see his face, judge his expression, watch the way his hands fiddle. Something.

"I've said too much," he says. "I'm hanging up."

"Wait," I say, but the call disconnects as he says, "You're so stupid, Elliott."

I look at the screen as it goes dark, my pulse thundering through my chest and radiating out with painful barbs with every beat.

And it's *beating* hard. Thrashing, really.

I don't know how Emma finds comfort in this chair. The rocking doesn't soothe me, and I get to my feet to go find some candy. Maybe some coffee M&Ms, though I'm already too keyed up.

I'm rummaging through my stash in the lower

cupboard beside the stove when Elliott's voice reaches my ears. "Ry? It's just me."

I stand up suddenly, my lungs seizing. I can't breathe, and my head feels like it's floating away from my body.

The back door opens, and Emma and Tahlia come in. "Elliott's here," Tahlia says needlessly, as the god of a man has just appeared in the doorway leading into the kitchen.

They're both wearing dresses, which means they went to church this morning, and Tahlia starts to unpin her hat as Elliott and I stare at one another.

"You're not drinking anything, are you?" he asks.

I blink, the perfect retort right on the tip of my tongue. But I can't get it to come out, and something loud and shrill shrieks through my head.

And my chest. By the time I realize it's my lungs crying for air, my legs are wobbly. I reach out to steady myself against the back of a dining chair, but I miss it.

And I know: I'm going to pass out.

As I do, my last thought is *Will Elliott and I ever get a date that starts normally?*

And the last thing I see is Elliott's panicked expression as he lunges toward me.

My ears have stopped working completely, and then blissful darkness swallows me whole.

————

"DID SHE HIT HER HEAD?"

"No."

"Didn't you see the way Elliott caught her?"

In that moment, I feel Elliott everywhere around me, and Tahlia's voice echoes in my head.

"She's waking up," Elliott says, and he smooths his fingers across my forehead, "Ry, sweetheart, wake up."

I want to do what he says, so I fight to open my eyes. I manage to do it too, and everything comes rushing back. I'm lying with my head in Elliott's lap, and his hands feel like they're *everywhere.*

"Whoa," I say as I try to sit up.

"Just stay for a second," he says, and I relax into him.

"I passed out."

"Yeah," he says. "Yep."

I focus on him though Emma is talking about getting me some orange juice, and Tahlia wants to know if I've eaten that morning.

He's wearing a sexy pair of bright blue glasses that have huge trapezoidal frames—and I barely passed geometry, so my junior high math teacher would be proud I know what a trapezoid is.

Ell didn't shave this morning, and while he's not smiling, his gaze is powerful as it locks onto mine. "You wanna sit up?"

I nod, and he helps me do that, scooting closer so I can lean on him if I need to. I don't *need* to, but I want to, so I do.

"I'm okay," I say. "I was looking for some candy, and I just stood up too fast." I wave away the muffin Tahlia offers me. "I had one. I just got lightheaded for like, two seconds."

Emma's poured two glasses of juice, but I ignore them as I let Elliott help me to my feet. He keeps one big hand on my elbow, and I like that.

"We can just—" He cuts off when I throw him a daggered look.

"I just need a jacket," I say straightening my dress. A bolt of mortification thuds through me when I have to pull the square neck into place to cover my shoulder and bra strap appropriately.

My legs tingle, like my skirt hadn't covered them right when I'd fallen, but I have no way of knowing that. I'm certainly not going to ask, and I let Elliott slide his hand into mine and lead me into the living room.

"Which jacket do you want?" He pulls open the front closet and looks inside. "Uh, I'm going to be useless here."

"Oh, this will be fun," I say. "Which one do you think is mine?"

He gives me a look filled with venom and faces the closet again. We all use it, and it's currently stuffed so full that not another thing will fit inside it. Tahlia added hooks to the back of the door, and various sweatshirts and sweaters hang from those—piled one on top of the other until another one won't stay on.

Elliott studies the various outerwear in the closet like it holds the secrets to all of the universe's mysteries. I find it absolutely adorable, and I giggle.

He turns back to me, his eyebrows drawn down. "Do I lose points if I get it wrong?"

"We're on a points system?" I scoff. "If so, I'm like, at negative-fifty for the hot chocolate spitting incident. Oh, and another fifty down for breaking a glass and splashing orange juice into your shirt." I cock my hip and fold my arms while his glare continues.

"And what's fainting worth? Negative one hundred?" I nod to the closet. "We work together and have for years. If you can't pick out *one coat* I've worn, ever, then, yes, we might have a problem."

He growls something under his breath and faces the closet again. "This one." He pulls down a red puffer coat I've thankfully worn before. Technically, it's not mine, but it's too small for Claudia now, and I adopted it.

"Thank you," I say as I put my arm in the first sleeve. He helps me with it, I grab my purse from the couch, and we leave the Big House.

"I want to just say something," he says. "And I can confess more in the car."

"Car confessionals," I say, grinning. "We do seem to do that a lot, don't we?"

He gestures to the driveway. "My mom hasn't gotten a new car in ages."

I blink as I take in the enormous—and I mean, like-a-boat-enormous—car sitting there.

It's a gold four-door Cadillac from probably the mid-eighties, and I have no words for it.

Because it's *gold*.

Claudia would probably call it Tarnished Trumpet, and that makes me start to laugh again.

I also now know why I heard him berate himself on our phone call. No way that thing connects to a device, and I lead us down the steps to the sidewalk.

"Come on," I call over my shoulder to him. "I can't wait to ride in this thing."

ELLIOTT

I should've just rented a car. I didn't think of it until it was almost time to leave, and then I didn't have time. And Momma had made me swear up one side of my own house and down the other that I won't "wreck her car."

Honestly, this thing would only benefit from a wreck. I could so make it look like an accident too.

I open the door for Ry, and it swings out so far, I nearly get knocked down. *My word*, I think. One of us falling today is more than enough, and Ry grins in a giddy way as she slides into the car.

"Bench seat," she comments. "Nice."

I slam the door on her Cheshire Cat grin and go around the back of the Caddy. The trunk is big enough to hold at least six bodies, and my momma says the "cargo room" is one reason she's held onto this car for so long.

The truth is, my daddy bought this car for her, for her fortieth birthday, and she can't stand to let go of it.

Since I have trinkets like that too, I don't give her much grief over the metallic vehicle that takes up the entire side driveway at my house.

I get behind the wheel, the plush seats beneath me almost too soft.

"This is *nice*," Ry says with a wide grin. She's having entirely too much fun with this, and I give her my strongest glare.

"Do you want to do this or not?"

She laughs, the sound pretty and joyous and full of festive cheer. "Yes," she says. "Take me for some peppermint hot chocolate, and I want to see this Living Bethlehem that Claudia's boyfriend won't stop talking about."

"Then buckle up," I say, concentrating on the old beast as I grip the oversized steering wheel. I crank the ignition, my arm muscle cramping with the effort, and the engine sounds like a dead dinosaur coming back to life. "This is the oldest car I've ever driven."

Ry leans against the armrest, her eyes sparkling. "It has character, Elliott. You just need to embrace it. Maybe give it a name."

"A name?" I chuckle but then seriously consider the suggestion. "Maybe it should be called Gold-zilla, since this thing is a real beast." I pull out of the driveway, and she giggles, her laughter washing over the awkwardness I've been feeling with her lately.

"Gold-Zilla it is." She watches out the window at the passing houses adorned with Christmas lights, the nearly midday sunshine illuminating her face in yet even more golden hues. "We could take a detour." She grins at me, and oh, I know that look.

"To where?" I'm determined to be a little grouchy today, because both Brandon and Momma—and even my fussy feline—ganged up on me and told me I better tell Ryanne about my vision impairment. And I know I need to. I do. I just don't know where the words are.

"Over the Muffin Top."

"I thought you ate a muffin at the Big House."

"Right. A *single* muffin, and I think you know how I feel about that."

"Muffins are like potato chips," I say, because I've certainly heard Ry say it five thousand times.

"You can never eat just one," she recites with me. She laughs again, and I release some of my tension. I don't have to be a grumpy-grump. In fact, I rarely am.

"Okay." She shifts in her seat, pulling her skirt across her knees. "Car confessionals."

And my bad mood is right back. "You go first."

"I don't have anything to confess."

"You fainted not ten minutes ago. You're lucky

Gold-Zilla doesn't stop by the ER on the way to your precious mini muffins and peppermint hot chocolate."

"You wouldn't dare." Her sunshine-y smile fades by several lumens. Seriously, lumens? What thirty-three-year-old knows what a lumen is? I so need a more exciting life.

I tap the leather steering wheel with gold stitching. "Sometimes this beast drives herself." I wish, because then I wouldn't have to squint to see the sign up ahead. Around me, Gold-Zilla hums like she hasn't been driven this much in years—because she hasn't.

"Start confessing," I say.

"You're so demanding."

"Well, I'm sick and tired of being the only one spilling his guts."

"Sick and tired?" She's teasing me, her eyebrows up and her smile toothy and so irritating. "Who says that?"

"A paper salesman," I shoot at her.

"You're not a paper salesman." Her face changes, and she looks away from me. "You manage the store."

"Co-manage." I make the proper turns, because I know where Over the Muffin Top is, and I know exactly what kind of pastry Ry wants.

Gold-Zilla clunks along, the tires feeling so grippy and rumbly against the asphalt, neither of us saying anything.

Finally, Ry says, "I'm worried my parents won't like you."

I side-eye her. "Because I'm a paper salesman."

She doesn't deny it, which is as good as a confirmation.

"Or, I know..." I say, flirting with real danger now. "It's because I live with my momma, isn't it?"

Ryanne pulls in a breath and whips her attention to me. I've never been happier for a steering wheel the size of a hula hoop and really old power steering, because I really do need to exercise all my attention to drive this beast.

"You live with your mom?"

"Technically, she lives with me." I glance over to her, but I can't meet her eyes. "It's my house. I own it. She moved in a bit back." I swallow, the walls of my throat sticking to each other.

At the same time, I've just experienced a true miracle: everything in my life weighs less now. If I wasn't trapped in this death trap of a vehicle, I bet I could float right up into the sky.

"I have a cat too," I blurt out, because I want to be able to have Ry over to my house without any other surprises.

At the same time, she absolutely can never come to my house and meet Momma. At least not for another six months. Momma will positively *bury* her with questions. Or me.

"A cat?" Ry asks. "Huh. I pegged you more as a canine-person."

"Cats need less attention."

"So you like kitty cats," she teases, and I don't need to vocalize anything for her to know I do. "A male or female?"

"She's a white and gray feline named Peppermint," I say.

"How long have you had this cat, pray-tell?"

She's enjoying herself too much, but it doesn't bother me. I *want* Ry to have a good time on our dates.

"I got her for my birthday this year," I say. "A present for myself."

"So you can buy yourself anything you want for your birthday," she starts.

"No," I say. "I have a budget."

"But anything less than...a thousand dollars." She raises her eyebrows at me, and I wave for her to go on. A mistake, as Gold-zilla immediately starts to pull to the left. I hurry to grab the steering wheel again and straighten out the car.

For all my joking about crashing my mother's car, I don't actually want to do it. The consequences of that... just no. I can't afford any more vehicular trouble right now.

"So you have a thousand dollars," Ry goes on, her voice taking on a thoughtful quality now. "And you love taking little bay cruises and going to movies, and..." Her voice trails off.

"That's my life?" I ask, somewhat horrified. "Going

to movies and taking harbor cruises." Said so simply, I can see why I look up the Mars rovers every day and use the vocabulary of an eighty-year-old.

"No," Ry says. "But you could've indulged in a lot of ways—and you get a cat?"

"I don't know," I say. "Felt like a good thing at the time."

"Do you love your cat?"

"I'm not one of the Mars rovers."

"When did your mom move in?"

Okay, so maybe Momma and Ryanne will get along great. They'll just fire questions back and forth to each other, and I won't have to talk at all. No answers will be given, but it won't matter. They can somehow ask something without needing an answer.

"After I got the cat," I say.

Ry reaches over and touches my leg. I nearly jump out of my skin, and Gold-zilla gets jerked to the right. She pulls away, because she has to lean too far over just to touch me.

I right the car, embarrassment heating my face.

Then she does a most surprising thing. She unbuckles her seatbelt—and the car doesn't even beep. No warning. Nothing. Just another testament to how old it is.

She slides across the bench seat and presses right into my side. "Seems like maybe you got a cat and had your momma move in, because you were lonely."

I don't see any point in denying it. "Maybe the cat," I say, and thankfully, we both get distracted by the appearance of Over the Muffin Top, and I have to use all my muscles to get Gold-zilla to turn into the teensy parking lot at this mini-muffin shop.

Even if she asked why my mom moved in, I wouldn't be able to answer her. I muscle the behemoth of a vehicle into the lot, and thankfully, there are two spots in the corner where Gold-zilla can rest while we got get sugared up.

I sigh as I bring the car to a stop, and then I grunt as I first pull the gear shift stick forward and then push it up into park. I look over to Ry, and I don't need to say anything more about why I got Peppermint. Despite the fact that I've had several girlfriends this year, I have been very lonely. Going out with someone isn't the same as having a real relationship with them, and I lean down to touch my mouth to hers.

And dang it, my stupid mouth only kisses her for a moment before I pull back and murmur, "I'm less lonely now that I'm with you."

And there's my car confessional, when I swore I wouldn't say yet one more thing to give away more of how I feel about her.

She kisses me again, which I now know is Ry's way of confessing the things she feels without using words.

RYANNE

I'm working the registers on Wednesday when Elliott enters the store. He carries a lunchbox, a backpack, and a smile to go with his khaki pants and the usual blue Paper Trail polo.

He raises his eyebrows, but I just reach for the five-pack of scissors the customer I'm helping just put on the conveyor belt. We've had a rush of lunchtime buyers in the store today, which is a bit odd for a Wednesday, but the closer we get to Christmas, the more random the gift-buying becomes.

People are desperate to have something for all the people they forgot to buy for, and they think a new desk chair or a printer, or apparently a thirty-pack of gel pens in every color under the sun, will convince the recipient that they're valuable. Thought about. Cared for.

"You okay up here?" Elliott asks, and I nod to Mindy across the aisle.

"Check with her. She's running the checkout team today."

Elliott nods, holds my gaze for another moment that sears the air between us, and then turns to talk to our coworker. Flames blaze through my bloodstream, and I realize now how stupid I'd been to think that everything would be the same at work when so much has changed between us outside of these walls.

I have five thousand things to do in the office we share, but I can't leave my people out to dry up here. So I keep scanning items, bagging them up, and taking payments until the dressed up and suited men and women rush back to their day jobs, lame office supply Christmas gifts in tow.

The store goes dormant then, and Mindy comes around with a spray bottle to clean the counters and belts, and I step out from behind the cash computer. "I locked it down."

"Thanks, Ry," she says. "I'll make sure I get the extra stations closed down, and I'll talk to Moose when he gets here for tonight."

I grin at her, the gesture falling from my face the moment I step by her. My goal is singular: get to the office in the back, so I can talk to Elliott.

The black door beckons to me, and I manage to make it through it without getting intercepted by another problem. Of course, one of those can come through my headset at any time. That's how I got notified of the frantic business-lunch-shopping, and I'd left my own midday meal half-eaten on my desk, along with my polar water bottle.

I left the office door propped open, and Elliott hasn't closed it. He's put away his lunchbox, and he sits in front of his computer, a forty-four-ounce cup beside his mouse. That'll have Diet Mountain Dew with mango syrup in it, and he reaches for it and takes a sip as I walk behind him to my desk in the opposite corner.

"Mad lunch rush?" he asks.

"Total chaos." I sink into my chair and look at my peanut butter and honey sandwich. The bread'll be dry now, and I don't really want the rest of it. I reach for my bag of Doritos, because it's always a good time for those.

"Have you checked your email?"

He looks past the fridge that stands between our desks. "Just opened it up. Why?"

"I got approved for my holiday vacation," I say, deciding not to make a game out of this. It is my job, after all, and even if Elliott and I don't make it, I need to keep my job. "Carmen said she'd do her best to approve you too, but she has to send down a regional manager, and..." I trail off, because I don't have to say it all out loud for Elliott to get it.

"Maybe I won't be able to come with you." He turns back to his computer. "I'll appeal."

"She'll get Barry House to come," I say, though it hasn't been confirmed yet. "We might not get to go for as long, which, honestly, is just fine. But Barry will come."

Elliott sighs as he leans back in his chair. It squeals, but I've heard it so much, I'm almost immune to it. I'm totally not immune to the way my pulse picks up speed when he grins over to me.

Last week, I'd have ducked my head and buried myself in my work, determined not to let him see my crush on him. Now, I simply smile back.

"Barry will come, huh?"

"Barry is fifty-seven, single, and his sister lives in Sugar Creek," I say. "So yes, he'll come manage the store for us while we're gone, because he'll get a homecooked meal and major store points."

"But maybe not the whole time," he says.

"Right," I say. "So we'll just go whenever we can get the time off."

"Hasn't your mom already bought tickets?"

"I told her to wait, but you know how she is." He actually doesn't, as Elliott's never met my parents. But he's listened to me talk about them plenty, especially my mom.

"This should be fun," Elliott says. "Changing flights at the holidays." He focuses on his computer again, sliding into his desk, leaning forward, and squinting through his glasses. He's got the font size set so big, I can read his email from across the room. So I see the email almost before he clicks on it.

He does that, bringing my attention to it, and he says, "I got it—no, wait. I have to be back on the twenty-seventh." He keeps reading, and I'm scanning his screen too, a sentence or two behind him.

"They are sending Barry." He throws me a look. "I don't know how you knew that."

I grin, because stuff like this irritates Elliott. "Now, all we have to do is pray everyone here will forgive us for inflicting Barry upon them."

"We'll have a staff meeting," he says.

"Yeah," I say. "Yep." Because I can't even imagine running a staff meeting with him, though we've done it loads of times. But we've never done it while we're holding hands and kissing, and I honestly feel like someone has tossed me out of a plane, and I'm desperately trying to pull my parachute before I hit the ground.

Before he can tease me about using his nervous language, a loud beep comes from Elliott's desktop, and I startle forward in my chair.

Then, the very familiar strains of *Happy Birthday* fill the office. It's just instrumental, but I smile as Ell gets up and closes the office door. He pulls the cord that flips the blinds closed—and that ignites my pulse in a way it never has before.

The song continues wordlessly all the way through,

and then, as it starts again, a high-pitched, robotic voice joins in with the words of the song.

I grin and grin, Elliott's expression matching mine. He extends his hand toward me, as if asking me to dance to a really romantic song, and I gladly put my hand in his.

I laugh as he pulls me to my feet and spins me around. Then, in that expertly graceful way Ell has always possessed, he pulls me right against his chest, our smiles in perfect alignment. He lowers his hand on my back until it rests right on my hip, keeping me flush against him.

"It's not my birthday," I say.

"You didn't finish your lunch," he murmurs, his eyes drifting closed. There's something a little antiseptic about him today, like perhaps he had to go visit someone in the hospital, and all that hand sanitizer smell stuck to him. "I could run next door to get you one of those pesto chicken paninis, and you can finish your break with something warm and one of your bags of candy."

"Mm." I close my eyes and lean into his strength, his arms around me so delicious and warm and ooey-gooey-wonderful.

"I know you have birthday cake M&Ms in that special cupboard of yours."

I do, but I usually save those for someone's birthday. Everyone here at the office gets a bag of them from me on their special day, and last year for Elliott's birthday, I baked him his favorite cake—vanilla—and frosted it with pure, pure white frosting. Then, I'd taken the pastel happy birthday M&Ms and beaded them around the bottom of each tier of the cake. He's the only person I've ever made a birthday cake for, and two tiers at that.

"I actually want the black forest ones," I say. "That feels more like what I should have with a pesto chicken panini."

Elliott's laugh rumbles in his chest, but he pulls away a moment alter and leans down. "I'm going to kiss you in the office."

"Scandalous," I murmur just as his lips catch mine. I so enjoy kissing him, and while he doesn't go on and on like we have over the weekend, there is a new thrill of something forbidden by doing this here.

He pulls away after only a couple of seconds and says, "I'll go get your panini, and I'll take the headset so you can have your lunch."

"Thank you." I tuck my hands in my back pockets as he ducks out the door, pulling it closed behind him.

I turn around, like Emma or Claudia will be there, and we can squeal together at the sweetness of my new boyfriend. Of course, there's just a cream-colored cinderblock wall, but my giddy squeal still comes out. Then I reached up to the cupboard above the fridge to get down my black forest M&Ms. I have to have them shipped from Frankfurt, Germany, and they're an acquired taste.

But one of my life's missions is to try all the flavors of M&Ms, from every country I possibly can. I've never traveled overseas, but I know big companies like Mars, Incorporated create different products for different markets.

For example, the cookie dough M&Ms aren't available in the US, but I can get them from Australia. Yes, maybe I spend too much time looking at M&Ms, and way too much money having them shipped to the Big House in small town Cider Cove, South Carolina.

They just bring me so much happiness, the way the Mars rovers do for Elliott. And I have the money for my candy addiction, so it's not a problem.

"I don't need to defend myself," I say to my half-eaten sandwich as I pick it up and stuff it back into the zipper bag. I toss that into the garbage can, because we empty that every day. And by "we," I mean Elliott. He does closing procedures, and I handle all the opening items.

A knock sounds on the door, and I glance over to it as I call, "Come on in."

The door opens, revealing James, one of our shelf stockers. "Hey," he says nervously, and I straighten and face him. He's in his early twenties and has some pretty severe learning disabilities. But he works hard, and he's meticulous in his accuracy with shelving and stocking. An ideal employee, really.

"Hey, Jimmy," I say.

"Miss Luckson." He smooths his hands down the front of his shirt. "I have to talk to you about the schedule over Christmas."

I turn toward the whiteboard where the next two weeks—including over Christmas—sits. "I didn't see a time-off request from you," I say. "What's the problem?"

"I know," he says darkly. "My mom thought I had until today to submit the time-off form, though I told her seventeen times it needed to be in last week."

I give him a smile, not doubting the seventeen times he told his mom. "If I can move things around, I will." I nod to the wall with all the employee names, all the jobs they do, and when they're scheduled to work. This is my Monday project every other week, and then I have to deal with employees when stuff like this comes up, family emergencies, personal sickness, and countless other things.

"We're going to my grandparents' house for the holidays, and I can't work Christmas Eve."

"Just Christmas Eve?" I focus in on that day. Elliott and I will fly out the day before that, and I sincerely hope no one comes down with anything—like a sudden invitation to dinner—for the days we're gone.

Thankfully, the store closes at three p.m. on

Christmas Eve. Elliott wouldn't have worked that day anyway, and he asked for the day off after Christmas, which he usually handles, as I bear the responsibility before the holiday.

"Yes, ma'am," he says. "I know you've got me scheduled for a few hours after we close, to get things ready for our Boxing Day sales."

"Yeah," I say. "But I can probably get Miles to come in, or maybe the holiday manager..." I'm musing now, and Jimmy doesn't need to hear any of this.

I turn to him as I pluck his name from the whiteboard. "I'll work it out. Don't worry about it. You can have that day off." I smile and tuck the slip of plastic in my pocket. "Do you need the day off after Christmas?"

"No, we're going on the twenty-second, and I didn't get scheduled except for Christmas Eve. We're coming home on Christmas Day, so I'm good for the day after."

"Great." I smile at him. "Thanks for letting me know so early."

Jimmy nods, his bushy eyebrows pulled down. He's dark from head to toe, with boxy shoulders that narrow to his skinny frame. "Thank you." He turns on his toe and leaves the office, pulling the door closed behind him.

"You bet," I say to the closed door, nothing going to ruin my amazing mood. I pull his name out of my pocket and turn back to the whiteboard. I definitely need a stocker for Christmas Eve, but the solution is easy.

"Joey." I pull my phone out of my pocket and send

him a text. If he can't do it, I can ask Miles, but he's already working a lot the week before Christmas.

That done, I settle at my desk and wait for my best-friend-slash-boyfriend to return with my panini. Maybe I can kiss him again, and that thought has me grinning from ear to ear.

ELLIOTT

THE AIR SMELLS LIKE FRESHLY PRINTED PAPER AND a hint of something far more delicious. I'm pretty sure it's the pesto chicken panini I'm carrying back to Ry, but it could be the lingering scent of her strawberry lip gloss still attached to my mouth. Mindy also likes to burn cinnamon-scented candles at the registers, and that smell makes my stomach pitch.

Now that I've thought of it, all I can smell is pesto, chicken, bread, and that sickeningly sweet-spicy Christmas cinnamon garbage back by the registers. The store does seem unusually busy today, but I'm a pro at navigating aisles to avoid anyone who might impede my progress toward the back office. A superhero feat, really, considering my vision issues.

My heartbeat thuds strangely in my chest, landing at the bottom and then pausing before it rebounds up again. I'm going to have to tell Ry about the encounter at the deli on the other side of the parking lot, even if the thought sends fear through me. Just a little.

One, the woman there—someone Ryanne has gushed over before named Lareesh—totally hit on me today. I guess she has in the past, but I've never noticed it until today. Until I imagined how Ry would react had she been at my side. Until she'd been so mad over the weekend about me even talking to those other women at the Christmas movie date-night, where we only stayed for ten minutes.

Two, I may or may not have told Lareesh that Ry and I were going to New York for Christmas. Together. Because we're together. The shock flowing from the other woman still sits in my throat the wrong way. And her words—*Oh, I didn't realize you and Ryanne were more than friends*—echo in my ears, my brain, and down to my toes.

Yeah, I didn't realize it either, until I did. And now she knows, which means it won't be long before everyone does.

"We have to have a staff meeting," I mutter, because the last thing I want to do is have an individual conversation about my relationship with Ryanne with every employee at Paper Trail.

The black door leading into the back of the store looms ahead, and I only have a few more steps until I'm home-free. I remind myself that we're at work, and I can't have a romantic lunch date with Ry the way I have the past several days. We do actually have work to do.

I make it through the black door and quickly stride around the corner—and very nearly ram into the closed office door. To save my nose from becoming bloody, I have to sacrifice the panini, and I grunt and groan as the soft sandwich smashes into the very solid door.

Multiple swears go through my head, all of them in the robotic voices of the Mars rovers. Leave it to me to try to juggle walking and carrying lunch, like that's a hard thing to do. I swear, everything I do ends with me wearing some sort of food product, along with a side of embarrassment.

"The panini isn't all over you," I mutter, though my hand definitely feels greasier than it had a moment ago. I fumble for the doorknob, finally grabbing it with my non-panini'ed hand, and practically falling into the room.

As I finally settle confidently in the office, I hold up the panini. Ryanne sits at her desk, blinking at me with wide eyes. "Wow," she says, her smile slowly crawling across her face. "Great entrance."

I grin, holding up the smashed bag like I've just run a marathon and come in first. "Chicken pesto panini, extra-pressed." I glance away, because surely she heard me ram the door only ten feet from where she's sitting.

"Did you get your discount?" she teases, her dark

ponytail falling over her shoulder as she leans forward to take her mutilated lunch. "Was Lareesh there?"

"No discount." I'd forgotten in the wake of all the flirting. "And yes, she was." I pass over the bag and hold my head high as I spin my desk chair around so I can sit. "And she totally hit on me, and I pretty much blurted out that you and I are dating."

"Ell."

I hate it when she gasps my name like that. Like I've just done something I'll never recover from. "We need to have a staff meeting. Or an office-wide memo sent out. Something."

"Yeah," she whips back at me. "Something."

"Did you think we wouldn't tell anyone here?" I throw her plenty of fire in my side-eyed look. I don't even know what work needs to be done right now. The scent of the panini is all mixed up with the chocolate and cherry-something of her M&Ms, which is all masked by Ry's rose-petally skin cream. I want to open the door, but I don't want the conversation to leak out of the office.

"Of course we're going to tell people."

"Should probably do it then," I say.

She grins, the corners of her mouth lifting into that smile that lights up her whole face. She takes out the smashed panini and unwraps it without comment. It seriously looks like I strangled it on the way across the parking lot.

"Well, you're doing a fantastic job of embracing the chaos our lives have become."

"Embracing chaos is my middle name," I say, nodding toward her desk. "Where did you put the headset?"

She's now staring at the panini like it's turned into a python. "What happened to this?"

"Oh, it's fine." I snatch it from her and wrap the white paper around it to hold it all together. Some of the chicken and cheese and pesto *has* seeped outside the edges of the bread. I take a big bite and go, "Mm, yes, this is so good," all around the food.

"You're going to eat my lunch?" Her midnight eyes shine with stars, and I hold it out to her while I finish my bite. She rolls her chair closer, but I pull the panini back.

"We have to send an email today about our relationship and the fact that there will be a temporary manager here over the holidays."

She sobers too, but none of the brightness in her gaze dims. "Fine."

"Those usually come from you, but I can draft it if you want." I don't know why I want the store to know about me and Ry, but I do. I want the world to know.

"You draft it," she says. "Now let me have a bite of my own lunch."

"That I bought." Grinning, and with a dose of heat flowing through my bloodstream, I hold the panini out to her, and she leans forward, her eyes never leaving mine. The whole room is going to light on fire at any moment, what with the fizzing flames between us. Finally, she takes a generous bite, her eyes closing in bliss.

A moan fills her chest, then the air, and my word, my skin breaks out in a sweat.

"Okay, this is delicious," she admits, her mouth full. "Even smushed like that."

"I aim to please," I say, trying to sound suave, but it comes out more like a lame pickup line.

She swallows, everything about her turning a little harder, a little colder. "Just remember that when we're in New York." Her eyebrows go up, all Miss Bossy Pants now. "I expect you to be just as charming when we meet my family."

"Oh, I will be," I assure her, though a twinge of nerves flares up in my stomach. "Just as long as you keep the M&Ms coming."

"Deal," she replies, and her smile softens as she swallows. "But seriously, I'm a little nervous about introducing you."

"Why? I'm not that scary." And I've met my previous girlfriend's parents before. Several times. I'm actually really great at parties.

She scoffs and lifts her panini again. "You have no idea how terrifying you can be."

"For your parents? Your siblings?" I do the scoffing now. "They won't be afraid of me."

"This isn't about that." She scoots over to her desk, and I recognize her way of hiding behind the fridge.

"It's about you being afraid to be with me." I fold my arms.

"No," she shoots at me, along with a venomous look.

I shrug, trying to keep the mood light, but there's a heaviness in my chest I can't quite shake. "I'm going for you, Ry, and you alone. I don't care what they think of me. It's going to be great." I turn to focus on drafting that email, because then I won't have to acknowledge the sting in my chest or the fact that she's blurred slightly now that she's further away.

After a few minutes with only the sound of my fingers tapping keys and the occasional shuffle of panini paper, she says, "My mom's lasagna is legendary. You'll love it."

"Lasagna, huh? That sounds promising. I hope she doesn't expect me to cook, though."

"We do a cookie baking contest." She sighs in an absolutely miserable way, and I force myself to keep working.

"Good thing you can read a recipe," I say. "Since I can barely make toast."

"It'll be fine," she says in that way that tells me she's trying to convince herself as much as me. "Anna will win. She wins every year, but don't worry. She's *not* my daddy's favorite." The last line is delivered with precise sarcasm that actually makes me smile.

"So we'll blow it on purpose," I say casually. "Try to make the most outlandish cookie on the planet, that will never possibly work."

She giggles and adds, "And we'll have to go around to like, sixteen different stores to find each specialty ingredient."

"Yep." I chuckle too. "Who cares if you win a family baking contest?"

"Don't say that out loud when we get there, okay?"

I mime zipping my lips, mostly because I'm about to blurt out another embarrassing thing. *I just want to be good enough for you.*

But there's no way I'm vocalizing that. Nope. Nada. Not happening.

Someone pounds on the door as it opens, and I jump in my seat. "Holy horses," I say, mimicking one of the old Mars rovers who no longer functions, as I spin in my chair. "What's the emergency, Darcy?"

She glares at me and then Ryanne, who has likewise frozen with her panini in mid-air. "I've called on the headset seventy-four times about a manager return." She surveys the office again, and I wonder what she sees. "What are you guys doing in here?"

"I'm coming," I say as I jump to my feet. I swipe the headset from Ry's desk before I turn to follow the dark blonde woman who's still swirling with a storm. "Hey, Ry," I call over my shoulder. "Check out that email when you finish lunch, okay?"

"Yes, sir," she parrots to me, but I hear the notes of disgust in her voice. She's not technically my boss, and I'm not hers, and we've always worked really well together.

I can't help it if I want things out in the open. We went from fake to real really fast, and I'm here for it. I want it.

I want her to know I'm here for it and want everyone to know about us. As I approach the customer service counter, where a disgruntled man in his fifties literally taps his toe at me, a voice rises within me.

I can't silence it while I type in my manager PIN and start his return-longer-than-thirty-days. I smile through the wail that starts in my gut and hand the gentleman his receipt.

"Thanks," Darcy says, lifting something from the printer.

"Yeah," I say. "Yep." My sign of nerves, because I know the real reason I want everyone to know about me and Ry is because I can't keep another secret from everyone. The things I'm hiding are heavy enough as it is.

And that's when the little voice becomes a shout as it says, *You better tell Ry the real reason your momma moved in before you go to Upstate New York.*

EMMA

ABOVE ME, THE FURNACE BLOWS SOFTLY AS I arrange the last of the holiday bouquets at Pretty in Petals. The scent of fresh eucalyptus and lavender seeps out of the back room, where I've left the door open as I brought out the prearrangements, mingling with the faint hint of vanilla birthday cake from the candles I've lit. I think a first impression takes place within the nose, and if a shop smells nice, people feel more welcome, will stay longer, and have a tendency to spend more.

I've only owned Pretty in Petals for a couple of months, and I've poured everything I have into this place. Literally every last dime, every spare minute, every ounce of strength. Fresh flowers naturally smell pretty good, though there are some varieties that don't have a pleasant smell, but I include a stick of vanilla incense in every arrangement that goes out the door, and my repeat customers come back more and more often with that simple change.

"There's just something magical about vanilla." I smile at my holiday displays, because I'm hosting the first-ever weekend floral fest in only one more day. All holiday pre-arrangements will be thirty percent off, and I have forty of them prepped. I've bought advertising on the radio, the Cider Cove Gazette, and in the flyers for the Christmas Festival, which is happening now, just down the street in the main square.

I've put flyers at several local businesses around town too, and I'm hoping to sell out of my pre-arranged flowers—and book up to thirty more before next Friday's holiday. After all, no table is ever fully dressed until there are flowers. They don't have to just be for funerals and Valentine's Day, though I'm already gearing up for that holiday—only seven weeks from now.

I pull out my phone and take some shots of the holiday display, being sure to get my wide splays for big family tables. "The display for this weekend's sale is ready," I say as my fingers fly over the keyboard on my screen. I add the details of the sale, and post to all my social media.

Satisfied and happier than I've been in a while, I lower my phone, a smile already on my face as the front door of the shop opens. "...in here, Mrs. Grindstaff," a man says. But an older woman hobbles through the doorway, her face set on Do Not Talk To Me Or I'll

Claw Your Face Off. I should know, because I was raised by a granny who wore this expression perpetually.

Still, my smile remains, because I love Grams with everything I have, and I can't wait to host her at the Big House for Christmas this year. We're actually having dinner at the house next door, where Aaron Stansfield lives. Hillary and Liam are coming from California and everything.

And Aaron himself walks into my shop next. Our eyes meet over Mrs. Grindstaff's head, and his smile lights the whole block. "Hey, Emma," he says. His light brown hair is tousled just right—probably done by the December wind—and I swear I've lost hours in his hazel eyes. They remind me of a forest—dark pine trees and shadows—and I seriously could wander around in them for a while.

He's wearing blue jeans and his bulky workman's boots, along with a dark gray sweatshirt that says *Stansfield Tools* across the front of it. He leans against the doorframe like he owns the place, which he practically does since his hardware store is right next door. "I found Mrs. Grindstaff next door, trying to pick up her floral arrangement."

With some difficulty—and a stern self-reminder that I am not feasting on males at the moment—I turn my attention to the white-haired woman between us. "Did you have a call-in order?"

"My daughter did it." She says this like having a daughter is the worst thing on the planet.

My smile doesn't slip. "What's the name?" Part of me wants to reach out and extend my hand to her, like she'll need help following me to the register near the rear of the store.

"Lucy Simons."

"Let me check." I've had a lot of orders for the holidays, and I walk back to the register, fully expecting Aaron to leave and Mrs. Grindstaff to follow. Her cane bumps along the floor, and I'm sure she's chased innocent children off her lawn, that staff waving angrily as she bellows at them not to come back.

And right at her side—Aaron. For some reason, the fact that he didn't leave throws me a little, and my mind blanks on the name she gave me. One, two, three terrible seconds pass, where I fear I'll have to show her how forgetful I am, before the name flies into my mind again.

"Lucy," I practically shout, now tapping on my tablet. The name comes up, thankfully—I really don't want to know what Mrs. Grindstaff would've done had it not—and I see she just ordered a couple of hours ago. My pulse flutters in my chest. "Oh, this arrangement isn't due for pick-up until Tuesday."

I look at Mrs. Grindstaff. "Were you supposed to...?" I trail off as the lines between her eyes deepen with her frown. I'm in so much trouble, because I really don't handle conflict very well. I'm a peacemaker, if Grams is to be believed, and it takes me a long time of knowing someone before I feel comfortable disagreeing with them.

"She said she ordered flowers," the older woman growls, and I'm not sure I've heard a female speak like that before.

"Yes, she did." I throw a look to Aaron. "For a Tuesday pick-up. Most people order them so they're really fresh for their parties."

"When is your family party, Mrs. Grindstaff?" he asks, taking some of the pressure from me. He holds my gaze, which I hope broadcasts my gratitude, for a moment before looking at her.

She actually stomps her cane on my hardwood floors, and I imagine the flowers and plants shrinking back in fright. I certainly jump. "She said she ordered flowers."

"Yes," Aaron says without missing a beat. He doesn't sound placating either. "But when does she need them? Today?"

"How should I know?"

"How about we call her?" Aaron's eyebrows go up, his smile starshine-bright. He looks at me, and I'm already reaching for the phone. With the number ringing, I extend the phone to him. He takes it and hands it to Mrs. Grindstaff.

Aaron steps closer to the check-out counter, his expression twinkling like fool's gold. I shake my head, trying to suppress the fluttering in my stomach. I am not dating right now. I'm not. I've had enough of men taking advantage of me, or me falling head-over-heels in love on the first date and getting my heart flattened.

Nope. I just need my flowers right now; not a man.

"It smells great in here," he says, glancing around. "Looks amazing too."

"Thanks," I reply, basking in the compliment—and not just because it came from him. "I'm hoping to sell out this weekend and book a bunch more pick-ups for next week before Christmas."

"Speaking of Christmas," he says, reaching for a pen I've wrapped with floral tape and made to look like a sunflower. "Are you going to the Christmas Festival tonight? I heard there's going to be a big tree lighting."

"I was thinking about it," I admit, though the thought of being around a crowd right now feels daunting. I've been avoiding social events lately, mostly due to the fact that I've worn all of Lizzie's cutest modeling clothes, it's super windy in the evenings, and I don't have anyone tall, hazely, and handsome to hold hands with. "I might just stay in and binge-watch holiday movies instead."

"It might be fun," he insists, his hazel eyes sparkling with mischief. "You can't spend the whole season hiding in the Big House."

"Why not?" I ask, my voice tinged with frustration.

"You can't tell me you want to stand in the cold with a bunch of people you don't know."

"If we go together, we'll be...together." His smile falls, and my heartbeat lurches against the thin walls of my veins. Is he asking me out?

"We don't need the flowers until Tuesday," Mrs. Grindstaff flings the phone at me. Yes, tosses it into the air as if I'm expected to catch it. I yelp; my hands fly up; I actually close my eyes. There's no way in the Garden of Eden I'm catching that phone, and I fully expect it to clobber me in the nose. Which will start gushing blood, and I'm already embarrassed as my fingers flap against empty air.

"Well, she's fifty shades of cranky," Aaron says, and my eyes fly open again. He's holding the phone and watching as Mrs. Grindstaff plunk-steps her way out of the flower shop. He turns his attention back to me, his adorable smile hitched back in place. He holds up the phone—a clunky, cordless thing that came with the flower shop.

I take it from him with a huff, which only causes him to laugh. "You looked like you were fanning butterflies," he says, his voice a bit tight. In the next moment, he bursts into laughter, and it's so much easier to reinforce my male fast when getting laughed at, even if Aaron is all kinds of good-looking and exactly my type.

"I don't suppose you're going to buy the rest of my poinsettias, are you?" I fold my arms and cock my eyebrows at the sexy hardware store owner. Well, almost-owner. He's taking over the shop from his daddy on January first, which is only a couple of weeks from now.

"No," he says. "But you owe me big for not ordering any this year and pushing everyone here instead."

"I owe you big, huh?"

"Tree lighting?" He actually smiles while asking again.

I don't want to dash his hopes. I don't want to watch him walk away, his tail tucked between his legs. I gesture for him to follow me into the back room. "Have you got a sec?"

"Depends," he says, but he steps behind the counter and comes with me. The back room is fifteen degrees cooler than the front of the shop, because this is where I keep all my fresh flowers before I arrange them into works of art. I usually wear a sweater or sweatshirt, and sometimes gloves, when I'm working back here for an extended amount of time.

"If you stay and help me get five more arrangements done," I say, indicating the vases up on the top shelf— where I can't reach. "I'll bring the bread pudding to Christmas dinner."

"I like how this sounds," he says slowly. "But it doesn't have 'tree lighting' anywhere in it." He clears his throat and moves over to the shelving that holds the vases. "It wouldn't be a date. I just want to feel like I'm getting out of the house, doing something festive."

"Do you have a tree in your house?"

"Not yet." Aaron reaches up and gets down the first vase. "Liam says there's stuff in the attic, but...I haven't had the gumption to get it down yet."

"So..." I take the vase from him and set it on the counter behind me. I like to line them up and let them talk to me about which kind of flowers they'd like to house. "Maybe we can just do a tree lighting at your place. I'll come over." I face him again, take another vase, and meet his eyes. I don't think he likes me as more than a friend, and I grab onto that idea. Of course I can be friends with a man. I *should* be friends with men.

"We'll get your place completely decorated and ready for Christmas dinner," I say with a smile. "Except for the flowers, of course."

"And you'll bring those—with the bread pudding?" He hands me another vase, and I turn to put down the pair I'm holding.

"Yes," I say decisively. "Five flower arrangements, and I'll come over tonight to help light your tree."

"Oh, boy." Aaron laughs again, the sound so free and so loud in this small room.

"That's not what I meant," I say as I swat his bicep.

He's good-natured and funny, and he lifts down the remaining two vases and puts them on the counter while he finishes chuckling. "I can order dinner or put in one of my sister's freezer meals. Come by around seven?"

"And it's not a date?"

"Not a date," he agrees. "I know you're not dating right now. I think I just need an excuse to try to enjoy the holidays. Things feel...hectic."

I nod, because when you own a retail establishment, the holidays definitely feel hectic. "Seven is great, and I don't care what we eat for dinner."

"Great." He sweeps into my personal space, one hand landing on my lower back as his lips brush my cheek. "See you at seven." With that, he leaves the cold storage room, which suddenly feels like it might burst into flames.

I've known Aaron for a while now, and never once—not one time—has he kissed me hello or good-bye. "It's a Southern thing to do," I tell myself as reason starts to fill my head again. "He said it wasn't a date."

But sometimes, men say one thing and think another. Ask me how I know.

RYANNE

THE PLANE TOUCHES DOWN WITH A JOLT, AND I GRIP the armrest tightly. I so hate flying, and while I've come home loads of times since I broke ranks and moved South, this time, it's different. I'm not just heading to a destination, where freshly baked ham and pumpkin pie await; I'm about to introduce Elliott to my entire family.

I can already hear the warbling sound of a drone, as my mom will no doubt hover around me and Elliott, throwing out a new question every other breath. He's told me he's used to a lot of questions. "No one beats my momma," he'd said with a chuckle. Still, I have a feeling mine will give his a run for her money.

"Welcome to Albany," the flight attendant announces, her voice crackling over the intercom, and I slowly let out the air I've trapped in my lungs. I turn to Elliott next to me, his dark eyes sparkling with excitement. He's been uncharacteristically quiet during the flight, but now I can see the corners of his mouth twitching upward in a smile.

"Ready?" he asks, his voice low and smooth, like warm honey.

"Not even close," I admit, glancing out the tiny window at the gray skies and the blanket of white snow covering the ground below. It's beautiful in a way that makes me remember why I had a good childhood, but it also reminds me of how different Upstate New York is from Cider Cove, South Carolina.

How different Elliott and I are going to be from everyone else. "You're going to hate me by the time we fly home."

He easily brushes his hand through his dark hair as the plane slows further. "I've survived worse."

"I'm sure you have," I say, rolling my eyes. "But this is—they can be... intense."

"You've told me all of this already." He takes my hand in his, his long fingers curling around all of mine. "Ry, it's going to be fine. We're still going to be friends after this, I promise."

I have told him about how my mom will be bouncing around like a small dog who's ingested crack-cocaine, and my dad walks around like he's got royal blood flowing in his veins. And I spent an hour the other night telling him about how Anna, who is the favorite and wins everything, has to one-up everyone in the family at every turn. It's like an infectious disease she can't control.

I nod, but I can't shake the nervousness curling around my stomach like a snake. I've wanted this for so long—a real relationship with Elliott—but now that it's here, it feels like the stakes have been raised. "I hope so. I just don't want to explain anything about when we started dating."

"Why not just tell them the truth?" he asks, quirking that sexy single eyebrow. "You know, that you've had three or four crushes on me this year, and you finally said yes to a date."

What he's saying is absolutely ridiculous. "I should've never told you about the crushes." I roll my eyes as he laughs, and I'm reminded of how happy-go-lucky he is and how kitty-cat-diva I am.

"Just stating facts, Ry." The chime sounds, and it's like a massive rush of unclicking metallic sounds as everyone races to be the first one unbuckled and standing in the aisle.

Elliott sits there like he's going to stay on the plane and return to Charleston instead of sticking by my side for the next several days.

My mother has already sent me an itinerary for the festivities happening in the Luckson family over the next several days.

Tomorrow is Christmas tree cutting, like, in the woods and everything. *Snowy* woods.

We always bake Christmas cookies on Christmas Day itself, after we have Belgian waffles with strawberries and cream, buttermilk syrup my sister will brag about at least fourteen times before she places a heated carafe of it in the middle of the table, and bacon.

Okay, fine, my mouth waters over the bacon.

The door of the plane opens, and that causes another round of excitement. I take a deep breath, ready to face whatever comes next. "All right," I say. "Let's do this."

If we make it through Christmas, my sisters, mom, and I will go shopping on Boxing Day, which this year, falls on a Saturday.

Sunday, we'll sleep late, go to church, and spend the afternoon making flavored popcorns, because my brother-in-law owns the largest flavored popcorn company in the country. Maybe Canada too. No matter what, it's a lot more than what Elliott and I do at Paper Trail.

Monday is my normal day off, so my leave got approved through Tuesday, and Elliott and I will fly home that afternoon. It's a short flight, and we don't have to cross any time zones, so we booked a late afternoon flight to be home at a decent time for me to get to work the next morning.

Elliott doesn't have to work Tuesdays, a fact I've been counting on for him to stay my friend. He'll have an extra day to recover, a whole day to himself after the craziness of spending twenty-four-seven with me for the next five days.

Not twenty-four-seven, I tell myself. Elliott will have the guest house all to himself, and he'll be able to escape from the Luckson Lunacy any time he needs to.

I won't have the same luxury, but I'm used to the insanity of my family. Sort of.

We gather our bags and shuffle toward the exit when it's our turn, the anticipation buzzing in the air. As we leave the plane and step onto the jetway, the cold air hits me like a blast from an industrial freezer.

I shiver. "Welcome to New York," I mutter, pulling my coat tighter around me.

"Feels breezy," Elliott says over his shoulder, and thankfully, I don't have to respond as we file up the jetway and into the terminal. "I've never been here before," he says once we're in the airport. "We go..."

"This way to baggage claim," I say, and I step slightly in front of him, as I've been here loads of times.

I lead the way through the busy, holiday-traveler airport, dodging families, strollers, and cleaning carts. "It's only about forty-five minutes to my parents' house," I say once we arrive at baggage claim.

Elliott doubles over and sucks at the air. "Are we trying to win a race?"

"Oh, stop it," I say. "You walk twice as fast as me."

"Not like that." He straightens and grins at me. "That was im-press-ive."

I look over to him and fix on my best eagle eyes. "Maybe my mom will time us."

He blinks and then starts to laugh. "You're not kidding."

"I wish." I glance at the offensive baggage claim, which has not started to spit out luggage yet, and then over to the restrooms. "I'm going to go to the bathroom and then get in line for the rental car."

"I'll get the bags," he says, and I take the first step away when he adds, "Wait. There's no way I can roll your bag around as if it's mine."

I turn toward him, my irritation and nerves combining into a dangerous cocktail. "What is wrong with my bag?" I ask evenly.

His smile is so dangerous—to my health and my heart. I also want to scratch it off his face. "It's bright purple with even brighter—neon—bubbles all over it."

"Yes," I say without moving my lips or even parting my teeth. "I'll see you over by the Enterprise counter." With that, I walk away, because my luggage is *cute*, and I'm not going to let my best friend, boyfriend, or any combination of the two degrade it. Plus, I need to go to the bathroom in a decent way, and maybe I jetted here in an attempt to text my mom that *yes! We're already at baggage claim!*

I don't know why I keep playing my mother's games. I need to take a page out of Elliott's book and make up my own. I don't have to follow her rules anymore. I don't have to race from my plane to her house in less than an hour. I can stop for coffee if I want to. Elliott and I can go to dinner.

My stomach clenches as the thought of showing up at my parents' house un-hungry, because I can guarantee Momma will have a feast on the table, waiting for us.

I still want some McDonald's fries, so I can go into the house in a better mood.

Twenty minutes later, I find Elliott sitting on a bench with his bag right in front of him and mine... loitering a few feet away, like someone might come by and grab it, ridding him of the fuchsia nuisance.

"Ready?" I ask.

Elliott looks up from his phone, and he's removed his glasses. For a moment, he seems so pure, so out of the moment, somewhere inside his head. "Good?"

"Yes," I say, holding up the key to the midsize SUV I rented for this trip. Both of my sisters and my brother said they'd come pick us up at the airport, but then we'd be trapped at the mansion, solely relying on my family for every single thing.

Trust me, a car is absolutely necessary. The way the wind howls down the sidewalk just outside the airport is so not, and I bend my head into the gale as we make our way to the appointed parking stall.

"It's that bright blue one," I say. "Can you handle the color of it?" I shoot him a pointed look, but he only smiles.

"Cars can be any color."

"I never have a problem finding my suitcase," I say as she rumbles along nicely beside me.

I let him put our baggage in the back as I get behind the wheel and adjust the seat, the steering wheel, the air, and the radio.

Elliott gets in the passenger seat beside me, looks at me, and then reaches for me.

"Don't be so stressed, kitty-cat," he whispers just before he kisses me. I can definitely get used to this type of delay, and I kiss him back until my phone shrills out my mother's text notification.

He pulls back too, and we both look down at my device. The text swishes away before I can truly read it, and I sigh as I look out the window. "We've been summoned."

"Let's join the royal party," Elliott says, and I fall in a little bit in love with him with those simple words.

ELLIOTT

"Wow," I say in a drawn out, over-exaggerated way. This isn't just a house. It's a whole...property. Estate. Something.

"I told you," she says, both hands gripped tightly on the steering wheel.

She has told me her parents are rich. Her dad works for a huge tech company here in the valley, and I've seen big houses and wealthy people before. Ryanne has just never struck me as anyone who once lived this way.

Maybe there's a reason why she doesn't live here anymore. And it's probably got something to do with the fountain in the circle drive, the perfectly spaced and hung Christmas lights on every edge of the house, and the individual stones in the driveway.

The driveway has those expensive lights along it, as do the upper story windows. Several cars are parked out front, and Ry navigates expertly and takes a spot between a full-sized SUV and a minivan.

"That's my sister's van," she says dryly. "Though she only has one child. She says it's way easier to load up a baby in a minivan, so my brother-in-law traded in her BMW."

"That's nice of him," I say mildly. I haven't been nervous about meeting Ry's family until this moment. But the thought of me walking into that mansion...I tell myself someone doesn't have to have money to be important and valuable, and that allows me to get my seatbelt unbuckled.

Ry, however, doesn't move, and I collect my backpack from the backseat and go around to her door. I open it and say, "You can't stay out here. I'm not going in there alone, and I don't think it's cold enough on this planet to keep your whole family inside."

She looks at me, and I offer her my best smile. "Come on. It won't be that bad." Even if I think it might be like walking into a ravenous lion's den.

I take her hand and help her out of the car, and she says, "Leave the bags. My brother will come get them."

"All right." Part of me wants to get the suitcases anyway, but I don't want to argue with anyone. Whatever anyone says for the next five days, I'm just going to do.

The double-wide front doors open as we walk up the

ornately bricked steps, and cheer, noise, and soft light spills out onto the porch.

"Oh, it's Ry," a woman says, and Ry jogs up the last couple of steps and into her mom's arms. Grace is smiling, and I attach the same gesture to my face too.

Her mother hasn't come outside even one inch, and Ry falls back to indicate me. "Momma," she says. "You remember Elliott."

"Of course." Her mom extends her arms toward me, but she doesn't move her feet. It's clear I'm to go to her, so I do. I give her a quick hug and a Southern kiss on both cheeks before I step back.

"Thank you so much for having me this Christmas," I say as diplomatically as possible.

"It's freezing in here," someone yells from further in the house, and that gets us to move the welcome wagon inside. With the final clicks of the door behind me, I definitely feel a tiny bit untethered.

Then Ry's hand slips into mine, and I'm completely anchored. I don't know if that means I'm falling for her, but I definitely feel something for her I haven't felt for anyone else before.

I squint as we go through the wide foyer, past a dark office, a closed pair of doors on the right, and into an enormous living area.

The family room holds two full-size couches, along with a pair of recliners, and a cushy-looking beanbag chair where a couple cuddles together.

The woman is clearly related to Ryanne, as is the one in the kitchen, wearing a dark blue apron without a single smudge on it. Beyond them, a man wears a pair of slacks with a pale blue business shirt with the sleeves rolled up mid-way on his forearms.

It feels like a scene from a movie called *Christmases of the Rich and Famous*, and Ry and I so don't belong.

"Daniel will get your bags and put them in the guest house," Grace says. "You did get my text about the shuffled sleeping arrangements, didn't you?"

"No," Ry says, dropping my hand so she can pick up a tiny dill pickle from an appetizer tray sitting on the end of the bar. "I can take my bag upstairs after dinner."

"Daniel will put it in the guest house." Her mother won't look at her, and Ry has frozen with food in her hand. Not just food. Pickles.

I swallow hard, my eyes flitting all over, trying to take in all the victims before Ry starts raging.

"I'm sorry?" she asks oh-so-politely. "I'm not staying upstairs in my old bedroom? I always stay upstairs in my old bedroom."

"I sent you a text about all of this," her mother says, clearly too busy using a pair of tongs to stir the salad—very attention-consuming, mixing lettuce and tomatoes together—to look over to us.

"Don't worry," Anna says, her smile hitched a little crookedly now. "Rob went out to get it warm a bit ago."

Ryanne looks at me. "I'm feeling a little like I need to get freshened up before dinner."

"It'll be ready in ten minutes," Anna says.

"I forgot to go start the fire," Rob says.

My focus gets thrown from person to person as they all talk right on top of one another. All I can think is, *Fire? The guest house requires a fire?*

With all this money, you'd think the Lucksons could afford a furnace.

"You took forever coming from the airport," her mom says. "I'm surprised you didn't freshen up there."

Ry stuffs the rest of her pickle in her mouth, picks up a handful more, and spears me with a look. "We need a minute."

She indicates me and says, "Everyone, this is Elliott. We'll do formal intros once we *freshen up* out in the guest house that we're now sharing because I got kicked out of the bedroom I always sleep in when I come home."

"Ryanne," her sister says, and her dad simply smiles as she marches toward him. "Hey, Dad." She hugs him without letting go of my hand, and then she takes me past the huge dining room table set with real gold chargers and fresh poinsettias and little cardinals that look like they could be real.

I think she'll go out the sliding glass door, but she's in hurry-up mode again, and it's all I can do to keep up.

She opens another door—a regular door that leads

out of the house and onto a sidewalk that parallels the patio.

The snow has been cleared here, so someone did something in anticipation of our arrival, and I find my stride the further we go. It's dark now, so I don't even try to look around and take everything in. It's too much work for my eyes anyway, so I focus on the destination— a bright light hanging above another door on a luxury shed.

"Is that the guest house?" I ask.

"Yes," Ryanne clips out. "And 'house' is a generous term."

"Good to know this is where I was always going to be staying," I quip.

She yanks open the door like she wants to rip it off the hinges—and she dang near succeeds. "It's like a shed. My dad even stores the wood out here." She takes a couple of steps inside and comes to a complete stop. "Yep. There it is."

A legit stack of chopped wood sits there, right against the wall, next to the door. "Easy retrieval for the house," I say, my voice pitching up too much.

The interior is about twice the size of my house, with a galley kitchen to my right that clearly never gets used— and it won't on this trip either.

A pair of mismatched couches stands in front of me, and the floor is one of those painted and sealed cement jobs, with paths of rugs across it leading to the bed in the corner.

A king-size bed.

A *singular* king-size bed. I may be going blind, but with every sweep of the guest house, I fail to see another bed.

I definitely hear Ry as she stomps away from me and says, "I can't believe I've been downgraded to the guest house."

She picks up a pillow and throws it. "It's like a *shed*, not a house. A *storage shed* for all the stuff my mom doesn't want anymore but also can't part with."

"And it's freezing," I say as I bring the door closed behind me. I suddenly know why this place needs a fire, as I spot the potbellied stove close to the bed and behind the couches.

"Freshen up," Ry mutters, and she opens a door, goes into the room beyond, and slams it behind her.

I've seen her mad before, so I know she'll calm down. Besides, she's not mad at me, so... I wander over to the bed, and my fantasies start to rage. Maybe I'll get to lie here and hold her while she complains about her mom. Or maybe she'll make me sleep on one of the couches that look like no one has ever sat on them.

"Knock, knock," someone says, and Daniel enters, pushing our baggage in front of him. "Dude, yeah, it's cold in here. Sorry about that."

He rolls the bags over to the couch, and then extends

his hand toward me. "Great to meet you, Elliott." He smiles, and he seems nice. "I'm Danny, Ry's brother."

"Great to meet you too," I say as I shake his hand. He has more red in his hair than Ry does, but his eyes are just as dark, with his eyebrows just as overgrown.

"You want to show me how to light this thing, so we don't freeze out here?"

"Sure thing." Daniel goes and gets some wood, then kneels down and pulls a basket of smaller kindling, newspaper, and long matches toward him.

"Sorry about Anna," he says as he puts a couple of logs in the stove. It won't hold much more than that, and then he lays another one across those. "She's a little crazy about her kids."

"I thought she just had the one daughter," I say, because Ry gave me a list of her family members, and I memorized it, so it would seem like we've been together romantically for longer than we actually have.

"Yeah," Danny says. "But she's pregnant again, and that means she has to get her daughter out of her bed."

"Did you know that's why Mom has king beds every-where?" Ry practically yells the words, and I startle as much as her brother.

"Yo, sis, we're right here."

"Because Anna and James couldn't sleep in a queen with Sariah. So Mom got all kings. And this one." She marches over to it and collapses onto it. "Wasn't good enough for their room. So Mom bought another one and shunned this one out here."

I turn back to her brother, and he seems as stunned as I do. "Yeah," he says slowly, and I decide starting a fire can't be that hard. *Yeah,* I think. *You won't think that when you're freezing to death in the middle of the night and you can't get the fire going.*

But I get to my feet and turn toward my girlfriend. I know it's strange, but I find her so attractive as she sits there with that murderous look on her face.

"Don't try to cheer me up," she warns as I step toward her.

"I wouldn't dream of it." I sit next to her, and in a very-boyfriend-like move, I put my arm around her. To be fair, I've laid in her bed with her and spooned her close, so this isn't scandalous or anything.

"I'm really sorry you have to be stuck out here with me."

"You're going to hate this too," she says, nudging me with her shoulder. "This was going to be your sanctuary away from everyone. Away from me."

"Ry," I whisper. "I don't need to be away from you."

"You say that now, but just wait until dinner. Oh, and then the Christmas tree decorating. The hot chocolate bar. Or, or, or—I know! Luckson family movie night, where you can't even pick what popcorn *you* want to eat, because you don't want my dad to feel back that you don't like his gross lime-ricotta-Tobasco popcorn."

"Ry, breathe," her brother says.

But Ryanne has started, and I know how this ends: when she runs out of things on her mind, and the woman never stops thinking.

It's one of the things I like best about her.

So I simply pull her against my chest and kiss her forehead.

"Or the cookie baking," she says. "The family lunch on Boxing Day. That's a real roof-raiser." She finally cuddles into me. "Trust me, Ell. This barn-shed-guest-house was going to be the only thing saving you from what is going to be a very merry mess."

"But it's *your* mess," I say, kissing her hairline again. "I'm going to be fine, Ry."

"You can turn your back on me out here and say, 'No talking until I'm sufficiently recovered.' And I'll be so quiet. Or I'll go back inside, no matter what whack-a-do thing is going on."

I smile at her use of *whack-a-do*. It's one of the first things she said when she started copying the things I say.

"Ry, that's not going to happen."

"Oh-ho, the crazy is guaranteed to happen."

"I second that," Danny says. "In fact, I wish I had this shed." He gets to his feet and slams closed the door on the stove. "It only takes about twenty minutes to heat this place."

He comes over with a giant grin on his face, and I want to warn him that Ry has gone into full diva-cat mode, and he's going to get his jugular ripped open. "Don't let her ruin your trip, sissy." He steamrolls right onto her, and I jump up from the bed before I become a Luckson sibling sandwich.

"I'm mad, Danny," she says, though she giggles next. "Get off. You're squishing me. I'm dying. My lungs!"

Her brother only laughs, and I really like the way they get along.

Her brother is sweet and tousled as he shimmies off the bed, pulling Ry with him. "Come on, you guys. Mom will not tolerate anyone being even two seconds late to dinner."

"Fine," Ry says as she smooths down her hair and then straightens her shirt. "But I'm not talking to Anna again tonight. A two-year-old does *not* need a king bed to herself. Like, not even a little bit. They could put a bed in that mega-master closet in the *suite* where they stay when they come."

"I so agree," Daniel says, exactly like I would've.

"Or, you know, their own house, which is only *ten* minutes from here. Ten. Minutes."

"We can keep hoping and praying," Daniel says, expertly guiding her toward the door. I trail along like a helpless puppy and my prayer isn't along the lines of Ry's sister staying home and just driving over for the holidays, but that I won't crash and burn at the first meal of the vacation.

RYANNE

"Ry, come help me carry the lasagna," my mom calls from the kitchen, just as I enter the house with Elliott on my heels. How she knows I'm here is beyond me, and I'm in the middle of a sentence as I brief Elliott on the finer points of Luckson family dinner politics. He meets my eyes, and he looks one breath away from fleeing back to the shed-guest-house and flinging my body to the hungry hyenas.

"I got this," he says, and some of the tension in my body melts away. "I'll be on the lasagna detail, and you save that salad from too much stirring." He grins and bumps by me, goes past the immaculately set dining room table, and enters the fray that is my mother and oldest sister.

"Ry," my next oldest sister says, and Cosette pulls me into a squishy hug. "Mm, it's so good to see you." She wears a smile in the words, and she's always been the buffer between Anna and me. Anna is high-strung, and I get crazy around her, while Cosette smooths everything between us. Danny is the youngest of us all, and if I hadn't brought Elliott, I'd be the seventh wheel in a big way.

My appreciation for him grows and grows—and then he yells, "I love Italian! Ry, come *look* at this lasagna!"

Cosette pulls away, her eyes searching mine before she bursts into giggles. I smile too, because Elliott sounded pretty sincere in his enthusiasm for layered pasta. I chuckle slightly as I head into the kitchen too, and he beams at me with the wattage of Times Square as he tilts the pan of lasagna toward me.

"You may want to dial it down a smidge," I mutter around a smile. "Mom, this looks amazing." I say louder.

My mother fusses over her famous spaghetti sauce, and at least ten layers of complex family dynamics lives in this dish. "It goes on the table, dear." She smiles at Elliott encouragingly, like he's a twelve-year-old who needs step-by-step instructions for how to walk a pan of lasagna over to a dining room table. She even has trivets all set out for him, and he goes in that direction while coughing the word, "Salad."

I grab the red-and-green striped bowl and follow him. Dad yells, "It's dinner time. Everyone to battle positions."

If only he were kidding. Elliott puts down the

lasagna and immediately searches for me. I place the salad bowl next to the lasagna and take his hand. "I sit on this side." I take him around to the other side, because for formal family meals, we sit in age order. Dad sits at the head, with Anna and Cosette and their families on his left. Mom is across from him on the other end of the table, and then me and Danny take up the other side of the table.

Since Danny and Katherine don't have kids, and Elliott and I are just dating, the four chairs fit just fine. Only Anna and James have a daughter, and her highchair fits easily between them and Cosette and Rob.

As the lasagna, garlic bread, and salad goes around the table, everything shines under the Christmas lights someone hung above the table. I take two pieces of bread, because of all the things Anna is, a bad cook isn't one of them. Then I squeeze Elliott's hand under the table, feeling less like a grumpy kitty cat and more like a loyal partner ready to have him at my side.

"Rob and I have news," Cosette says as Danny places the bread platter back in the middle of the table. She's shining like all the stars in the sky, and my mom gasps like she's just inhaled a handful of breadcrumbs and needs to cough them out.

"Don't say—"

"Mom, just let her tell the news," I say, which earns me a glare from my mother.

"Yes," Anna agreed. "It's her news to tell."

Mom softens instantly, which only ignites my irritation, and she gestures to Cosette. My sister looks at Rob, who smiles back at her and puts a large forkful of pasta in his mouth. "This lasagna is so good, Grace," he says.

What a suck up. Cosette says, "Rob and I are going to have a baby next year."

My mother shrieks like she's suddenly been possessed by a train approaching a busy intersection. Congratulations start to go around, and my dad gets up to pour drinks.

"Scotch?" he offers to Elliott, and though I've never seen the man drink, he nods and says, "Absolutely, sir. Thank you."

"I bought some bubbly, hoping someone would have news like this," Mom trills out, which is one of the truest things she's said. Danny and Katherine have been married for a couple of years now too, with Cosette and Rob pushing up against five. I'm the only outlier in the group, and there's no way she bought pink champagne thinking I'd announce an engagement.

She knows I hate the stuff, and I wave away her offer of a pretty flute of drink. A tornado of conversations blow into the room then, all of us attempting to keep up with each other. The subsequent chaos makes me want to curl up in a ball—Christmas just seems so hectic with my family all in one room.

I glance over to Elliott to see how he's faring now that I've learned Cosette is due in June, which means I'll need a couple of weeks off at that time. Everything in my life keeps changing, and while this is a happy one, it just adds to the weddings I'll probably be attending this year for my roommates. Weddings and babies—everything I want but don't know how to get.

"Okay?" I lean toward him as I speak, and he nods as he reaches for his drink. Except it's not his drink. It's a squat evergreen-scented candle—because my mom does not allow our Christmas tree to be set up until Christmas Eve, and it must come from the forest a little north of here.

Yes, the jar is a similar shape and size to Elliott's scotch glass, but it's got a flame flickering from the top of it. Surely he'll notice, but he keeps bringing the jar toward his lips like he'll take a sip of the melted wax.

"You know that's a candle, right?" I ask.

Elliott's eyes fly to it just as it starts to tip, and he swears as he hurries to set it down. A flush floods his face, and I can't help it: I start to laugh. And laugh, and laugh.

Thankfully, Elliott grins too, but he doesn't reach for his drink. I take a bite of bread and watch him for a moment. "What?" he finally asks, his voice quiet and meant only for me.

"I haven't seen you take a sip of your scotch."

He leans toward me, and I do the same to him, my mind already imagining what sleeping in that bed in the guest house will be like. "That's because it's disgusting."

I grin. "Don't let my dad hear you say that."

"What should I do with it?"

"It's rude to whisper at the table," my mom says. "Do you two have news?" Her eyes glint as brightly as her pearls do, and I give her one of my severe diva-cat looks.

"No," I say as Elliott's hand lands on my thigh. I dang near jump out of my own skin, but I manage not to buck in my chair. "Thanks for the dinner etiquette, Mom." I force my smile wider and then wider still as I swing my attention to the other end of the table. "And Dad, Elliott says this scotch is great."

"I'm glad he likes it," Dad says, and I nod at Elliott, who seems to get my message to move the glass of scotch closer to me. I won't drink it, but I am an expert at getting rid of things I don't want to eat or drink and making it seem like I have. So, as the meal progresses, I have to get up several times, first to get a new knife after I drop mine, then to get more marinara sauce to dip my bread in.

Every time I do, I take the glass with me and splash a little more down the sink, so by the end of the meal, it seems like Elliott has enjoyed his scotch, the lasagna... and even pine-scented wax.

THE LAUGHTER and chatter from the dinner table and subsequent lounge-by-the-fireplace fades as I finally pull the door closed behind me. Maybe Anna is still in the middle of a sentence. I don't know. What I do know is that I'm done. The night is pitch black and freezing cold, and I hurry after Elliott.

"Are you really going to go Christmas-tree-cutting with them tomorrow?" I ask when I finally catch him. He's a fast thing when it's cold, let me tell you. He pulls open the door to the guest house and ushers me inside, quickly sealing the winter out. Thankfully, the stove has done its job in the past few hours while we've been feasting inside the main house, and my muscles instantly start to relax.

I'm exhausted, as I usually am after dealing with my whole family, and I want nothing more than to change into my pajamas and climb into bed. But I eye it like it might turn into a Tasmanian devil and whirl toward me, ready to claw my face off.

Elliott stands right next to me. "What are you thinking?" The glow of the decorative fairy lights in the corners casts a soft golden hue across his face, and I don't imagine the playful sparkle in his eyes.

"I'm thinking about how you have no idea what's coming tomorrow." An evil little smile breaks out across my face as I imagine Elliott standing amidst the dense pine forest and the men in my family, armed with chain-saws and winter gear.

His brows furrow, and I can't help but crack up.

"What did I get myself into?" he mutters, a mix of dread and humor dancing in his tone.

"You'll have fun, I promise. It's your first Christmas with a Luckson, after all. Every year comes with its own set of chaotic traditions."

His charmed expression fades as he sinks deeper into the cushions of the couch. "You're sure I need to be a part of the tree cutting?"

"Yes. Your initiation is due." I bump him with my hip. "Didn't you hear my mom? It's a *fam-i-ly trad-i-tion.*" One females aren't invited to attend. Oh, no. The men go out in the morning to cut the tree. We decorate it when they bring it back. Mom and Anna will cook and bake all day, and no one ever goes hungry, that's for sure.

He moves over to his suitcase and hefts it up onto the couch. As he unzips it, he says, "Performance evaluation."

I sigh as I walk over to my suitcase. "Pure perfection, as always, Ell."

"You think so?"

"I'm sure they're all talking about you," I say as I sit on the opposite couch. I'm not sure why I let the negative things infect me the way they do.

"Us," he corrects. He turns toward me with a wad of clothes in his hands. "You're going to miss the scent of bacon and yeasty waffles in the morning, aren't you?" He comes to sit by me, and he puts his arm around me, creating a space where I belong. Where it's okay to be a little grumpy I got kicked out of the main house. Where it's okay to be myself, just as I am.

Hot tears press into my eyes. "What are we going to do about the sleeping arrangements?"

He bends his head and nuzzles my neck, sending shivers and sparks—cold and hot—through my body. "I'll do whatever you want, kitty-cat, but have I mentioned I have a bad back? And wow, this couch feels so lumpy."

I nudge him with my shoulder, because he does not have a bad back. "Seriously."

"And my suitcase is over there already," he continues, his lips made of glitter and hot candle wax, as they leave a tingling trail along my neck and up toward my ear. "No way I can lift that thing again. And bending over every time I need a pair of socks? *So* bad on the back."

"It's a big bed," I say.

"We'll just sleep in it."

The moment lightens as I reach over and take his hand. Our fingers entwine, the warmth of his skin mingling with mine, grounding me to this place at his side. "Midnight confessional?" I suggest next.

"As long as it's you and not me," he murmurs. "I don't have anything else to confess right now."

"There's always something to confess."

"I just said I wanted to share a bed with you," he says. "Trust me when I say there's nothing else right now."

I turn and look at him, which is hard with how close he lingers. "There's going to be a pillow wall between us."

"I look forward to it." He gets to his feet and grins. "Now, the door to the bathroom has been closed, which means it's going to be freezing in there. You better change into your pjs fast...and get building, because I'm gonna be back out here in under sixty seconds."

I yelp as he turns and jogs—actually *jogs*—around the couch and toward the bathroom. I jump to my feet, looking frantically from the bed to my unopen suitcase as the bathroom door slams shut. Three precious seconds are lost while I try to figure out what to do. Then I say, "Wall first. I can change in the bathroom after him."

"It's below zero in here!" he yells.

Still, I throw myself into pulling the pillows from the bed and making a line of them down the middle. Elliott has severely underestimated me if he thinks I can't construct a wall in less than sixty seconds.

ELLIOTT

THE GUEST HOUSE CREAKS AND GROANS AROUND US, the wind outside pressing against the old wood beams like there's a secret it must extract. The air itself is charged with expectancy. I've already climbed into the bed, while Ry dashed into the bathroom after me, saying, "Don't you dare break down my pillow wall, Ell."

I've been tearing down all her other walls, that's for sure. "She's been kicking down yours too," I mutter with a quick glance over to the still-closed door. I've put another trio of logs in the stove, and that should keep this place snug and cozy until morning. I hope.

I look up to the ceiling, only the glow of the fairy lights shining down on me. My stomach clenches and churns around the delicious Italian meal I consumed. "Hey, at least you didn't drink candle wax." I scoff up to the ceiling, the ridiculousness of picking up that jar flowing through me. I literally couldn't tell the difference between it and a tumbler of liquor.

I press my eyes closed, because they hurt so much. It's so much better when I'm not straining to see, and my pulse fires from the front of my face to the back of my skull. I should've taken some painkillers tonight, but the bathroom door opens, and the possibility of me getting out of bed right now zooms to zero when I open my eyes and look over to Ry.

Ryanne's pajamas are a pale cream, almost white, with bright green pine trees on them. They're blurry, but I can see enough to tell. She puts one hand on her hip and cocks it out, a bright smile on her face. "Well?"

"The pjs are spectacular," I say. "Very festive." I'm wearing way more than I usually do to bed, as I have on a t-shirt with my gym shorts.

She grins as she comes toward the bed, and her step is shy as her smile fades. "You left the wall."

"I know how to follow directions," I say, though I want to grab every pillow she strung from the headboard to the foot of the bed and fling it out the front door.

The bed jostles a little as she sits down, her back to me. Then she exhales as she leans over and unplugs the string of lights above us, plunging us into blackness. Then she lays down, the comforter moving as she pulls it over her.

I have to say, three weeks ago, I'd dreamt of something like this. I had no idea it could actually happen. "Midnight confessional," I whisper. "Starts now."

She rolls, and though I can't see, I sense the pillow between our heads moving. Then Ry tucks it against my side and eases into my arms. I sigh right out loud and whisper, "I've laid with you in bed before."

"As friends," she whispers back. "This is different."

She's not wrong, so I don't argue. "I'm serious about this, Elliott." Her voice is a soft murmur, reminding me of velvety rose petals.

The air hangs heavy between us, my heart rate picking up slightly as I shift my weight to hold her closer, that darn pillow still wedged between our bodies. "About what?"

"Me and you." She runs her hand up my arm and right under the sleeve of my tee. "About us. This relationship. I want to continue it after the holidays."

I feel the warmth spreading through my chest, and I can't help but grin. "You mean this is more than just a fun holiday fling?"

"When have *fling* and *Ryanne* ever gone in the same sentence?"

"Never," I whisper, but my chest fills with ice.

"I know you don't really want serious, but—"

"I'm working on it," I say, and it's so much easier to talk to her in the dark. "There are things—there's a reason." The ground has disappeared beneath the bed, and I'm floating out in very dangerous territory now.

Can I tell her about my degenerative condition? Will she treat me differently?

Of course she will, a tiny voice says in my head. It grows bigger and louder, and I swallow back my midnight confessional. This isn't about me. Not tonight.

"I feel crazy for this confessional, but here we are. I'm scared."

"I am too," I whisper. "But Ry, you've become more than my best friend. Surely you know that."

She softens in my arms, and I press a kiss to her hairline. Here comes my confessional, and I keep my eyes closed as I say, "You light up the darkest parts of the night for me, the blackest parts of my soul."

She hums quietly, everything about her calm and demure now. A minute passes, then two, my mind racing with disorganized words. I have to tell her about my vision, and now feels like a great time. She can't see me, and I won't be able to witness her horror when I tell her I'm going blind, and that's the reason I've sworn off serious relationships.

"Ry," I whisper, the words nowhere near ready. I'm just going to open my mouth and say whatever comes out. Then, Ry snores softly, and I realize she's fallen asleep. I exhale slowly, letting all the tension and fear go with my breath.

"I'm going blind," I whisper, the words ready and eager to come out when she can't hear me. Of course. "I won't be able to see in oh, probably five years. That's why I don't date anyone seriously. I'm not going to saddle them with taking care of a blind man for the rest of their lives."

Now that I've said it, though she didn't hear me, I truly relax. After all, holding Ry is about as close to heaven as I'll ever get, and I don't have to see to make this incredible non-sight memory.

———

I PULL on my thick winter coat and tuck my scarf down into it as I glance out the window of the guest house, the snow falling gently in soft, fluffy flakes. "It's snowing," I say. Ryanne sits at the tiny table at the end of the couch and galley kitchen, and she stands up, the chair scraping the cement floor.

"Are you sure you want to do this?" Ryanne's voice is laced with concern as I zip up my coat. "You're not obligated to join my family's tree-cutting tradition just because you have a Y-chromosome."

I pause for a moment, my heart flipping over her as she comes nearer. She tucks her arm through mine and leans her head against my bicep. "It's going to be fine. They go every year."

"Doesn't mean you have to."

"And I'll what? Hang out here while you ladies gossip and bake?" We went to breakfast, the scent of waffles and bacon hitting me square in the face the moment we'd opened the guest house door. Ry had huffed, but she'd not complained about it again. And I got the itinerary for the day: Men—tree cutting. Women —cooking and chatting.

Honestly, both aren't great options for me, but I can't be the only one who doesn't go out in the forest. I just can't.

Her light laugh dances around the room, a sound that instantly brightens my day. "Just promise you'll come back unscathed. That means no climbing trees, no stubbornly trying to get the tallest one, and absolutely no lightning bolts."

"Lightning bolts?" I scoff. "You've been watching too many holiday movies, Ry."

"I'm just saying—trees can be dangerous."

"Flying pigs might be next," I tease. I step toward the door. "I'll be fine."

She rolls her eyes and stands there, arms crossed, a mixture of pride and worry etched onto her face. "Don't let my dad say anything rude."

"Okay."

"Don't pay attention to Danny either. He always says things will take twenty minutes, and that's never true."

"Ryanne," I say, turning to take her by the shoulders. "I'll be *fine*."

"Kiss me before you go."

"Oh, beg me." I grin at her and lean down to do what

she asked. She clutches the collar of my coat in a needful way, but I'm already late, and I can't be caught kissing her when I should be gathering on the porch with her brother, dad, and in-laws.

So I kiss her quickly, say, "See you soon," and walk out to the frosty morning while she stays inside, probably taking a few minutes to ground herself before she joins her sisters and mom. Everyone in this house seems *so* excited to partake in the Luckson family traditions, and I won't deny it makes me nervous to be the new guy in this massive family gathering.

The crisp air fills my lungs with a sharp bite, invigorating and terrifying all at once. The world is completely still, blanketed in winter white, and thankfully, the snow seems to be slowing. I go around the garage, and sure enough, everyone's waiting for me already.

"Let's get this over with," Danny calls from the front porch. That's right. I'm on a Christmas-tree-cutting mission with Ry's dad, her brother, and her brothers-in-law, Rob and James. All the classic manly men ready to reclaim their territory as they tame giant trees with chainsaws. I join them, my excitement weaving in and out with my nerves.

"What are we looking for in the perfect tree?" I ask Danny as we begin to walk down the driveway toward the edge of their property. He's bundled up in an oversized coat and a beanie, his breath puffing out in clouds of vapor, and the expansive snowy field stretches out before us, interspersed with various evergreen trees standing tall against the winter sky.

"Depends on who you ask," he says with a cheerful grin. "Me? I like something symmetrical. My dad wants something with good girth." When he says nothing about Rob and James and their opinions on what makes a good Christmas tree, I know my place.

"We'll be out for half an hour at most. Dad says he's spotted a good one already."

"Down by the creek," Leo says, and I throw a smile to Ry's dad. I have no idea where the creek is, but I know it's further than I probably want to walk in the snow. Up ahead of us, Rob and James carry black sacks over their backs, and I wonder what's in those, as Leo's pulling a sled with rope, the chainsaw, and a couple of axes on it.

"We'll be back to have hot chocolate before lunch." Danny grins, and his enthusiasm over pine trees is slightly infectious, if we're talking fatal diseases.

"Sounds like a solid plan," I reply, quickly looking around, hoping to catch a glimpse of this mysterious creek that'll have us out and back in less than thirty minutes.

"Snowshoes," Rob says when we reach the end of the road, the trees closer and taller now. Looming. And it's the middle of the day, but I swear it's almost as dark as nighttime in the forest.

"Snowshoes?" I ask as he and James drop their bags and start pulling out this new development. I've literally never *seen* a pair of snowshoes, let alone worn them. They do know there's no snow in South Carolina, don't they?

I watch as Danny steps into a pair and pulls the straps tight over his boots. Even with slightly blurry vision, I can do that, and before I know it, the five of us are properly equipped for the next leg of our journey.

No one seems to notice that I wait for all of them to go ahead of me, and I step into Leo's footsteps and the sleigh tracks, my focus completely on the ground only a few feet in front of me. My breath starts to come quicker, and I pause to take a moment to look up and around me. The trees are magnificent—tall, lush, their branches heavy with soft white snow. My excitement builds as patches of light filter through the trees, illuminating the men in front of me.

It's literally the most perfect Christmas forest scene in the world.

But we keep passing trees. Perfectly good pine trees. Tall ones. Short ones. Symmetrical ones. Girthy ones.

And there's no freaking creek anywhere.

I focus on my feet again, the soft squishy-crunch of snow beneath my feet the only sound. Images of Christmas Future stream through my mind, and as crazy as it might sound, Ryanne is in every one of them. She wants serious, and her midnight confessional rings through my head. I want to tell her. I *need* to tell her.

"You're going to tell her."

My voice almost sounds foreign among so much silence, and that's when I realize...there's so much silence.

I come to a stop again, because I can barely walk and look around on flat, dry ground, and I certainly can't do it in a fluffy snowbank. When I look up, I expect to see Ryanne's dad only a few paces ahead of me, with Rob, James, and Danny in front of him.

There's no one. Only me. The realization sends a rush of adrenaline coursing through me. "Hey," I call out, my voice battling against the stillness of the trees. "Where you at?"

My own words echo teasingly against the towering pines. The air feels colder now, sharper, as if the forest itself is beginning to close in around me. I take a few hesitant steps forward, scanning left and right to catch a glimpse of my companions, but nothing moves beyond the trees. Thankfully, I can see their footsteps, but I have no idea if I can catch them.

"Guys?" I step deeper into the snow, the crunching noise reminding me of just how little traction I have on these snowshoes. "Leo. Danny?"

Just then, a distant sound—a burst of laughter filtering through the branches—meets my ears, and I follow it, my heart hammering. I trust Ryanne's family, but this is insane. Have they completely forgotten about me already?

"Elliott!" Danny's voice pierces the winter sky, and a

small wave of relief washes over me. I pick up my pace, briefly forgetting how difficult walking with snowshoes is. I'm winded in mere moments, but I reach the edge of a stand of trees and see the Lucksons another hundred yards in front of me.

How do they move so fast? My word. I need a Mars rover companion to press down the snow and make walking easier.

Danny waves both hands above his head, as if I can't see him. He yells something, but I can't make it out.

I suck at the air and take another step, my feet immediately slipping despite the snowshoes. Panic strikes, and I fight to maintain my balance, my arms windmilling to grab onto something solid, but there's nothing but air.

"Stay there!" Leo yells, but that's not going to happen.

I'm already falling.

I tumble forward, my snowshoes tethering my feet awkwardly in the deep snow, pitching me headfirst into a bank of the cold stuff—which is so not as soft as I imagined it to be. I sink deep into it, flailing my arms to push myself out, but it keeps shifting, never solidifying. My face brushes against an icy solid, and I sputter, catching an unexpected mouthful of snow as I gasp for breath.

When I finally can push myself up, I can't see anything. Just whiteness everywhere. Funny, I've always thought the world would be black once I finally go blind.

Then, the worst thing in the world happens—worse

than me falling face-first into the snow in front of Ry's family. Worse than this horrible weather and devilish activity. Worse than going blind.

The enormously strong scent of a skunk hits me— right before I get sprayed.

RYANNE

I'm up to my elbows in cookie dough when I hear the commotion outside. My mom and sisters chatter away about Anna's pregnancy and Cosette's upcoming baby shower, but I tune them out as I strain to hear what's happening on the front porch. Something bangs, and that gets my heart pumping.

"What in the world?" my mom says, interrupting my sister for the first time ever and moving to the mouth of the hallway. "They're back already? That can't be true."

I wipe my hands on a dish towel and rush past her, my goal the front door, my heart racing. Something's wrong; I can feel it. As I fling open the front door, I'm hit with a wall of cold air and the most putrid smell I've ever encountered.

"Fish and chips," I gag, covering my nose with my sleeve. "What *is* that?"

And then my dad moves to the side, and Elliott emerges. He looks like he's been through a war with nature itself, and he's being half-carried, half-dragged up the steps by Danny and Rob. Snow and pine needles cake his clothes, and there's a nasty-looking scratch across his cheek. But worst of all is the smell. A skunk has definitely decided to use him as target practice.

"What happened?" I demand, glaring at my dad who's already on the porch, looking sheepish.

"Well, honey," he starts.

But I cut him off with, "I can't believe you." I swat at his chest, and he has the decency to flinch away from me. "You—let—a—skunk—spray—him?"

"It was an accident."

"Like someone would want to get sprayed on purpose," I fire back.

"I can't believe he didn't see them," Rob said as he helps Elliott over to one of the chairs on the porch. "It was a whole skunkeriffic family."

"They were pretty plain," James agrees. "Black against white, you know?"

I don't see how this is helping. "Wasn't he with you?"

"He'd, uh, fallen behind," Rob says. They have no Christmas tree on the empty sled, and the four of them stand there like they don't know what to do next.

"Close the door," Mom says behind me. "It's

freezing—oh, it's a skunk. Turn on the fans; get out the candles."

"Mom." I spin toward her. "We have to clean up Elliott."

"Guest house," she calls as Anna literally closes the door in my face.

I turn back to the men in my family. Dad offers a tiny smile. "We have to go back out and get the tree, so..."

"Fine, go." I play a drumroll on Danny's chest too. "You—I trusted you to take care of him."

"He's fine," Danny said, though he casts a worried look over to Elliott. He still hasn't moved or spoken, and he stares straight ahead, his glasses sitting a little askew on his face. "You know the drill."

"And good news," Dad says. "All the skunk stuff is in the shed—uh, the guest house."

"Perfect." I fold my arms, my internal temperature falling rapidly. I'm not wearing a coat, and an apron certainly isn't adequate protection against a New York winter.

They go, and I turn toward my boyfriend. "Elliott," I say softly as I approach. "Are you okay?"

He looks up at me, his eyes a bit unfocused, and manages a weak smile. "I'm fine, Ry. Just had a little... encounter with the local wildlife."

I brush his hair off his forehead. "Okay, let's get you cleaned up," I say, trying to keep my voice calm even though I'm seething inside. How could they let this happen?

He'd fallen behind.

I scoff at the lack of care the males in my family offered to Elliott. "Can you stand?"

He nods and slowly rises to his feet. I help him out to the shed-guest-house, then ease off his coat at the corner of it, wincing at the smell that seems to have permeated every fiber. "I think these clothes are a lost cause," I mutter.

"Definitely," Elliott agrees, his voice muffled as I help him pull his sweater over his head. He gets off his own shoes, socks, and pants, and we leave everything stinking on the sidewalk as I hurry him toward the door in only his boxer shorts.

Once inside, I try not to stare at his bare chest, focusing instead on the task at hand. "Okay, um, you should shower. I'll get the de-skunking supplies and meet you in there."

"In the bathroom?"

"Yes. Open the window and use lukewarm water. Don't wash your hair or anything yet. I'll mix up the vinegar and baking soda, and I'll come in and cake it on your skin and hair." I peer at him, the door open behind us to keep the guest house ventilated. We have to sleep here, after all, and I can stoke up the fire and warm it up easily later.

"Did it get in your eyes?"

"No," he says. "I buried my face in the snow at the last second. I think it just hit my back—so it's all in my hair and all over my clothes."

"Easy peasy then," I say as brightly as I can. "We're so eating M&Ms and watching the Mars rovers after you get out of the shower." I smile, though there's nothing smile-worthy right now.

He nods, still looking a bit dazed. "Thanks, Ry." He moves toward the bathroom, and I rush over to the kitchenette to get the supplies I need. I can't remember the exact ratio of vinegar, dish soap, and baking soda off the top of my head, but I make a pretty decent mixture of the stuff. It's blue goop, and I stare at it as the winter wind continues to air out the guest house.

When I arrive at the bathroom door, I lean into the seam and hear the shower running. I knock and call, "I'm coming in."

He's standing in the shower, the curtain all the way open, as water streams over him and his boxers. I take the bowl of detergent and say, "Point the stream down. I'm going to get this all over you, and it has to sit for ten minutes. Then you can shower as normal."

He says nothing, but his teeth chatter. I don't blame him a bit, because he's got the window open, and he's wet. I work as quickly as I can, scooping up big handfuls of the blue goop and spreading it over his shoulders and up his neck into his hair. It only takes a few minutes, and I fall back, wet and goopy and cold too.

"Ten minutes," I say, pulling the curtain closed. "You can warm up the water now."

I leave the bathroom door open and go close the front door of the guest house. I wash up and clean out the bowl, leaving it to dry in the dish drainer before starting a timer for eight minutes on my phone. Then I build up the fire so it's crackling and raging, and I close the door on the potbellied stove. Turning, I spot Elliott's suitcase, and I step over to it to find him some new clothes.

My parents are so buying him a new coat and sweater. "Jeans too," I mutter as I pull out a pair of dark gray sweatpants and a T-shirt with three triangles stacked inside one another on the front of it.

The timer on my phone goes off, and I rush over to the bathroom. "Ten minutes, Ell."

"Okay," he calls back, his voice sounding a bit stronger. "Thanks, Ry."

I reach for the doorknob. "I'll be right outside if you need anything," I say before pulling the door closed to give him some privacy.

As I wait, I pace between the two couches, noting no one has come to see if I need any help. We have a Luckson family text, and I feel like giving them all a piece of my mind. The only reason I don't is because we still have four full days here with everyone, and my mom will just tell me to calm down anyway. Like I need that right now.

"Ry?"

I spin toward the sound of my sister's voice as Anna enters the guest house. "We have some soup and bread for you guys." She enters with a bright red crock and sets it on the narrow counter in the kitchen.

Cosette follows her with an extra loaf of garlic bread from last night. "It doesn't smell so bad in here," she says. "I'm just going to bag up the clothes and throw them in the bin."

"Okay, yes," I say. "I got him cleaned up; he's in the shower." An idea forms in my head, and I seize onto it. "We're just going to hang out here until the tree decorating." I lift my chin, daring them to argue with me.

Anna steps over and hugs me. "We figured." She gives me a kind smile, which confuses me for a moment. It's not like we're best friends, and we've definitely had our share of disagreements over the years. She's always right, and everything is her way or the highway. So this feels...a little weird. "He'll be okay."

"Yeah," I say as I pull back. "Thanks for the food."

"Text me if you need anything else," Cosette says. "I made sure there's hot chocolate stuff in the cupboards here."

"Oh, I haven't looked."

"It's there." She grins at me and gestures for Anna to leave with her. They do, sealing me back in the guest house with a skunky Elliott.

"Ry?"

I spin again, my adrenaline getting a workout today. "Yeah?"

"Clothes?"

"Yeah, yep, I got them for you." I hurry over to the couch and swipe them up.

He exits the bathroom, a fluffy blue towel tied around his waist. "Smell me."

"An interesting demand," I say.

He grins too, though he seems…dimmer than usual. More subdued. "I have plenty more where that came from." He leans down. "I can't tell if I still smell. It's like my nose is ruined."

"Skunks can do that." I lean one palm into his shoulder while I press his clothes to his chest and tip up to smell his hair. "Not bad," I say.

"Just what every man wants to hear," he says dryly. "You don't smell bad."

"It'll only last a couple of hours," I tell him. "And my sisters brought food, and the fire's raging. We're just going to lay in bed and eat M&Ms and put something on your phone that'll make you forget about skunks."

Elliott looks at me for a long moment, then takes his clothes and goes back into the bathroom. When he comes back out a minute later, I indicate the bed. "No pillow wall."

"It's my lucky day." He's salty, but he takes my hand and lifts it to his lips. "Thanks for taking care of me."

"And we're just getting started," I say, and that finally—finally—earns me a smile.

———

THE AFTERNOON SLIPS AWAY in a haze of hot chocolate, M&Ms, and Elliott's favorite Mars rover videos. By the time we emerge from our cozy cocoon in the guest house, the sky has darkened to a deep blue, and the twinkling lights strung along the eaves of the main house cast a warm glow over the snow-covered yard.

"Okay?" I ask Elliott as we approach the back door. He's looking much better now, the scratch on his cheek less angry, and the skunk smell has faded to almost nothing.

He squeezes my hand. "Let's deck some halls."

We step inside to find the living room buzzing with activity. The enormous pine tree—which was obviously cut down after the skunk incident—stands proudly in the corner, waiting to be adorned. Boxes of ornaments are scattered around, and my family members are bustling about, untangling lights and sorting through decorations.

"There you are," my mom calls out, waving us over. "Elliott, dear, how are you feeling?" She rushes at him and pulls him into a hug.

"Much better, thank you," he replies politely. When he returns to my side, and retakes my hand in his, I give it a reassuring squeeze to remind him I don't care if everyone in my family loves him or not.

My dad approaches, looking sheepish. "Elliott, I want to apologize again for what happened earlier. We should have been more careful."

Elliott waves him off. "No harm done, sir. Well, except to my pride maybe."

Danny comes closer with a box of moss-covered ornaments. "And your face." He grins and extends his fist for Elliott to bump.

I shoot my brother a glare, but Elliott chuckles good-naturedly and does the bro-fist-bump-thing. "That too."

"Well," my mom interjects, clapping her hands together. "Let's get this tree decorated, shall we? Elliott, why don't you and Ryanne deal with the white balls?"

Elliott looks at me. "That sounds exciting."

I grin at him and point to the others who've clearly already been assigned a task. "Rob and Cosette are on the cloth ornaments. My grandmother sewed the whole nativity set before she died, and we decorate the tree with it every year."

"Your dad's on lights, obviously," he says.

"Obviously." Dad looks like he might lose his battle with the white lights for the first time in years. "We all stand here and wait for him, and he refuses to start early so we don't have to." I look over to where Anna is crouched down with Sariah. "Anna and James are doing the metallic balls."

"Even more exciting."

I shake my head and nod over to Danny and Katherine. "They're doing all the picks."

"I don't even know what a pick is."

"Red, white, and blue poinsettias," I say. "Fake flowers. My mom cuts them so they just have a long stem—like a pick. They just poke them into the branches to fill the holes."

"And your mom?" He glances around, but she's not in the living room.

I turn him toward the kitchen and dining room. "She's finishing dinner and laying out presents. We each get one on Christmas Eve, and we open them at the table, before we eat."

Elliott nods and twists back to face the living room. He's quiet for a moment, and then he says, "Your family traditions are nice."

"Are they?"

"I think so."

Warmth fills me, because I suppose it is nice to be able to gather here, all of us, and enjoy something familiar and fun. My dad finally finishes with the lights, and we kids descend on the tree with our various ornaments. Elliott and I fall into sync easily, with him threading the hooks through the tops of the white orbs and holding them out to me to place on the tree.

"To the left," he says, and I find the hole he sees from further away. Our dance is fluid and natural, and when our ornaments have all been hung, I step back to his side and cuddle in close.

"You're pretty good at this," I murmur, taking in the grandeur of the tree as it blooms into Christmas glory right before my eyes.

He grins. "I have hidden talents."

As Danny and Katherine finish up, they come to stand beside us, a feeling fills my chest that has nothing to do with the crackling fire or the hot cocoa or the magic of Christmas. Fine, maybe it's some of the magic of Christmas.

Elliott's arm sits easily around my waist, and he laughs at something Danny just said, and I realize with a start that this is exactly what I've always wanted: someone who fits so naturally into my world, who can weather the storms—or skunks—and still come out smiling.

"Okay, everyone," Mom says. "Oh, look at it." She pauses, and I appreciate how much she works for the holidays to be so seamless, so perfect, so wonderful. She's not perfect, but she's very, very good, and I smile softly over to her as I catch her swiping at her eyes as she gazes at the Christmas tree.

Dad steps next to her and puts his arm around her too, and standing there with Elliott, I finally feel like I fit inside the Luckson family. I lean into Elliott's side, breathing in the pine scent of the freshly cut tree and catching just a hint of vinegar, but no skunk.

"Okay," Mom says again. "It's time for presents. Everyone take their spot behind their chair."

"We open the gifts standing up?" he asks as everyone files into the dining room, and no, no one pulls out a chair to sit down. Ornate gifts sit atop each place setting, including Elliott's. When we arrive at the same spots as last night, he glances over to me. "I didn't—"

I shake my head, and he cuts off. I'm sure my mom started shopping the moment Elliott texted her that he'd be my plus-one for the holidays. Dad says, "Ry, why don't you go first this year?" and I reach for my present. The box is small and square, and I suspect jewelry as I pull off the silver paper with blue glittery snowflakes.

It's definitely a black jewelry box, and I open the top to find a delicate silver charm bracelet inside.

"It's lovely," I breathe out, admiring the tiny charms —a book, a palm tree—the state tree of South Carolina— and a little house that looks suspiciously like the Big House back in Cider Cove. I look up and smile genuinely over to my mom. "Thank you." Then I touch my palm to my heart and look at my daddy. "Thank you so much."

There are new pajamas for Sariah, a fancy bottle of cologne for my dad, and a beautiful scarf for my mom. Dad then says, "Elliott," next, and he stands there still and silent.

"Ell."

He startles at the sound of my voice and reaches over

the top of the dining room chair and picks up a long, rectangular box wrapped in rich, red, wrapping paper. He acts like he's trying to unwrap glass, and when he finally opens the top on the clothing box, he reveals a soft, forest green scarf, hat, and glove set.

"We thought you might need it for future tree-cutting expeditions," my dad jokes, earning a laugh from everyone.

Elliott wraps the scarf around his neck and grins as he pulls the hat over his non-skunky hair. "It's perfect. Thank you all so much." He beams around at everyone, and I scan my family too.

And cookie dough M&Ms, he's charmed them all. Completely.

No wonder my sisters brought soup and bread to the guest house earlier today. Elliott is *in*.

And while I'm thrilled by that, I wonder what will happen to me inside my own family if we can't make something real and serious stick after the magic of Christmas wears off.

ELLIOTT

I wake up to the sound of Ryanne's soft breathing, her head nestled against my chest. Even though I can't see her face clearly in the dim light of the guest house, I can feel the warmth of her body pressed against mine, and my heart does a happy little flip. I've never woken up next to a woman before. Well, I did yesterday, but not with the feeling that I could stay here forever, holding her close, listening to the gentle rhythm of her breath.

I ease my arm out from under her, careful not to wake her. The fire in the potbellied stove has died down to embers, and I shiver as I get out of bed. The cement floor is freezing beneath my bare feet, and I hurry over to the woodpile and grab a couple of logs. I get the fire going again, then head to the tiny kitchenette to make coffee.

I'm halfway through measuring the grounds when Ryanne moans, "Being...too...loud," in her true kitty-cat fashion.

"Go back to sleep for a bit." Then I can shower and get dressed, and we'll have coffee before we have to face her family again.

She rolls and pulls the blanket up over her head, and the lumpy shape of her in the bed makes me smile so hard. I will say that Christmas Eve dinner bordered on perfection. Decorating the tree while her mom put the finishing touches on dinner and gifts. The way they all seem to know when to settle down and when to get each other going again.

Her mom and sisters are good cooks too, and a powerful wave of missing my own family bulldozes through me. I set the coffee to brew, and I rummage through my suitcase for an appropriate outfit for Christmas Day. Ry's said her family does a big huge breakfast, then gifts, and then the cookie baking competition begins. I certainly don't have to wear slacks and a jacket for that, and I pull out a pair of khakis and one of what my brother calls my "old man sweaters" and head for the bathroom.

I'll call Momma as soon as I'm ready, and I hurry through getting cleaned up so I can make sure she's having a good time with Brandon and Shirley. She was taking Peppermint over to my brother's house last night, so they should be waking up together this morning. "I can't believe she's meeting Shirley before me."

But I'd already committed to coming to New York with Ry, and I can meet Brandon's girlfriend any time. I'm out of the shower, dressed, and pouring coffee in the kitchenette when my phone rings. Ry's gone into the bathroom, and she won't want to talk until she's properly caffeinated.

I glance at the screen, and my heart skips a beat when I see Momma's name flashing there. "Hey, Momma," I answer, my voice pitching up too much. I take a deep breath to settle the missing back down in my stomach and add, "Merry Christmas."

"Merry Christmas, son." She sounds a little breathless, like perhaps she just ran a mile. "How are you? How's Ryanne's family?"

"Everything is great," I say just as Ry comes out. She's wearing a red, white, and green plaid dress, which makes me feel perfectly dressed in my khakis and dark blue sweater with tiny snowflakes on it. We're both nodding to the season; hers is just more festive than mine.

She sweeps into the kitchen area as I ask, "Have you met Shirley yet?"

"Oh, it's your mom." She pours herself a cup of coffee as Momma starts to gush over Shirley and how amazing she is. "I'll give you a minute." She sweeps her lips across my cheek and heads out the front door of the guest house, leaving me in privacy to talk to my family this morning.

"Anyway," Momma says. "She's a real sweetheart, and I do hope Brandon can get his ducks together to propose."

I grin and say, "I hope so too, Momma."

"Anyway," Momma says airily. "We have some amazing news for you too." The giddiness comes through in her voice, and my stomach pitches left and right.

"News for me?"

"Hey, bro," Brandon yells, and it sounds like he's on the phone now.

"It's the best Christmas present in the world." Momma sniffles, and now I'm all worked up. Is this good news? Or not?

"Paws For a Cause called," Brandon bellows. "You won the guide dog this year!"

"I—what?" bursts from my mouth. My pulse hammers in my chest, and I'm so glad Ryanne went into the mansion instead of lingering out here. I turn in a full circle as Brandon laughs and Momma shushes him. My legs feel like crutches someone has attached to my body, but I manage to walk over to the non-suitcase-holding couch and sit down on it.

"You're going to get her on January fourth," Momma says. "They called me this morning, saying you'd won their annual guide dog Christmas gift, and they have the perfect canine for you. I accepted, of course, and—"

She keeps talking, but my ears have timed out. They're full, and I can't take in any more. Yes, I'd known my mom had applied for me to get the guide dog from Paws For a Cause. I never believe in a million years I'd get chosen.

"Why aren't you saying anything?" Momma asks. "They offer classes so you can learn how to work with Luna, so there's nothing for you to worry about."

"Luna," I say. Seems fitting, what with my obsession with space, planets, and the moon.

"Now, I know you've taken a bunch of time off to go up to New York," Momma says, ever pushing ahead. "But we have to go to Michigan the first week of January, so I'm going to text you all the details—"

"I have them in an email, Ell," Brandon cuts in over her. "I'll forward it to you."

"You're yelling," Momma yells at him. "Talking right over me."

"Well, you don't need to text him details," Brandon says. "It's all in an email."

I smile, though my stomach still feels like I've swallowed boiling battery acid. "I'll check my email, and I'll put in to get work off." I swallow, wondering how I'm going to get down Belgian waffles with strawberries and cream when I can't even get my saliva down.

If I put in for work off, Ry will want to know why. Suddenly, I have a very loud clock ticking over my head, and I really wish she hadn't fallen asleep so soon the other night.

Finally, the call ends, and I lower my phone, staring at nothing across from me. "You have to tell her," I tell myself. "Today, Elliott. You're going to tell her today."

Not only because she deserves to know as my best friend and girlfriend, but because getting a free guide dog is *huge*, and Ryanne is the one I want to share this good news with.

I stand and leave the guest house, intending to find her and drag her into the nearest room with a door and just...tell her.

The mansion is once again hopping when I enter it, this time with the scent of bacon, coffee, and butter-scotch hanging in the air. You'd think with their proximity to New England, the Lucksons would be bathing in maple syrup, but no. Anna has a recipe for buttermilk syrup, and it's more butterscotchy than mapley, and I've taken four steps toward Ry when she lifts her fork with a bite of dripping-with-buttermilk-syrup waffle.

"Eat this," she says with the biggest smile I've ever seen her wear.

So I take the bite, having her feed me one of the hotter things we've done in front of other people. The tangy taste of butter and salt hits my taste buds first, followed by a quick chaser of caramelly sugar. I can't suppress the moan of delight that lunges out of my throat, and Ry tips her head back and laughs.

"Right? It's so good." She cuts off another bite, which she takes, and then she indicates an empty plate sitting on the counter. "There's lots," she says around her food. I'm clearly not taking her out of here without causing a scene, which is the last thing I want. So I pick up the plate to get some breakfast, trying very hard not to feel like a coward, or like I'm doing something wrong, or like this is the last time I'll ever have to tell Ryanne about my vision impairment.

I still have time, I tell myself as I ladle buttermilk syrup over a crispy Belgian waffle, my mouth watering with all the goodness in front of me.

———

A COUPLE OF HOURS LATER, breakfast has been cleared, and the instructions for the cookie bake-off about to happen gone over and over. And over. The Lucksons are a fun group, but my word. They need every little detail planned out, or, in Ry's words, "Danny will cheat," or "Anna will spin things to her advantage," or "Dad will change the rules in the middle of the game."

What's even funnier is that none of them accused of doing nefarious things even try to defend themselves. It's like they know who they are, and they don't deny that they've cheated, spun, and changed things in the past.

"So we'll draw names now," Grace says, which was also a wrench in the cookie bake-off that Ryanne argued against for a good twenty minutes, all the while eating the leftover bacon until it was gone.

I exchange a look with Ry, because we'd planned to be partners for the bake-off. Apparently, in past years, they'd never drawn names before. I raise my eyebrows, hoping she'll understand my question. *Are we still doing the silly stuff?*

She grins and nods, then turns her attention back to her mother as she draws the first name out of a cookie tin covered in gingerbread men. I swear, the lengths this family goes to to Christmasify everything is mind-blowing. "Danny," she reads, and for some reason, that gets everyone to go, "Ooooh."

Laughter ensues, and then Danny gets paired with Rob. "Can we forfeit?" Rob asks, and he's grinning but not kidding.

"No," Grace says firmly. "We already discussed this."

And they'd made a rule that couples can't be paired together, and if they're drawn, it will have to be redone.

"Elliott." Grace gives me a kind smile, and I return it before glancing nervously around to everyone else in the room. I know I can't draw Ry, and I don't know anyone else all that well. Ry and I each have a list of things we're trying to work into our cookie bake-off; things like one of us singing the chorus from *Annie*, or faking a fingertip being cut off, or getting one of her pregnant sisters to say, "My word, you're going to put me in labor."

After the skunk incident, I'm not sure I'm brave enough to pull out all the silliness card, but then I'll lose to Ryanne. *If there's anyone you're willing to lose to, it's her.*

Then my gaze snaps back to Grace as she reads, "Anna."

My heartbeat tumbles down to my new socks—a lovely, woolly pair from Anna and her husband, in fact—and my gaze flies to Ryanne's oldest sister. Now, my vision is pretty far from twenty-twenty. I'm the first to admit that. But even I can see the expression of irritation, then distaste, and then how she smooths everything over, meets my eye, and smiles like she'd have picked me over everyone else if given the chance.

Oh, this is going to be so fun.

———

AN HOUR LATER, Ryanne has been paired with her mom, we've planned world baking domination after we snuck away to the guest house for a quick minute, and now, it's my and Anna's turn to "shop" from the pantry for our recipe.

"I still think we should do something *tropical*," I say

loudly. Maybe I do have some of Brandon's yelling capabilities. Who knew? "Like with dates and stuff. Do you think your mom bought any *dates*?" I step up to the shelf in the garage, where Grace has set up a series of shelves with a variety of baking goods on them. It's legit like going to the grocery store, but since it's Christmas Day, and we don't have that option, Grace has prepped this "pantry" for us.

"Dates?" Anna says as I wander down the row of ingredients. It's not exactly warm in the garage, and every pair gets ten minutes to shop for their ingredients. I currently have nothing in my basket, and I can feel the seething displeasure emanating from Anna behind me. "We're not using dates. We agreed to do Linzer window cookies."

She steps up to the shelf too and plucks down a box of baking soda. "We need this. Can you grab the almonds? I'm pretty sure I saw them down there."

I do not see almonds anywhere, and I can't remember the last time I ate a nut that wasn't first covered in chocolate and candy coating that only melts in your mouth, not your hand. "Almonds," I mutter. "Almonds...almonds...almonds." I pick up a blue bag of nuts, and I lift it closer to my eyes so I can read the words. "Oh, these are walnuts."

And just like stink on a skunk, Anna is suddenly on top of me. I practically throw the bag of chopped walnuts back onto the wire shelf. "Not walnuts," she says, swiping up another bag. "Almonds." She tosses them into my basket but doesn't back up a single inch.

"That bag of almonds was literally ten inches from your face."

"I was getting—"

"You didn't see them."

"Yet. I hadn't seen them *yet*."

"You didn't see the skunks." Anna comes around me, and all the things Ryanne has told me about how intense she is. How much of a pitbull. If she sinks her teeth into me, I'll never get away. "You literally picked up a candle last night, thinking it was your drink." Her eyes search mine, and I see all the dots lining up.

"Anna," I say, but I don't know what comes next.

"Elliott, can you see?"

I try to turn away, but the shelves are there. Anna's boxed me in the other way, and I'm now stuck. "I need new glasses."

"Five minutes," Grace calls from the doorway which leads into the kitchen. Anna turns toward her, temporarily distracted, and I back up a couple of steps.

The door slams closed, and Anna barks, "Elliott."

"I'm fine," I say. "What else do we need?"

"Does Ry know it's this bad?"

I spin to face her, something igniting through me now. "No, okay? Can you drop this, please?"

Anna opens her mouth, then closes it, her eyes wide and only getting wider. "You just need a new prescription." She's not asking a question, and I just need someone to know.

I shake my head. "I do get a new prescription every three or four months, but...my vision is going to continue to get worse until I can't see at all."

She sucks in a breath, and all the things Ryanne has told me about how dramatic Anna is bloom to life right in front of me. "I'm still trying to figure out how to tell Ryanne," I whisper. "I'd appreciate it if you could keep this to yourself until I do."

The ticking clock in my life booms with every move of the second hand. I'm running out of time, and everything suddenly feels so heavy.

"Of course I will," Anna whispers, and she does something I never thought she would. She puts her arms around me and hugs me. "I can't believe Ryanne hasn't noticed yet, but she's probably blinded by your charm and good looks." She pulls back, her smile kind for one, two seconds. Then she takes a deep breath and adds, "Now, come on. We have less than five minutes to get everything."

She grabs sugar and flour and drops it unceremoniously into the basket. I grunt, and she gives me an eagle-eyed look I've seen on Ry's face plenty of times. "And you're just going to do everything I say in the kitchen, Mister I-Need-New-Glasses."

"Oh, come on," I say. "Haven't you ever heard that song from *Annie*?" I take a deep breath as Anna moves down the shelf, probably looking for salt or vanilla extract. "The sun'll come out! Tomorrow! Bet your bottom dollar that tomorrow, they'll be sun!"

I may be going blind, but I have perfect pitch and the will to win this contest between Ry and I.

"More peppermint," Mom declares, shaking the red and white container over our bowl of melted chocolate. Tiny flecks of crushed peppermint candy rain down, and I slap my hand over the bowl.

"Mom, stop it." I pull the bowl closer to my side of the counter, narrowly avoiding a white chocolate and peppermint avalanche. "You are going to poison people."

"Oh, you can't poison people with peppermint." Her eyes twinkle with mischief, and while I could've definitely drawn someone worse to bake with, Mom is a bit too serious for my taste. "In fact, you can never have too much peppermint."

I look over to where Elliott peers into the big silver bowl my sister has parked him in front of. "You can *definitely poison people* with too much peppermint," I yell.

Elliott looks up, his hazel eyes glowing from within.

Yep, that's a point for me. Of course, he burst into the theme song from *Annie* before he and Anna had even come in from the garage, so he's for sure ahead in the game.

"It's Christmas," Mom says, and I gasp as a drop of liquid hits the back of my hand. She is legit adding more peppermint extract.

"Mom, my eyes are burning." I snatch away the bottle of extract, holding it high above my head. "You have got to stop."

"They're *peppermint* logs, Ry," she says so matter-of-factly. "The last thing we want is for them to be bland."

I wipe tears from my eyes. "Not gonna happen, Mom." I give her one of my kitty-cat glares. "How much *Food Network* have you watched to come up with that line?"

Mention a TV show. Point for me.

Down the counter, Elliott says in an overly loud voice, "I had no idea you could grind nuts into flour."

Making a flour—point for him. I knew he'd get that one the moment Mom had drawn Anna's name after Elliott's. My sister is no-doubt making her famous Linzer cookies, and she'll make the jam from scratch too. I should insist I get double points as a handicap for his partner being the Baking Queen.

Mom reaches for the peppermint extract bottle, and she nearly gets me while I'm distracted. "Please," I say. "I'm taller than you." It's a blatant lie, but Mom just laughs that tinkling laugh that always makes me smile, even when I'm trying to be annoyed with her. "And second? We're *not* making straight-up peppermint patties."

I glance around the kitchen, where three of the five teams are now baking. "I have peppermint extract *abuse* happening over here. Who can take this bottle to save us all?"

"One bottle to save them all," Elliott says, coming to my rescue. He grins at me, earning some points as he takes the offending bottle, and then he bounds back over to his station, exactly the way a golden retriever would.

Movie quote, put in baking context. He's too smart for me.

"Oh, this is a little watery now," Mom says, and I force myself to focus back on our cookies. We need to get them in the oven in the next twenty minutes, or we'll run out of time during the decorating phase. Just the fact that I've thought the words "decorating phase" tells me how far I've fallen into my family traditions, and I don't hate that.

"Yeah," I gripe at her. "From all that *liquid* peppermint extract."

"We'll just add a bit more flour," she says.

"Mom, that's not how baking works." I grin to myself as I pick up a rubber spatula to see what I can do with this batter. It should definitely be more fudgy, as we'll need to roll it out like gingerbread, cut rectangles, and roll the cookies before they bake. "I didn't ace algebra," I say loudly. "But even I know what a trapezoid is."

"Trapezoids are the building blocks of cookie-making," Elliott says.

"What are you two talking about?" Anna asks, and it's all I can do not to burst out laughing. I deliberately don't look over to Elliott, or our little ruse will be discovered, and Anna will launch into what Anna does best: lecture.

"Just bonding over geometry," I say sweetly, deciding we can add a little more powdered sugar to the batter. I dump some in with a little too much gusto. Point—make a powdered sugar mess. "Oopsie!" I yell, as that earns me another point. "Got a little too much snow over here!"

Elliott scoffs, but that's only what it sounds like. He's really trying to stifle his laughter. "Anna," he says, and my sister thankfully returns her attention to him. "What's jam made of?"

Oh, my word. I duck my head as my laughter starts, my shoulders shaking uncontrollably as Anna starts to boss him around the stovetop, where he'll stand stirring the raspberries as they cook down into jam.

"What's a trapezoid?" Mom asks, her cheeks flushed pink as she sets down her mug—that so has spiked eggnog in it. "I thought we just needed the rectangle cutter."

"Yeah," I say. "Yep. You didn't mention you'd be eggnogging during our bake time."

Mom only laughs a little, and I decide I have to be a little bit more like Anna. "Okay," I say. "You're going to start on the decor while I get these cookies rolled, cut, and in the oven." I nudge her down the counter and point to the white melting chocolate. "Candy canes, Mom. Go wild with the peppermint."

"Fifty minutes!" Danny calls from the living room. The kitchen has already seen two teams put together their concoctions, and there are mounds of sprinkles, globs of frosting, and even edible glitter remnants from their time.

It's pure cookie chaos, this bake-off. And I sort of love it.

I glance over to where Elliott and Anna are meticulously rolling out their dough, a picture of baking bliss. Seriously, how does he do it? "My grandmother's secret recipe involves singing to the dough at midnight." He grins at Anna and then me. "I guess we don't have time for that, though."

"Singing at midnight?" Anna asks, her confusion absolutely priceless. "What does she sing to...the dough?" And she's making things too easy for him. It's so not fair.

"Oh, you know," Elliott says. "Brittney Spears. Backstreet Boys. Yeah, yep. My granny *loved* boy bands."

"Boy bands," Anna repeats as if she doesn't understand those two words in that order.

"Yeah," I say. "You know, Anna. Bye, bye, bye—bye-bye!"

"What?" she asks, but Elliott's eyes sparkle like all the stars in the sky.

"It might sound crazy, but it ain't no lie...bye bye!" he belts out. "You know, like that." He delivers the last line with a perfectly straight face, and he is so winning this competition. I don't even care if he does. This has been the best cookie bake-off ever.

"Well," I say with my mouth curved upward. No matter what I do, I can't straighten out my smile. "Our cookies have been blessed by a unicorn, so they're guaranteed to be magical."

"Please," Anna says. "Unicorns aren't real."

"You sure about that?" I ask, and Cosette turns from the counter behind us.

"Can you guys stop it? You're giving me a headache."

"I have the perfect remedy for that," I say, nodding to Mom. "Peppermint."

"Or dragon scales," Elliott says, and I can't stop myself from tipping my head back and laughing right out loud.

———

I JOG the last few steps to the guest house, giggling. My glee is off the charts, even if my stomach aches a little from all the taste-testing I did. "That was *awesome*," I say as Elliott and I burst into the warm interior of the house.

"Incredible," he says through his chuckles. He lets out all his breath and adds, "I totally won too."

I can't argue with him, so I just grin at him and say, "You absolutely did." I laugh again.

"When you burst into that N'SYNC song, I seriously thought I was going to wet my pants." He laughs too, and I sure like the sound of it. As we sober, our eyes meet, and I move over to him. Or maybe he moves closer to me. It's probably simultaneous.

"You're incredible," I say just before he kisses me. His lips are chilly, touched with mint, and I simply can't get enough of him.

Elliott dips his head, breaking out kiss, and murmurs, "I'm going to go change."

"Yeah." I step back and tuck my hands in my back pockets. "Yep, me too."

He ducks away from me, and I watch him grab his shorts and tee from his side of the bed before going into the bathroom. Then I fly, hurrying to change into my pjs before he comes out. He's in there for a couple of minutes, and I'm sitting in my spot in bed when he comes out.

He sighs as he climbs right over me, and I go, "Hey. What—? What is this?"

"The floor is cold." He flops onto the bed and pulls

the blanket out from behind his back. "It's your night to build up the fire."

I stare at him as I swipe up on my phone. Then I look back at it, but I don't want to be in a kitty-cat mood. "You know what?" I say. "Today was so awesome." I slide down under the covers too and roll toward him. He opens his arms to me, and I easily move into them.

"I'm surprised Katherine could carry your dad like that," Ell says, his voice quiet as his breath wafts softly over my forehead. Katherine and Dad won the cookie bake-off which surprised no one except Elliott. Katherine has always been the quiet one, but she can bake like a champion, and her mint brownie cookie bars were pure perfection.

"She's a good baker," I say. "I nearly stole the victory from you."

"Yeah, if your brother hadn't called time, you'd have put your whole hand in that bowl of melted chocolate."

I grin and grin. "Best day ever," I say.

"Merry Christmas, Ry," he whispers.

"Merry Christmas, Ell." I tilt my head back. "Hey, did you talk to your family today?"

"Yeah," he says, swallowing. "This morning."

"You miss being there with them."

"Sure do." He holds me closer. "But Ry, I wouldn't trade this time with you for anything."

I smile, and if he's not careful, he'll make me think he's getting really serious about our relationship. He dips his head closer and touches his lips gently to mine, and oh, he's not going to be careful. My feelings for him multiply, and I can't help it—I fall for him even more.

I shouldn't. I know I shouldn't. But he's so warm and so good and so funny that I can't help myself.

He pulls away and says, "Okay, I'm going to put on the next episode of that murder mystery, and I believe you promised me the coveted coconut M&Ms if I won our little contest."

———

THE RHYTHMIC THUMP of the bass reverberates through my body as I lean closer to the window display, my breath fogging up the glass. My eyes widen at the outrageous price tag on a pair of sparkly red heels.

"My word." I shake my head and turn to my sisters. "Who spends that much on shoes?"

Cosette lets out a low whistle. "Someone with a lot of credit card debt, probably."

"Or," Anna adds, her gaze glued to her phone. "Someone with a sugar daddy."

I wrinkle my nose. "You're both terrible."

"And you love us anyway," Cosette says, linking her arm through mine and tugging me toward the next shop in this quaint outdoor row, all of which have racks out front with their Boxing Day sales.

We're in downtown Grayson Falls, and though the

temperatures should be keeping us all inside, the sidewalks teem with people. The crisp winter air does little to dampen the festive spirit, and I find myself getting swept up in the excitement of the holidays. It's exhilarating, being here with my sisters, a sense of camaraderie settling over me that I haven't felt in years.

Maybe it's the Christmas spirit, or maybe it's the fact that we're all a little bit older now, and while there's still some competitive vibes between us, it's nothing like when we were younger.

Anna tucks her phone away and links her arm through my other one. "I sure like Elliott, Ry."

"Do you?"

"Yes," she says crisply as Cosette says, "He's pretty great, Ry. Funny. Smart. Looks at you with stars in her eyes." She laughs and nudges me with her hip.

"Sexy in those glasses," Anna adds, giving me a side-eyed look I can't interpret before Cosette squeals.

"Anna," she chastises. "What a thing to say."

"Please. I heard you telling Rob he should get his eyes checked in the New Year. You want him to get some sexy glasses like those blue ones Elliott wore to breakfast."

I whip my attention back to Cosette, who holds her head high and shakes her hair over her shoulder. "I *suggested* the visit to the optometrist, because we have to use our flexible spending money before the end of January." She rolls her eyes. "So there, Anna."

"I do like Elliott's glasses," I say as Mom opens the door to a clothing boutique none of us but her will like. We'll still go in, because that's what we do on Boxing Day. We stick together, and we go into any shop anyone wants.

"I told him that he needs to invest in some better winter wear. The man wore a T-shirt to a Christmas tree cutting." Anna shakes her head, then stops in front of a rack with plenty of what she speaks of.

"He's from South Carolina," I remind her. "It's not like he has a closet full of winter wear."

"Well, he'll need to invest in some." She casts a knowing look my way, and I wonder what she sees when she looks at me and Elliott. And just when I think she's going to launch into one of her big sister lectures about how she always knows best, or how she can see things I just can't, she simply pulls out a puffer vest and says, "I think James would like this."

She's chill today, which is especially surprising since she and Ell didn't win the bake-off. Her Linzer cookies were delicious, but the jam was a little lumpy, and she didn't have time to roll them all out to exactly the same thickness.

"Please. Your husband doesn't need any more winter wear." Cosette takes the vest and replaces it back on the rack. "Plus, I've seen him wear the other puffer vests you've bought for him, and just...no."

I giggle but duck my head as I pretend to look at a

ghastly sweater that Lizzie would swat my hand away from. I can hear her saying, "No, Ry. No stripes."

Mom comes over to us and pulls out the exact sweater I'm looking at. "Ooh," she says, holding it up to her body. "This is cute." She looks at me, her eyebrows up, and I can't keep a straight face.

"Ew, Mom, no," Cosette says, and I let my laughter fly. It sure is nice to be out shopping with them, and for all the things that rub me wrong or make me roll my eyes about them, I do love my sisters and my parents.

Sometimes it just takes a very merry mess to remember why.

Now, all I can do is hope that the merry mess doesn't continue once Elliott and I get back to Cider Cove. Elliott's MO is to break-up with women when things get too serious, and while he's said he'll try with me, I'm simply not sure what will happen once we're back to real life.

ELLIOTT

THE LUCKSON FAMILY ROOM BUZZES WITH excitement as James unveils his annual popcorn extravaganza. I stand back, taking in the sheer magnitude of it all. Bags upon bags of fluffy white popcorn line the coffee table, accompanied by what seems like miles of flavored powders in every color imaginable.

"Holy popcorn balls, Batman," I mutter under my breath, earning a giggle from Ryanne beside me.

"James takes this very seriously," she whispers, her breath tickling my ear. "It's like his Super Bowl."

I nod, trying to make sense of the chaos before me. Anna and Cosette stand together, chatting, while James, Rod, and Danny move around the counter, putting out labels for all the powders. Those are definitely going to come in handy. Ryanne's parents are working on the hot drinks--spiced apple cider, hot chocolate, and a coffee bar. It's a whirlwind of activity, and I find myself swept up in their post-church family traditions.

"All right," James says, and that seems to be enough from the man who doesn't seem to have a lot to say. In fact, he steps back as his wife eases away from her sister and to her husband's side.

"The popcorn bar is now open," Anna says. "I just want to remind everyone that it's not a competition. You can make yourself a dozen flavors if you want. Or make a big bowl for others to try. Or just try the concoctions of others. It's just popcorn."

It's so much more than that, but no one argues with her.

In fact, they simply surge forward, a line forming immediately. James steps back to the counter to open the industrial-sized bags of already-popped popcorn, and my mouth waters. "What if I just want all the butter and salt I can get?" I ask Ry.

"Then have all the butter and salt you want," she says. "But how many times are you going to have access to powdered essence of truffle?"

"Truffle popcorn?"

She grins at me. "It's not just a salty snack, Ell." She takes my hand, and I find her so bright, so shiny, so much fun. I'm free-falling through space with her, and I don't mind at all that there's no ground beneath my feet. As long as I have Ry's hand in mine, everything will be fine.

"I need to see all the flavors first," I say, and Anna lifts her eyes to meet mine. "Can I just go around and read the labels?"

"Of course," she says as she delicately taps a spoonful of green powder over a small bowl of popcorn. "I like making caramel apple." She smiles and moves expertly to the next bowl of flavoring she wants, which is the caramel. It's going to take me ten times as long to read all those signs, so I ease away from Ry, deciding to join the line last. Maybe then everyone else will have their preferred flavor and be ready to start the movie.

I guess that's what the rest of today is: movies. Ry says sometimes they get into a real argument between them, as they try to come to a nine-way consensus about what to watch next. This year, ten-ways.

"I'm making a lime coconut," Cosette says. "I love the tropical flavors on popcorn."

I've literally never thought of that, and she's made a big bowl for sampling. Others have too, and they're set up at the end of the countertop, crammed in by the last little bowls of powders.

There are your classics—butter, salt, cheese, both cheddar and parmesan. Then we move into the more adventurous territory—ranch, barbecue, sour cream, onion, ranch dressing powder—condiments. I've had barbecue chips, but never barbecue popcorn, and I spy the Tabasco Ryanne told me her dad used one year.

The powders then move into the sweet territory.

Chocolates, which are drizzle-able, come in chips or as a powder, marshmallows—which are teeny tiny little things that I can just toss into my bowl with my popcorn, and tiny pretzels. Maple, butterscotch, cinnamon, caramel powders and bits. There are mini M&Ms, and I'm not surprised one whit when Ry adds a scoop of those to her bowl, along with one of pretzels. She's making a popcorn-style trail mix, which I find brilliant and just so Ry.

Then come the fruits, and there's everything from passionfruit to dragon fruit to banana. I don't even want to think about banana popcorn, and I move past the fruits pretty fast. The chatter is constant, punctured with laughter as everyone partakes in the merriment.

At the end, we get into the weirder stuff. Bacon bits. Cajun spice. Soy sauce powder. Rosemary. I've never thought of herbs going with popcorn, and now it's all I can think about.

I want to make a sweet and savory popcorn, but I'm no chef. I can barely make toast and pour milk on cereal. But I think of my favorite things to order in a restaurant—pork chops and applesauce, orange chicken and noodles—and I want that with some popcorny crunch.

"Popcorn is a blank canvas," James says when I finally get in line. He wears a smile and holds out the clear plastic scoop. "Take three or four if you want to make a tasting bowl," he says. "Then it's usually one scoop of flavoring per scoop of popcorn, but Ry does double."

"Well, she likes her tongue to be tingling when she eats."

"I like what?" Ryanne demands, but I only smile at her.

"You do like strong flavors," James says in his even-keel way, and I take the plastic scoop and a small bowl.

After I put in one scoop of popcorn, I take another half and smile at him. I'm very aware of everyone watching me, and I carefully and deliberately pick up another small bowl and put in another scoop and a half of popcorn.

"What in the name of Colonel Sanders are you doing?" Danny asks.

I grin at him, and he's holding a single bowl of popcorn that looks like he added six scoops of cinnamon sugar. Gross.

"Is it a one-bowl limit?" I ask.

"Have you made flavored popcorn before?" He grins like a cartoon animal, like I don't know what I'm getting into when I dump a scoop of butter powder over popcorn and shake it all together.

"No," I say. "How hard is it?"

"It's not hard at all," Ry says, coming to my rescue. "Didn't I tell you not to listen to anything Danny says?"

"Nothing?" he asks incredulously. "*Nothing* I say?"

Ry takes one of my bowls and slides it into the

microwave. "You just heat it up slightly, Ell. Then the powder sticks better."

"What did you make?" I ask.

"Chocolate-drizzled popcorn mix." She whips my bowl back out of the microwave, and there's no way that got very hot. "What are you going to make?"

"I'm going to do a maple bacon one," I say, moving down to the maple powder. I add the real maple sugar too, then move down to the poor, lonely bacon bits, which no one has touched.

"Of course," Ry says, and I take one of the plastic lids and cover the bowl, then shake it up and down, down and up, vigorously to combine all the flavors.

The moment I take the lid off, Ry dips her hand into my popcorn bowl and lifts a couple of perfectly popped pieces out. It's barely touched her tongue before she says, "Mm."

I smile at her, then take a bite for myself. The cheap, fake bacon flavor isn't my favorite, and I say, "This needs real bacon. Or bacon salt."

"I have bacon salt," Grace says, and I turn toward her.

"Is it allowed to start over?"

Ry nudges a full bag of popcorn that hasn't even been opened yet. "Gee, Ell, I don't think we have enough for that." Then she takes the bowl from my hand and opens a cupboard behind her. It's got wine glasses in it, but she tosses my maple bacon popcorn in there and slams it shut.

"Ryanne," I say, grinning.

"I'll get the bacon salt," Grace says without commenting on Ry's disposal of my fake bacon maple popcorn.

"Here's another bowl." James hands me another small bowl with probably the exact number of popped kernels in it as the first one I had. I smile around to all of them, and Grace returns with the bacon salt.

"Real bacon," James says, his voice thoughtful as I go about warming my popcorn and adding the flavorings again.

This time, when I taste it, the smokiness is less, and the offensive crunch of the bottled bacon bits is gone. "Much better," I say, and I tilt the bowl toward Ry to try. James takes a handful too, and I can't even imagine how much popcorn he tastes.

"It's good," he says, and for some reason I feel like I've won a major award to have gained his approval.

"I'm making you a buttery, salty one," Ry says.

"Yeah?" I slide my second bowl into the microwave and tap the same button Ry did.

"Yes," she says. "I know you want that."

"I'm going to make a savory one too."

She gives me an easy, soft smile. Something that tells me she already knew that, something that means we know each other well enough for her to know that. "I figured," she says.

"Something's burning," James says.

I turn in a full circle, getting back to facing him right as he lunges for the microwave. "It's this." He pulls out my bowl, yelps, and drops it immediately. "Ow! That's hot."

I back up, like perhaps someone else snuck into the kitchen to make a bowl of popcorn, as all eyes come my way.

"I...thought I pushed the same button Ry did." I look at the microwave, but it's not like I can read the teeny tiny lettering on the small buttons.

"Sorry," I say, going into full Lambert-the-Sheepish-Lion mode.

"Again, we have more popcorn," Ry says.

"But it reeks in here now," Danny adds. "Mom's going to say something in three...two...one..."

Grace pops up from where she's sitting on one of the huge couches, the TV in the living room already on. "It stinks," she says, twisting to look into the kitchen. "Someone burned their popcorn."

I surely can't be the one person who's ever done that, though in this family, maybe I am.

"We got it under control, Mom," Ry calls. She hands me another bowl of slightly warmed popcorn and nods down to the sweeter components on the counter. "Go make your savory bowl, baby."

Her Southern drawl comes out on that last word, and I sure like such a pet name—for me—coming from her.

"Okay, yeah, yep," I say, feeling a little out of sorts. I face the row upon row of flavored powders, my mind a little blank as to what I was going to do before the microwave incident.

We go home tomorrow, but I wonder how many more things will happen that I'll be able to label "incidents."

Hopefully none.

Then I move down to the more savory flavorings, and I put in a half-scoop of soy sauce powder, a half-scoop of orange powder, and a whole scoop of lemon-pepper.

I put on the lid and shake, shake, shake, and Ry walks toward me with a tray with three bowls built in.

Two of them hold the popcorn flavors I've already made, and I dip my hand into the oriental orange chicken popcorn I've just made.

It's not precise, but it's pretty dang good.

"Can I try it?" Ry reaches for it without waiting for my permission, because she knows she doesn't need it.

I love that about us—and I realize that I am dangerously close to loving Ryanne.

Her midnight eyes brighten, and she nods. "Yes, this is good."

I grin at her and sweep my arm around her waist. I

chuckle as I hold the bowl of popcorn out to the side as I press her close, close, close.

"Thank you for having me here," I whisper, and then I don't care who's watching, I kiss Ry standing right there in her parents' kitchen.

It's sweet and over a moment later, but the ground beneath our feet shifts violently. Or maybe that change is just inside me.

Ry tucks herself into my chest, and then Danny calls, "The movie's starting. Bring over all the popcorn and let's do this."

Ry looks up at me, and that's when I see it—something has shifted for her too.

"Let's have James try this." Ry takes the savory popcorn in one hand and mine in her other. Then she leads me into the living room, hands the popcorn to James with the words, "Try that," and then pulls me onto the remaining bean bag with her.

I have a very real feeling that I'll go wherever Ry wants me to and do whatever she wants me to—and I've never been in this spot before.

It's as terrifying as not being able to see, but I tell myself I've survived a skunk-spray and maybe, just maybe, I can survive falling in love with my best friend.

"Holy cow," James says, because he's not a Luckson and doesn't curse in the name of Colonel Sanders. "Who made this, and what is it?"

"Good or bad?" Danny asks, already reaching for a handful of my oriental orange chicken popcorn.

"Amazing," James says, and that's how I know I'm not getting my bowl of popcorn back. "If you ever need a job, Elliott, let me know."

Ryanne grins at me, but I just shake my head, despite the warm glow moving through me as Anna says, "I'm not sure why I can't stop eating this. It's funky, and yet...delicious."

RYANNE

"I LOVE YOU SO MUCH," MOM SAYS AS SHE HOLDS ME tight. I hug her back, tears flooding my eyes.

"I love you too, Mom," I say, my voice caught and stuck and tight. "Thank you so much for having me and Elliott."

Our bags are in the back of the rental car, and all we have left are these good-byes. Anna and James left with Sariah about an hour ago, and Cosette and Rob pulled out twenty minutes ago.

Danny and Katherine left last night, as Danny had to get back to work, and it has been just me and Elliott with my parents for a little bit now.

It's been nice.

The moment I step back, I swipe at my eyes, and Elliott sweeps into my mom's arms.

He's laughing where I'm crying, and my mom

giggles as Elliott lifts her right up off her feet. "You are the best hostess in the whole world," he says. He steps back and takes my dad's hand in his. He pumps it hard, his smile absolutely huge.

Almost Joker-like.

"Thank you, sir. It's been an amazing time here. Really."

"You're welcome back anytime," Dad says, and that only confirms what I've been suspecting since I went shopping with my sisters on Boxing Day.

Elliott has charmed my whole family.

I beam at him when he glances over to me. "Ready, sweetheart?" he asks.

"Yes." I hug my mother one more time, then square my shoulders and turn to leave the porch. Elliot comes behind me, and the moment we get in the car, all the tension between us lifts. It's been this way every time we escape to the guest house too, and I sigh as I buckle my seatbelt and look over to him.

"We survived."

"I really enjoyed that," he says, his boisterous personality still pinned in place.

"It's just me."

"Tell me you didn't have fun at your parents'." He folds his arms, and as I start to drive, the seatbelt reminder beeping begins.

"There were some interesting moments," I admit.

The beeping continues, and I glare over to him. "Can you put your seatbelt on?"

"Not until you admit you had fun. That you miss them. That you *love* your family." He grins at me.

My eyes fill with tears again. I can't speak, but the beeping is going to drive me insane.

"Ryanne," Elliott says.

"I love my family," I say, and my tears spill out of my right eyes. Of course, the one closest to him.

"They're pretty great," he says as he pulls his seatbelt across him and snaps it in place. Thankfully, the beeping stops.

"It's okay for them to irritate you sometimes and for you to love them at the same time."

"You're right," I say. "Thank you for coming."

"I had an amazing time," he says, and he settles back into his seat. "Best Christmas ever."

"I'm sure that's not true," I say.

"Listen." He clears his throat. "There's something I have to tell you."

I glance over to him, because he's deflated back to regular-Elliott. "Okay," I say.

"It's about this present my mom got me for Christmas," he says.

I know he's talked to his family several times while we've been here, but he hasn't told me much. "Is it a good gift or a bad gift?" I ask. "Because you look like you're going to throw up."

Before he can answer, my phone rings through the car. "It's Tahlia," I say, and I glance over to him. "Can I get it?"

"Yeah," he says, and I tap to answer the call as he adds, "Yep."

"Hey, Tahlia," I say before I catalog that Elliott has used his yeah-yep on me. I glance over to him, but his attention is out his side window. "What's going on?"

"Claudia says you'll be home about seven-thirty. Is that right?"

"Yes," I say. "If the flight goes as planned."

"Great, can we do mic-night at eight?"

"We want to hear all about your holidays," Emma calls.

"And everything with Elliott," Claudia adds.

"He's in the car with me," I say. "And you know you won't get everything." I look over to him. "I don't tell them everything."

"I know," he says at the same time Claudia does.

"I have so much baking left over," Tahlia says. "And Lizzie has some news."

"And I need some help too," Emma says. "Man help."

"Oooh, boy," I say, a smile filling my face.

"See you soon," Tahlia says. "We miss you!"

"Miss you!" the others chorus, and the call ends with more love than ever.

"Miss you too," I say, and I sigh happily. I take a deep breath and look over to Elliott. "Okay, it's—"

But his eyes are closed as if he's asleep, and he's leaned his chair back slightly. So I cut off, and I let him rest until we get to the airport.

———

"I'M HOME," I call as I pull my suitcase up and over the step, and into the Big House.

"Ry's here," Lizzie calls, and then she and Emma both meet me in the foyer of the house. They mob me and form a big group hug, with Tahlia and Claudia joining in.

"I wish Hillary were here," someone says, and that's something we've all said at least once since she moved to LA a few months ago.

"I have news with that," Tahlia says, and that breaks up our huddle-hug.

"News?" I demand.

"Yeah," Claudia says just as sharply. "What news?"

"She'll tell us when we get her on video," Tahlia says with a smile, and she pushes her blonde hair out of her face. "Now, come on. Ry's a little late, and Hillary is calling right at eight."

We all file into the living room, leaving my suitcase in the hallway, where Tahlia turns on the TV and hooks up her work computer to it.

While she does that, the rest of us gab about Christmas with our families—nothing major, just things that are funny or of little consequence.

Tahlia's already laid out her baking, which ranges from pies and cakes to cookies and sweet breads.

"So, when are you going to see Elliott again?" Claudia asks.

I glance over to her. "I guess this isn't necessarily roommate-newsworthy."

"You *are* going to see him again, right?" Claudia glances over to Emma. "I shouldn't have asked. I thought this would be mild."

"It is mild," I say. "Five days together is a lot." And I haven't even told them about the sleeping arrangements yet. "So I told him that I'd see him at work on Wednesday. His day off is tomorrow, so he won't be at the store, and I'd be mad if he brought me lunch or whatever." I shrug and reach for a coconut cookie half-dipped in dark chocolate. "He agreed."

"He agreed, huh?" Claudia asks, and she hides so much in her dark eyes.

"Are you surprised by that?"

"Hillary's calling," Tahlia says, ending the conversation. "Quiet down, everyone."

Lizzie and Emma are giggling over something on Emma's phone, but she quickly shoves it away as our long-lost roommate's face fills the screen.

She's alone, as she usually is when we do these calls, though her boyfriend lives in LA near her.

She smiles and smiles and then she starts to cry.

"Oh, wow," I say, setting aside my half-eaten cookie. "This is serious."

"It's just so good to see you guys," she says.

"I thought she and Liam were coming for Christmas." I look over to Emma, who shakes her head.

"His momma and sister went out there, so Hill stayed. Last-minute."

I hadn't known, and I watch one of my best friends wipe her tears and keep smiling through them.

"I don't think we need the mic for her," Tahlia says, and even her voice is choked. "Tell them, Hill."

She breathes in deep and wipes her face with both hands again. "Okay." She exhales slowly, obviously trying to find her emotional center.

I'm not usually a sympathy crier, but right now, I am. I dab at my own tears as she takes another breath, and this time, she says, "The documentary is done filming. Now, we just have to edit it and put it out."

"How long does that take" three of us ask at the same time. Hill's news is always about Liam or work, and since they're so intertwined, it's usually both.

"Our final edit date is March first," she says. "And then Liam and I are going to come back to Cider Cove to...get married."

Tears leak down her face again, and she wipes them

away. "We'll come back here for the premiere, but we don't have to live here once edits wrap."

She grins and laughs through her emotion. "So I'm moving back onto the third floor in March, and Liam and I are going to get married one day in April when his orchards are at the height of their bloom."

"This is so great," I say.

"Amazing news," Lizzie agrees.

"So you're not going to set a date," Claudia says, and it's not a question.

"We'll have a few days' lead time," Hillary says defensively, pinning Claude with a darker look. "I want all the blossoms, and Liam says that depends on the weather, the rainfall, lots of things."

She shrugs. "I have a dress. Our families are there. No one needs to travel all that far. I promised my parents I'd give them a three-day lead-time, as if they can't come the day-of. My daddy's retired, for crying out loud."

Her joyous emotion hardens slightly when she talks of her parents, but that quickly dissolves away too.

"Liam says the trees bloom at the end of March or beginning of April. I want you all there, so I guess clear your schedules for then?"

"I wouldn't miss it," Claudia says, and I nod in agreement.

Tahlia gets to her feet and holds up the pink sparkly microphone, which is really just a paper towel tube with a tennis ball attached to the top of it. The whole thing has been painted bright pink, and it looks like it got a facelift since the last time we used it.

"All right," she says. "I'm holding the mic, but I don't have any news. My life is very boring."

She holds out the mic among our protests, and I say, "We'd all starve to death without you."

"Truth," Claudia says, while Lizzie says, "Someone needs to be *stable* in this house."

"Stability is a better term for it, yes," Emma says.

"Stability, blah-bility," Tahlia says, shaking the mic. "Who's next? Claudia? Engagement news? Ry? We want a full report on the holidays. Emma? You specifically said you had something."

I don't want to go first, so I look at Claudia beside me, then Lizzie, then Emma. Claudia sighs like she has the migraine of the century, then gets up and takes the mic from Tahlia.

"No news," she says. "Beckett is all moved out at the office, though, and he's not working this week until he starts next week. I've likewise taken this week off, and we're going to...do something."

"Do something?" I ask, seizing onto the color of her face as it goes deeper into the maroon category. "Do what?"

"That's what I want to know," Emma says.

Claudia sighs like this is a federal interrogation. "It's just a simple road trip."

"Sounds like it," Hillary says, and I gesture to the TV.

"We're going to Orlando," she says. "Gonna ring in the New Year at Walt Disney World." A smile finally touches her face, and oh, there it is.

Of course, I know she's in love with Beckett, but it's still so beautiful to see on her face.

I panic as I think about how I have a lot to tell. Will my roommates be able to tell that I'm in love with Elliott?

Am I even in love with Elliott?

My phone buzzes, and I glance down at it while Claudia passes the mic to Emma. *New Year's Eve?* Elliott has asked. *Me and you. A pretty dress for you, and I'll wear something nice too. Dinner and sitting outside without freezing to death.*

I smile, because I love getting asked out. *Absolutely,* I tell him.

"All right," Emma says. "I'm having a bit of a flirt-fest with a man, and I'm not sure if it's like, a crush on his part, or if he likes me, and I'm, you know, on this male-vacation, but he's really cute, and..."

She sighs. "I don't know what to do."

"Are we allowed questions?" Tahlia asks.

"Yes." Emma sounds pretty miserable about it, but she is one of the more emotional roommates.

"How long has this been going on?" Claudia asks.

"A couple of weeks," Emma says.

"Are we allowed to know who it is?"

Emma surveys the room, holding my gaze for a few heartbeats of time, just like she does everyone else.

And I know this is going to be big.

"I wish to remind everyone that only the person with the mic can talk," Tahlia says.

"She said we could ask questions," I say.

"I'm more worried about the upcoming reactions." Tahlia quirks her eyebrows at me, and she's probably not wrong.

Emma actually holds up the fake microphone to her mouth and says, "It's Aaron Stansfield."

There's a momentary beat of silence where the four syllables of the man's name hovers in the air between all of us.

Then Hillary says, "The boy next door," right before the rest of us erupt into more excited questions or actual cheers like, "Yes! I knew he liked you."

And ah, it's so good to be home.

ELLIOTT

I FLOP ONTO MY COUCH, EXHAUSTION SEEPING INTO my bones after the whirlwind holiday weekend with Ryanne and her family. Oh, and the sleepless night after I chickened out and didn't tell Ry about my eyes.

Peppermint, my fluffy gray and white cat, immediately jumps up and settles on my chest, purring contentedly. I scratch behind her ears, grateful for the familiar comfort of home.

"You missed me, didn't you girl?" I murmur. Peppermint responds by kneading my shirt with her paws.

My mind drifts back to the past few days—the laughter, the chaos, the warmth of being included in Ryanne's family traditions. It felt so natural, like I belonged there. Her parents and siblings sure seemed to like me, and it was all Ry could talk about on the drive home from Charleston.

Anna says your glasses are sexy.

Cosette thinks you're smart and funny.

My mom has never taken to one of my brothers-in-law the way she did you.

And Ryanne...my heart swells two sizes just thinking about her. I sigh, something the Mars rovers can't do, but I think of that Pixar robot movie with the robots, and Eva an WALL-E sure do seem to have feelings. So maybe I've been a robot for a lot of my life—at least the past six years since I got my diagnosis. It really has made things easier.

The buzz of my phone interrupts my robot-thoughts. It's an email from Paws For a Cause with more details about Luna, my soon-to-be guide dog. I skim the message, excitement and nervousness battling for space in my brain. This is really happening. Just next week, if I confirm, I'll be partnered with a dog specially trained to help me navigate the world as my vision continues to deteriorate.

I need to tell Ryanne. The thought sends a jolt of panic through me. "I need to put in for time off."

I can imagine how that conversation will go.

"How about this? 'So, hey, Ry, funny story, I'm going blind, but don't worry! I won a guide dog for Christmas and surprise! I need more time off. Want to go steady?'" I say sarcastically to my feline companion. Peppermint blinks at me slowly, unimpressed. In fact, her eyes squinch shut in the next moment, and she circles, turning her back on me.

How very diva-cat.

I can only pray Ry won't do the same when I tell her. I sigh and reach for my phone again. I can start with something easy and maybe just type out the blindness issue as a test. My thumbs hover over the screen as I contemplate what to say.

Me: *Hey beautiful. I need to make reservations for New Year's Eve. I want to take you to one of your favorite places, so a list of your favorite places would be much appreciated.*

I hit send before I can erase the "much appreciated." I mean, I'm not seventy-four years old.

Her response comes almost immediately. *My favorite places. That's awfully generous of you, Mr. Huston.*

Me: *What can I say? I'm a giver.*

Ryanne: *Hmm... this sounds suspiciously like what you do when you're going to break-up with someone. Take a woman exactly where she wants to go right before you "break the bad news."*

The air whooshes out of my lungs as if Peppermint's punctured it with her claws. But Ry's not wrong about my past behavior with women. But what she doesn't know if that that's what I do with women I'm not serious about.

As I type that out, my phone rings and Ry's name sits there.

"Hey," I answer, unable to keep the smile out of my voice.

"Hey?" she repeats. "I...politely asked you to take today to detox." She sounds mad, but it's a restrained anger I usually only see when we're at work. Maybe there are people around. "I didn't realize part of that was going to be you planning your exit strategy."

...And there's the familiar bite I'm used to.

I want to chuckle, but my chest is still leaking air. "I'm not planning my exit strategy."

"No?"

"I mean, if I have to try any popcorn flavor Danny makes again...but I think we're safe for another year."

She says nothing, which means she's feeling silly for jumping to conclusions. I hope. "Just a minute," she says to someone on her end of the line. "Yeah, I'm coming."

"I really did just want a list of your favorite places." It's getting pretty late to make reservations for New Year's Eve, but I have to try.

"You should see this place," Ry says, and I recognize her ranty-tone. "Barry-House-the-Temporary-Manager rearranged the whole thing. Cardstock is on aisle six, and I've been running around all day, trying to locate the sticky notes. Do you *know* how many people want sticky notes to write their New Year's resolutions on?"

She's grumpy, and I should hang up. Or better yet, get dressed and get into work to help her. "I can—"

"You're not coming in," she says. "I just need to vent." Something scratches on her end of the line. "Yes, Jimmy, I want everything that used to be in this aisle returned. Fans, printers, shredders, please. Joey! All desk chairs back on the floor."

"It's that bad?" I ask. "He moved the desk chairs out of the furniture section?"

"His note said, and I quote, 'A line of desk chairs down the middle of the floor looks cheap. Put them against the back wall.'"

"He realizes he was there for four days, right?"

"Apparently it was pretty bad." She sighs. "I've spoken to every employee today, either in person or on the phone, and while I thought we might have the very merry mess in New York, it turns out, it was here."

"Let me come in then."

"No way," she says. "You'll have to deal with this crazy tomorrow. I'll leave you a note."

I sit up, the word vomit that needs to come out choking me. I certainly can't be lying down while I say it all. "Listen, Ryanne, I need to talk to you about something important." I said the same things in the car while we were leaving her parents' house, but we'd been interrupted.

"Go on," she says, but something doesn't feel right, and I hesitate.

"Oh, pink pixie dust," she swears. "Hold on a sec." Her voice goes muffled as she covers her phone, but I still hear her talking to someone in the background, something about how we can't leave small appliances outside overnight. "Sorry, Ell," she says. "This is a nightmare."

"Then I'll talk to you tonight."

"I'm sorry."

I force a smile to my face. "It's fine. Go."

"Mindy!" she yells right over me. "There's water leaking back here!"

Instead of making her talk to me some more, I simply hang up. She has plenty to do, and I don't need to burden her with an about-to-be-blind boyfriend on top of it.

Peppermint meows at me, and I reach over and pat her. "Yeah, I know. Massive fail."

And that about sums up everything that's happened since Ry and started dating. At the same time, it's been three of the best weeks of my life. Nothing makes sense.

My phone chirps, and I reach for it, because it's my momma. I know what she wants before I read her message. *Have you put in for time off at work?*

Yes, I tell her, though I haven't. It's just one more thing I need to do on a long list of things that are going to cause me to crash and burn with my boss, best friend, and girlfriend. So sue me if I don't want to do it.

Good, Momma says. *Have you confirmed the pick-up of Luna?*

Not yet, Momma, I say. *I need to wait for my approved time off. They said they'll keep her until I can come.*

Okay, she says. *I'm stopping by the store on the way home from work. Requests?*

"Yeah," I mutter. "Can you stop by Paper Trail and explain to Ryanne Luckson that the reason I can't be with her is because I'm going blind?"

Because that would be great.

Oh, and *some hazelnut cream for my coffee would be nice,* I text to my mother.

AARON

I STAND AT THE FRONT WINDOW OF MY BEST friend's house, where I live. The sun has risen in beautiful colors today, and I lift my coffee to my lips slowly, as if my life is simple and easy, made of sunshine and marshmallows and women who text me back within moments of me sending them a message.

I actually scoff right out loud.

I've made the coffee too strong, and I set it on the side table next to Liam's couch. I should've left the house an hour ago to go work on my place before I have to be at the store, because when my best friend returns from California, I'll need somewhere to live.

I bought my grandfather's house in the middle of Cider Cove after he moved into a home for those sixty-five-plus, but the house needs a lot of work.

I've ripped it down to the studs, and I'm slowly

rebuilding the walls, floors, plumbing, and everything in between. Literally.

And you know what? I'm tired today, and I just want a lazy morning before I have to go into the hardware store where I've worked since I was nine years old.

"Twenty years," I say, and I'm honestly surprised my daddy is letting me take over for him before I'm thirty.

Of course, he fell last year, and he can't really keep doing what he's been doing at the store. And he doesn't need to. I'm capable, and I love the store. I know every detail of it, and it's a legacy I want to continue.

"So you'll ask out someone else," I tell myself. Because the gorgeous Emma Newberry has not been taking my flirting as well as I hoped, and no one wants to keep getting rejected over and over by someone they have to see on a regular basis.

So fine.

I look away from the blue sky and gold sunshine and down to my phone. Surely there are the names and numbers of women in here that I haven't made a fool of myself in front of.

"There has to be," I mutter.

The Christmas Festival is over now, so those "easy dates" are gone, but it's New Year's Eve in a couple of days, and that has to be super simple to get someone to go to dinner with me.

Right?

Frustrated, I put my phone away, because there's not

going to be anyone in it I want to spend more than thirty minutes with.

I texted Emma yesterday, and she still hasn't responded. I tap over to that conversation and reread what I sent her.

Hey, wondering what you're up to for New Year's Eve. I got invited to a party at my sister's house, and she's planning a game that requires couples. I just need a partner to go with and thought you might be interested. Let me know.

She has not let me know. Sam has texted me two more times, and if I don't answer soon, she'll invite someone else.

"So *you* invite someone else," I say, and I turn to take my coffee back into the kitchen. I have to get to work anyway.

Liam's built his garage behind the house, so I leave through the back door and go down the sidewalk there. The orchards extend beyond that, dormant right now as we approach January.

He's got several vehicles in various states of completion, but there's space for my truck. I get in it, and driving is just a mindless task at this point. I pull out and start down the dirt lane that leads to the road that'll take me in front of Emma's house and then on to Main Street, where the hardware store is.

I'm determined to look straight ahead until I get to

the store—and that alone saves me from hitting the pretty woman standing in the road.

I slam on the brakes and grip the steering wheel, while saying right out loud, "Dear Lord, don't let me hit her."

Thankfully, the truck comes to a stop, a cloud of dust billowing up behind the back tires.

I meet Emma's bright blue eyes through the windshield, and then I'm flying out of the truck. "Are you okay? Did I hit you?"

She doesn't look hit, and she's wearing a blue plaid dress that flares at the hip and has a full skirt that falls to her knees. White sandals complete the look, and she is so stinking pretty, I can't stand it.

Nuts and bolts and washer fluid too.

She looks down at her clothes, and that's when I notice she's holding something in her hands.

"I'm fine," she says, lifting her eyes back to mine. She swallows visibly and raises the paper plate. "I brought you some cookies."

I can't just snatch them from her hands and grump my way back to my truck. So I don't move at all.

"Thalia made them," she says. "So they're pretty good, even if they're the no-bake kind."

"I like the no-bake kind," I say, but they're not why my mouth is watering.

"I can go to your sister's party with you," she says, and it feels like the sky has opened and a whole herd of unicorns has flown down on us. Or do unicorns fly in a flock, like birds?

I shake the glittery thoughts out of my head. This is so not the time for them.

Then I mess it up with, "It's okay. You don't have to."

Emma tilts her head, her eyes falling slightly shut. "You asked someone else." And she's not asking.

"I mean," I say as casually as I can. "I'm waiting to hear from a couple of people, and I'm sure—" I cut off, because I just can't stand to lie.

"Fine." I look away, across the expansive lawn and toward the Big House, where Emma lives with her roommates. "That's not true. I haven't asked anyone else."

I'm not sure how brave to be. Emma has been very clear with me; it's not that I'm confused, it's that I'm frustrated she doesn't seem to like me as much as I like her.

She flirts back with me, but she never takes it a toenail further.

"It's not a date," I say. "We can go as friends, because we're...friends," I finish lamely.

She nods. "Okay," she says, her smile brightening slightly. "What time should I be ready? Is there a dress code?"

"It's eating junk food at my sister's house," I say. "No dress code. And we'll go over about eight, otherwise it'll feel like we've been there for half our lives by the time the ball drops at midnight."

Emma nods, and she takes quick steps toward me and hands me the plate of cookies. "I remembered you said you liked these."

"Thank you."

"Are you going to kiss me?"

"What?"

"On New Year's Eve," she says. "People kiss at midnight."

"Do you want me to kiss you?" I realize what I'm saying as it comes out of my mouth. "Do *not* answer that. Of course I'm not going to kiss you. Friends don't kiss each other. That's a very *un*friendly thing to do."

She nods, just once, and almost robotically spins and walks away. "Okay," she says. "I'll be ready to go by seven-thirty."

"Okay," I call after her. "See you then."

And because I don't want her to text me later and cancel, I stop staring and get the heck back in the truck.

RYANNE

I SIT ON THE CLOSED TOILET SEAT, MY EYES CLOSED
as Lizzie masterfully does my makeup. I'm saving all my
conversational capability for my New Year's Eve date
with Elliott in less than an hour.

"So the store is mostly back to normal?" Lizzie asks.

My eyelids flutter before I remember to keep them
closed. "Almost," I say. "I honestly don't know what
Barry was thinking, especially since he'll probably never
step foot in our store again."

Both Lizzie and Emma had come over to Paper Trail
this week to help me and Elliott get things put back the
way they've always been. Our store has earned several
awards from the corporate office, and I honestly wonder
if the temporary manager they sent while Ell and I went
to New York had been tipping back eggnog by the
gallon.

During the staff meeting I'd held, Mindy, who usually acts as our supervisor on the days when Elliott and I aren't there together, said that "he just started, and it was so chaotic, that we just ran with him to stay alive."

I'd filed a report with corporate, but I haven't heard anything back yet. The store isn't open tomorrow, but I'm taking Tahlia, Lizzie, and Emma to finish the stationery section. Then, everything will be done moving into the New Year.

I love the beginning of a new year. It's so exciting, with dozens of doors open and plenty of enthusiasm for making changes. Good changes. I can't help but think that this year will be pivotal in my life, and that so much of that has to do with Elliott.

My stomach clenches, and I try to push the thoughts and feelings away, because I really shouldn't hook my happiness onto being with another person. I've worked hard to find out who I am and to make life choices that will make me happy, regardless of if I'm single, with someone, at home in New York, who my roommates are, any of it.

But I've entertained feelings for Elliott for such a long time, and he's such a big piece of my life, that I don't know how to box him out. I don't know how separate him from me, especially not now.

"Okay," Lizzie says. "You're ready."

I open my eyes to find her smiling at me. "You have

the best bone structure," she says. "What did you decide to wear tonight?"

"Tahlia pulled out her black dress." I stand up and sigh. "Thank you, Lizzie." I hug her quickly and then we leave the bathroom on the second floor.

"I'll get the shoes and come help you zip," she says, ducking into her room ahead of me.

I continue to my room and look at the dress that Tahlia has hung on my closet door. It holds a curvy shape, with glittery fabric, and I simply love the one-shoulder look. It is hard for me to get into on my own, but I get started by taking it off the hanger and stepping into it.

I shimmy it up over my hips about the time Lizzie enters my bedroom, and she helps me get the strap in place and the dress zipped. "Let me just tuck this..." She flits around me, making sure every little string and flap is in the right place.

Then she sets the shoes out and offers me her hand, so I can step up into them. She grins at me and hugs me, something falling on her face in the moment before her cheek presses against mine. "You're so beautiful. He's so lucky."

"You think so?"

"Absolutely." She steps back and wipes at her eyes. "I can only hope to meet someone like Elliott."

"You will," I say.

She nods, her smile watery and shaky. "Does he make you happy?"

I think about her question, because it's not one I've considered before. "Not like a bag of mocha crunch M&Ms," I say thoughtfully, which makes a bursting laugh come out of her mouth. I grin and shake my head, sobering. "But yeah, I think he does. In a totally different way than candy ever could."

"I hope this New Year is everything for you." She tucks her hair and adds, "Okay, I'm going to go join that dating app, because I can't be the last one to find a boyfriend and get married. Once Tahlia does, she'll want this house for her family."

Her smile feels fake, but I don't have time to ask her anything or reassure her that Tahlia isn't going to need five bedrooms and three floors of rooms the moment she meets her One True Love. Lizzie turns and leaves my bedroom while I'm still absorbing what she's said.

My phone rings, and the ringtone tells me it's my mom. I step over to the desk and swipe up my device, seeing that this isn't the first time she's called tonight. I'd left my phone in here while Lizzie had made me up, so I swipe to answer the call. After all, I don't want her to come on my date tonight, and she obviously wants to get in touch with me.

"Hey, Mom."

"I finally got you."

"I'm getting ready to go out," I say. "I have about ten

minutes." I really have about thirty, but I don't want to be on the phone right up until the moment I need to head downstairs, stress-eat whatever Tahlia's left in the kitchen, and then drink a gallon of water before Elliott shows up.

I can't believe I'm still nervous to go out with him—and I'm not. Not really. But tonight feels like a big date for some reason.

"So what's up?" I ask my mom.

"I just wanted to wish you a Happy New Year," she says. "I call every year, remember?"

"Oh, sure," I say with a smile. "Happy New Year to you and Dad too. Are you guys doing anything fun tonight?"

"Oh, let's see. Anna's bringing Sariah over for a little bit while she and James go to dinner. I suppose we'll fall asleep by ten-thirty, the same as always." She laughs, and I let myself giggle with her.

"What about you and Elliott?" she asks. "I assume you're going out with him."

"Yes," I say. "I don't know where we're going to dinner. But we're going to dinner." I sit down on my bed, needing to test how the dress does while I'm seated. It's great. "After that...I don't know. I think he said I could come meet his mom and cat. So we'll probably end up at his house."

"Are you driving then?"

My brow furrows. "No," I say slowly. "He's coming to get me."

"Mm, and you think that's safe?"

Alarms ring in my head as confusion builds beneath my breastbone. "Why wouldn't it be safe?"

"Oh, well, maybe it's fine," she says airily. "I just didn't realize Elliott could see well enough to drive at night."

Air leaks out of my lungs, and my brain and body have gone on vacation, so it's not getting replaced. "I—"

"I'm sure it's fine."

I pull in a big breath. "Why do you think Elliott can't see?"

She says nothing, and I seriously don't have time for this. "Mom," I bark.

"He just didn't seem like he could see very well," she says. "And you always drove when you two were here. I suppose I just assumed, what with the glasses."

"Did he say anything to you?"

"No, dear." She sounds like I'm the one being difficult now.

"He wears glasses," I say. "But he can see just fine."

"Anna mentioned that she noticed some vision issues too."

Aaaand there it is. Anna's got her nose somewhere it doesn't belong. "Okay," I say, my tone hard as rocks. "Well, I have to go finish getting ready."

"We love you, Ry. Christmas was so fun with you and Elliott here."

"I love you too, Mom. Say hi to Dad." The call ends, and I let my hand fall to my lap. My heart beats irregularly, and I can't figure out why. Is it racing? Skipping beats? It seems to be doing all of the above, and I press my free palm to my chest in an attempt to calm it.

But my hand isn't a weighted blanket, and my heartbeat thrashes against my ribs. Angry now, I pick up my phone and text Anna.

What did you tell Mom about Elliott's vision?

I don't care if she's out with James. Her gossiping might ruin my date too, so she can take thirty seconds and answer me.

Nothing much. Elliott asked me not to say anything, and I haven't.

My chest grows cold on my next breath, like I've inhaled dry ice and the air burns instead of replenishes. I tap to call her, and Anna answers with, "We just got to the restaurant, Ry."

"Two minutes," I bark. "Elliott asked you not to say anything about what exactly?"

"What has he told you?"

"Nothing," I say. And it really irritates me that she knows something I don't. There aren't enough M&Ms in the world right now, especially when Anna sits there, silent.

"You should ask him," she says. "I'm assuming you'll see him tonight."

"Yes."

"Then just ask him."

"Anna—"

"I have to go. Love you, Ry." She hangs up on me. Like, legit hangs up on me, and I scoff out a "What?" as I look at the dark screen of my phone.

My mind whirs and spins and races. Scenes from the holidays blitz through my mind, one after the other. The fact that he didn't see the skunks—black against white, and he didn't see them.

The burnt popcorn...he claimed to have pushed the same button as me, but he hadn't.

"The candle..." He'd picked up a *burning candle* and thought it was a glass of scotch.

How have *I* been so blind?

The doorbell rings, and I jump to my feet. Well, I'm wearing heels, so there's no jumping, but I stand and immediately move toward my bedroom door. Emma's already left to go to a party with Aaron; Claudia is over at Beckett's aunt's tonight, and Lizzie and Tahlia have a movie date together on the couch downstairs.

So Elliott has to be here. I haven't had time to stress-eat my candy or cure my dry-mouth, but my swirling emotions and thoughts propel me down the stairs, where I find Elliott standing in the doorway leading to the foyer, laughing and chatting with my roommates.

His eyes come straight to mine though I haven't said a word, and the electric zip between us sends a charge through my bloodstream. As if I need another reason to be worked up.

"Hey," he says, his gaze dripping down my body. "Wow, wow, wow, Miss Luckson." He looks at me again. "You're incredible."

I can't speak, because I don't want to say something I'll regret in front of Tahlia and Lizzie. I really appreciate the fact that he hasn't commented on how I look. No, he's complimented *me*, as if *I'm* incredible, and that causes a warmth to burn within me.

I move toward him and kiss him in a slow, welcome kiss, then take his hand in mine.

"Ready?" he asks.

I nod, smile the best I can at Tahlia and Lizzie, and lead Elliott out of the house. If I can get to the car, I'll be able to ask him whatever I want.

"You okay?" he asks as we start down the steps. The front door is closed behind us, but I'm not sure we're out of range of the doorbell cam. My hand tightens in his, and we keep going.

As I approach his car, I slow. "Do you want me to drive?" I finally turn toward him. "New Year's confessional: Can you see?"

His mouth opens, and his eyes turn wide and round. "I...I'm wearing my night-driving glasses."

"But can you *see*?" I look over to the rock—the huge,

decorative boulder marking the edge of the parking space in front of the Big House. He hit that rock...as if he hadn't seen it.

"Let's get in the car," he murmurs, and he opens the driver's door for me and indicates that I should get behind the wheel. So I do, and my hands shake as Elliott goes around the back of his own car.

It takes him at least thirty seconds, and I know something major is happening by the time he pulls open the passenger door. He slides in and says, "Car confessional: I have a degenerative vision impairment, and no, I don't see all that well most of the time."

"Elliott," I say.

He faces me fully. "Can we please go to dinner? I had to negotiate the reservation, and I don't want to miss it."

I turn the key in the ignition and look at him. "I don't even know where we're going."

"Coleman's." He looks out the passenger window, his voice barely his.

I don't know what else to say, and the words *degenerative vision impairment* have been put on a pedestal in my mind, spotlighted, and they rotate slowly while I try to make sense of them.

I know what degenerative means, and it's not good.

I drive us to Coleman's and park, and Elliott practically leaps from the SUV as if it's caught fire. He comes and opens my door, and when I stand, he pulls me directly into his arms. "I've tried to tell you a couple of times."

He has told me he had something we needed to talk about. Something always interrupted us, and then things at the store have been so chaotic after we returned from my family's house.

"I'm sorry," he says, and he takes my hand and leads me into the restaurant. It's extremely busy, and Elliott leaves me near the door to go check-in, and he really has worked some magic, because he returns for me only a minute later, secures my hand in his again, and draws me through the crowd like a pro.

We get a booth against the window, with a view of the downtown Cider Cove Christmas lights. I smile out at the twinklingness, which is something that has always lifted my spirits.

Elliott smiles at the waitress when she comes to get our drink orders, as if this is just a normal date. I'm not sure what to do either. Coleman's is hard to get into, and I'd only given him the list of my favorite places three days ago. I want this date—this whole year—to be filled with magic and sparkles and kissing Elliott, so I don't know what to say either.

We're not even talking about work, and I've drunk half my lukewarm water before the soda pop shows up.

"I'll order for us," Elliott says, looking across the table and raising his eyebrows at me. "Okay?"

"Sure." My throat feels so dry, and I'm not sure how

much I can speak. I tell myself it's not me who needs to talk, so I let Elliott order the burrata appetizer I like, as well as the chicken pesto pasta that makes my mouth water, as well as his French onion soup and the mushroom-smothered steak for himself.

The waitress grins at him, then me, and says, "Great choices," before she leaves.

That's one of my pet peeves, but I don't comment on it tonight. Instead, I look at him, everything I want to ask streaming into the silence between us.

Elliott stares back at me for several long seconds, and then says, "The bottom line, Ryanne, is I'm going blind."

ELLIOTT

THERE. IT'S ALL OUT NOW. WELL, NOT REALLY, BUT the most damaging things. I throw my hands up as if tossing confetti to welcome the New Year. "I go get a new prescription every couple of months, but my vision is getting worse and worse."

"Degenerative," she finally says, and I hate that that's one of the few words she's spoken tonight. She looks down at the table and back to me, open vulnerability in her expression. Sympathy—which I so don't want. In fact, it lights a fire in me I know will rage out the things I need to tell Ry.

"How...long?" She swallows. "I just want you to talk. I don't know what I don't know. I don't know what to ask." She pulls her mocktail closer and takes a hearty pull on the straw.

"I know what you're asking," I say, so many things

inside me shaking. Every cell vibrates, and I can't look at her. I focus on the coaster in front of me, my eyes burning burning burning.

I really don't want to cry tonight, but I fear it's a battle I'm going to lose.

"When I was diagnosed five years ago, I was told it could take twenty or thirty years to go completely blind." I take a breath, because I can only get one out at a time. "That we wouldn't know until time passed. So I go to the doctor every two or three months, even now, and well, we have a pretty good trajectory now."

I look out at the window, my throat so tight. "Right now, it's predicted that I'll be completely blind by the time I'm forty." My voice cracks, and I drop my head again, this time taking off my glasses and shading my eyes as if it's bright in here.

I close them, because they hurt, so I don't see Ry leave her side of the booth and slide onto mine. She's simply there, right at my side, and my immediate reaction is pure love for the woman.

I lean into her as the tears slip down my face. I wipe my eyes while she's just...there. She links her arm through mine, and she's shielding me from the rest of the dining room. I take a breath, so much more needing to be said.

"So that's it," I say, and thankfully, my voice doesn't sound too nasally. "That's why I don't have serious relationships. That's why I stay at Paper Trail."

"They have free vision insurance," she whispers.

"They pay for everything for my eyes," I confirm. "I have no desire to leave and find another job. I just want routine. I want something I can do even if I can't see, and I don't know if that's possible at Paper Trail or not, but I figure I can stock shelves...with some help."

I glance over to her, but I can't maintain eye contact as my emotions surge again. "I really didn't bring you here to break-up," I say. "Honestly. I *don't* want to break-up with you, but I also can't—" My voice breaks. "I can't do this to you."

I am nasally and weepy now, but I don't care. I shake my head, my eyes hot and tight and wet. "I won't doom you to a life of being a caregiver."

"Elliott."

"No, Ryanne." I glare at her now, and honestly, the anger is so much easier than the pain and turmoil raging within me. At least I know what to do with anger. "No matter what you say, it won't be right. You haven't sat with this at all, and you need to. I've just given you a death sentence, and you can't sit here ten minutes later and say it'll be okay. It's not okay."

She pulls her arm back. "Okay."

"You asked me to take Tuesday to detox from spending twenty-four-seven with you and your family, and I'm asking you to process this. Really process this."

She nods, and I do too.

"I'm going blind," I say. "I *will be* blind. And I really

don't want to subject anyone to having to care for me, and I thought I could control my feelings for you." I shake my head, pure embarrassment and shame showering me now.

"But I let my crush get out of control. I let myself become part of your family. I allowed myself to fall in love with you, and I shouldn't have."

"Don't say that," she whispers.

"I can't stand it. I can't stand how good it feels to be in love with you, but also how much it hurts. I will not hurt you. I will *not* saddle you with my problems for the rest of your life. It's not fair to you."

I meet her eye again, and I can't really tell what she's thinking or feeling. Her starry-starry eyes simply gaze back at me, and she says, "Life isn't fair."

"No," I say. "It's not. And it's not fair for me to be in love with you, and I hate that that's what's happened." I take a deep breath, the core of my debate about to spill out. "I'm no good for you. I'm the one going blind, and I can see that."

"Ell—"

"All right," the waitress says, and I quickly turn my face away from her. I wipe my hand across my face as Ry slides to the end of the bench and gets up.

"You know what?" I face the waitress too. "Something's come up, and we have to leave. Can you box this all up for us?"

"Elliott."

"Oh." The waitress has just set down my soup, and it looks amazing with melty, Swissy cheese and the rich, salty aroma of French onion soup. "Yeah, uh, sure. Let me..." She looks over her shoulder, and I take the moment to get up.

"Ry." I extend my hand toward her. "I'll walk you to the car and come back for the food."

"I'll go tell them to fire the mains," the waitress says, and she practically runs off.

Ryanne stands, and she's so beautiful and so amazing, and I can't believe I've let myself get to this point. I take her into my arms and whisper, "I'm so sorry, sweetheart." Then I lead her out to the SUV, where she looks up at me with soulful eyes.

"I really didn't mean for any of this to happen. I'll be right back."

Ryanne has said very little, and I sigh as I walk back into Coleman's to pay and get our food. I have no plans for the rest of the evening, when an hour ago, I'd been hoping for an amazing, hopeful start to a new year.

She hasn't said how she found out, but it had to have come from Anna. I honestly can't blame her—no, the only person who can carry that blame is me.

I have to wait about ten minutes for our food, but I get it, pay, and head back to the car. I get in the passenger seat and blow out my breath. "You want to go home and change?"

I can't imagine inviting her to come meet my mom or

my cat. That's what a girlfriend does, and now Ryanne and I are in a weird, in-between place where I don't want to break-up with her, but I don't see how I can be with her.

"We can just eat out of the back," she says, and I nod. "I'll drive us up to Lakeshore Lookout."

I lean my head back and look out the windshield, but since I'm not driving, I don't have to try to focus. I don't see much, because it's dark, and I eventually just close my eyes. We arrive, and I gather the food and open my door. Ry meets me at the tailgate, and she lifts it.

I steady her as she climbs up, and then I get up beside her and reach into the bag. We've eaten like this before, out of the back of one of our cars, behind the office supply store. It feels like what we've done at best friends, and I honestly need this tonight.

"I'm sorry," I say again, wishing I could say it enough times for it to mean something. For those words to ensure that Ry won't be hurt by the past month.

"I don't want to break-up either."

I nod as I hand her the cardboard container with her burrata in it. The stinging scent of the balsamic vinegar makes me smile, because Ry's said she could drink it she loves it so much.

"You have to think about this for at least twenty-four hours," I say. "Probably a lot longer." I had to go through the entire grieving process—and some days I'm thrown back a step or two or three and have to move through them again.

Ryanne will have to do that too.

"I want you to take that time," I say. "I want to answer whatever questions you have that come up." I clear my throat and pull out my soup. "And, uh, I need more time off in only a couple of days. I'll put it through the system in the morning."

"Why?" she asks.

I smile and chuckle, though the sound is without merriment. "You won't believe this, but there's this organization in Michigan that gives away a guide dog to one person every Christmas. The ultimate Christmas gift. My mom put my name in, and I won."

"Ell, that's amazing."

"Yeah." I glance over to her. "My mom and I are going to go pick her up." I look out into the night, the town lights of Cider Cove below us and creating a scene from a perfect picture book. "I'm really sorry, Ryanne."

"I've heard you say it the other ten times," she says.

"I can't say it enough." I finally take a bite of my soup, and the croutons are soggy now, but the flavor and salt are still prevalent. I moan and nod. "Yes, this is good."

Ry reaches over and pats my forearm, and I give her a small smile in return. It's all I can do right now—oh, and hope and pray and cross all my fingers that Ryanne will at least still be my best friend now that she knows about my vision.

RYANNE

"So he broke up with you?" Hillary asks.

"Semi-break-up," I say miserably. I reach for another candy from the bead container where I've dumped out multiple flavors of M&Ms. Some of them are so big, only a few will fit in the square compartment, and others hold dozens and dozens of treats.

I eat one flavor at a time, one at a time, and I pick up an almond M&M and pop it into my mouth.

"I don't know what a semi-break-up is," Hill says.

This New Year hasn't started the way I would've liked, and though it's only been about twelve hours since Elliott dropped me off last night, I feel like I've been through an array of emotions.

Right now, I feel calm and demure, almost sedated, and everything seems soft and spongy around me.

"He wants me to really think through what he's said."

"And?"

I glance at my computer and see the fiery best friend I miss so much. "I don't know, Hillary. It's complicated."

The boxiness of her shoulders deflates, and she nods. "I'm sure it is."

I look up and out my window, the candy coating on the M&M finally giving way so I can get to the chocolate underneath. I don't just bite into a nutty M&M like a savage. I savor them, going layer by layer, so all the flavors mix.

And mixing flavors reminds me of Elliott and his delicious orange chicken popcorn.

"Have you told everyone else?" Hillary asks.

I shake my head, simply watching this January first day as it drifts by over the lawn here at the Big House, which gives way to the orchards at Aaron's next door. "I've always loved this view," I say.

"Do you love Elliott?" Hillary whisper-asks, drawing my attention back to the screen.

"I don't know," I say. "Friendship and love got all mixed up." Tears prick my eyes, and I shrug one shoulder as I reach for the next compartment, and the M&M there. It's caramel, which aren't my favorite, but they're eatable.

"He said he loves me," I say next, and it's the first

time I've said it out loud. But Elliott said he loved me four times last night. Four.

"I don't know how it's possible, but—"

"Stop it," Hillary says. "Of course you're possible to love, Ry."

"But by him?" Tears seep out of my eyes, and I brush them away. "You should've seen him at Christmas, Hill. Everyone in my family loved him, even my dad. He and Anna baked together flawlessly, all of it."

"So you fell in love with him too."

I sniff and roll my arms. "Oh, I've been in love with Elliott forever." I look at her again, and I can't stop the tears from leaking out again. "What should I do?"

"We need to get everyone on-board," Hillary says. "Tahlia will have a good idea."

"I have a good idea," Liam says, and Hillary moves the camera so it's trained on him. "Hey, Ry."

I blink, because I hadn't known he was there. He sets down his cereal bowl and leans toward the computer. "What did I do when Hillary was leaving town? Did I just let her walk away? Leave me in the dust?" He starts shaking his head before he even finishes talking.

"No," I say at the same time as him.

"No," he repeats. "Once you decide you don't care about him eventually being blind, then you show up with the plastic bins, and you make sure he knows you're not going anywhere. That he can't run from you."

"Tahlia might have some good ideas for how to do that, I meant," Hillary says, and she grins at Liam. When she looks back at me, she keeps her pretty smile. "Or Lizzie. She's pretty pro at make-ups."

I nod, my nerves starting to buzz at me again as I cycle from a down period to an up. I pick up a few minis and throw them in my mouth at the same time. "I'll talk to them tonight."

But I'm not sure I will. I kind of just want to sit with this, the way Elliott suggested, and see how it feels.

"Love you guys," I say. "We'll talk later." The call ends, and I stare up to the ceiling.

Last night, the moment I stepped in the Big House and the door closed, the only emotion I had was anger. Pure, unbridled anger. The only reason I didn't rip the dress off my body and throw it in the trash is because it's Tahlia's, not mine.

I'd cried. Felt betrayed. Paced my room. Finally fell asleep after the clock had struck midnight without any celebration from me. No kiss from Elliott, because he sort of broke up with me before we'd even eaten dinner.

I haven't left my room yet this morning, and for New Year's Day, that's not abnormal. I am going to have to face everyone at some point. They'll all have questions about my date, and unless I'm willing to put on a giant beach hat and sunglasses, Emma will suss out the fact that I've been crying without me saying a word.

I want to make this decision on my own. I'm a grown

woman, and as I snap the lid closed on my M&M assortment and lay back onto my pillows, I take a deep breath. I don't want the frazzled, irate me to take over this more subdued quiet thinker-me.

I need her to help me figure out what to do about Elliott.

"His vision doesn't matter," I whisper. "*He* matters, and he's the same whether he can see or not."

A while later, I open my eyes when someone knocks softly on my door. "Ry?" Tahlia calls, and I manage to sit up before she cracks the door. "Are you—uh oh." She gestures over her shoulder as she enters the room, and everyone comes rushing in.

Tahlia arrives at my side first, and she pushes my limp hair back off my forehead. "What's wrong?"

"Are you sick?" Emma asks, crowding onto the floor in front of me.

"Are we still going to the store?" Claudia asks as Lizzie joins me on my other side.

I've forgotten they were going to come help me finish out the store. "Yeah," I say miserably. "It'll give me something else to focus on."

"What happened last night?" Lizzie asks. "Is this an Elliott thing or...something else?"

It's only my whole life, but that sounds so dramatic inside my own head, so I don't say it out loud. "I found out why he doesn't do serious."

Tahlia gasps. "He broke up with you?"

"Only kind of," I say. "He has a degenerative eye condition that's causing him to go blind slowly. He doesn't think it's fair to, and I quote, *saddle* someone with the responsibility of taking care of him."

No one says anything, which is about how I'd reacted to the revelation. "Let's go get the store done," I say as I stand. "It'll get me out of my room and doing something good."

"How does someone kind of break-up with someone else?" Lizzie asks, and none of them have moved. Claudia does come to my side and wrap me up in a side-hug.

"He said I need to take some time to think through it all, you know, to see if I really want to deal with his health problems for the rest of my life."

"That's what 'in sickness and in health' means," Emma says.

"Yeah, but they're not married." Tahlia gets to her feet, her eyes full of concern as she fixes her gaze on mine. "Tell us what you're thinking."

"He told me he loves me, but that it was a mistake. He shouldn't have let himself do that." I wipe angrily at my tears, because I'm so tired of crying. "I'm going to figure out how I feel and do what he asked—really think about what a life with him will truly be like."

"Ry," Claudia says quietly.

"He asked me to," I say, my mouth contorting as I fight my emotion. "I'm at least going to do what he asked." I give her a sharp look and start to peel off my pajama top. "I'll change, and we'll go. Sorry I forgot."

"You're allowed," Tahlia says. "Come on, guys. Let's wait for her downstairs."

But no one leaves, not even Tahlia. I sniffle through changing my clothes, and then I survey the four of them. "I'm not going to ask you what you'd do if you were me."

"Of course not," Claudia says. "This is something only you can decide."

I nod, and then I lead the way out of my bedroom and down the length of the second-floor hallway to the stairs. Once we're all in my SUV, Lizzie says, "Blindness, wow."

"He won't be able to drive," Emma muses, as if she and Lizzie have rehearsed this conversation. "You'd have to help him with that."

"With everything," I mutter at them, thinking of how I really enjoyed helping him get cleaned up from the skunk spray. But blindness is a far cry from assisting with a one-time accident.

"There are a ton of resources for the blind," Tahlia says. "Guide dogs, personal assistants, audiobooks..." A moment passes before she gives a little giggle. "I don't know where audiobooks came from."

I shoot her a smile. "Seemed a little random, I'm not gonna lie."

"He'd have to have someone read him a menu," Claudia says. "Or he can learn braille, I suppose."

"Name the last place you went where their menu was in *braille*," I say, giving her another glare in the rearview mirror. "And he won a guide dog for Christmas."

"What?" all of them ask at the same time. "That's incredible," Lizzie says. "He can learn how to navigate the world while he can still see a little bit. If he's somewhere familiar, I bet he won't have trouble getting around at all."

"Besides the driving," Emma says.

"Right, besides that," Lizzie agrees.

I start to wonder how grandiose my life needs to be. I don't mind driving Elliott around. We work at the same place, and if we were together, that wouldn't have to change. He can stay in his house, and...why can't we have an amazing life together?

I let my roommates continue to talk, because we all process things differently, and it actually helps me to hear them work through some of the challenges a blind person encounters in a seeing world. Things I wouldn't have thought of, and I enjoy listening to them banter gently back and forth about how This Thing or That One isn't really that big of a deal as we get the scrapbook papers back where they go, the adhesives back under their sign, and sort through the rolls of wrapping paper we have left over from the holidays.

"I just need to check my email," I say, and I dash into the office to do that. Still nothing from corporate about

Barry rearranging our whole store. But I do have a time-off request from Elliott, and my stomach settles heavily in my body as I click to open it.

He's requesting time off from January fourth to the eleventh—which is only three days from now. Right there on the reason is: Medical leave for ADA – blind.

I can't deny a medical leave under the Americans with Disabilities Act. I can ask Mindy to help me manage the store, so I quickly hit approve and pull out my phone to text her.

All of those days? she asks.

If possible, I say. If she can't do it, we'll get by. It's not the end of the world, and we don't have major sales in January.

I think I can. I just need to double-check when my doctor's appointment is.

Let me know.

There's nothing else of importance, and I head out to where my roommates wait in the car. Once I'm behind the wheel, I start it but don't pull out. "Okay, let's say I decide I don't care about the blindness. That I want to be with him. What's a good way for me to do that?"

"Tell him?" Claudia guesses.

I shake my head. "No, he knows I'm mad he didn't tell me. I had to find out from Anna."

Tahlia actually gasps again, which tells me I was right to be upset. "Sort of," I qualify. "She knew, but she told me to ask Elliott."

Another round of humiliation fills me, because I should've seen the signs. "I can't believe I didn't know he couldn't see." I shake my head and flip the vehicle into drive.

"I had no idea," Tahlia says. "How could you possibly know?"

"I don't know." I brush at my eyes again. "So let's say I want to make up with him in a big way, so he knows I don't care about the eye condition. I only care about him." As I say it, I know it's true.

I only care about him, and I'll do whatever I have to do in order to be with him.

Now I just need a way to show him, so there's no doubt whatsoever.

ELLIOTT

"This way, baby," Momma says, and while I'm irritated that she has to guide me through the airport, I go with her, because I need her to guide me through the airport.

We've flown into Detroit, and I've never been here before. I've rented a car, and we'll head out of the city and to a smaller suburb called Mayflower. Paws For a Cause operates on a farm in the more rural community, and they raise, train, and sell their guide dogs from one of the quaintest places on earth.

Well, that's at least what it looked like online. I've spent the past week or so confirming the pick-up of my dog, getting the name, phone number, and address of the person I need to contact when I get to Paws For a Cause, and looking at the services they provide to people like me.

People who can't see.

A quiet excitement builds within me, because I'm finally taking a step beyond wearing glasses to admit I can't see. Once I get back to Cider Cove, Luna and I will go everywhere together, and she'll be wearing a harness and handle to show she's a service dog.

More than that.

A guide dog for the blind.

I'll be here for a few days, learning the same commands Luna has been trained with, and we'll work together with the help of her trainer and handler, and then...she's mine. She's coming home with me, and Paws For a Cause has already connected me with a center for the blind and visually impaired, so I can continue to get assistance with Luna, and with my own visual disability.

I stand with my mom as we wait for our bags, and when they come, I pull them from the belt. I handle everything at the rental counter, and twenty minutes later, we're loading everything we brought to Michigan with us into the back of a mid-size SUV.

Ninety minutes later, I make the turn from the highway onto a quieter road, and after one more left turn, a well-kept sign announces our arrival at Paws For a Cause.

Momma has been unusually quiet since we left the Charleston airport, and now, she reaches over and pats my leg. "I'm so excited for you, Ell. Are you excited?"

"Yes, Momma." I stop to read the sign at a fork in the road. "Which way to Candidate Parking?" I ask.

That's where my directions said to go, and Momma points to the right as she says, "To the right, son."

I haven't had to give up driving yet, and I told her I want to keep doing things I can until I can't anymore. After much nagging, which she's earned multiple Gold Medals in, she finally agreed to stop asking me if I can see. I know when I can and can't, and this drive out here hasn't been too bad.

Candidate Parking is empty, with only a couple of cars down on the end, parked in reserved spots.

As we step out of the car, I feel the cool air wrap around me, invigorating yet slightly intimidating since I've never been to this place before. "Let's do this thing," I mutter, mostly to myself.

Momma gives me a gentle squeeze on my shoulder, a silent show of support that I really appreciate. "You ready for this?" she asks, her voice laced with excitement.

"Definitely," I reply, trying to sound more confident than I feel. My heart beats a little faster as I follow the signs—all of them decorated with some version of a guide dog—leading to the "recruitment center," my mind filled with thoughts of Luna and all the possibilities she brings to my life.

I open the door for my momma, who enters first, a

rush of heat coming out into the winter where I still stand. I wish I didn't feel like I'm standing on a teeter-totter. So many good things in front of me on the one side, with Luna and a bright new way of living for the next several years.

Alone.

A bright new way of living alone. I can just hear the Mars rovers saying such a thing, and it makes me sad, because I want Ryanne in that bright new future. She weighs everything down, and I wish I could share this with her *and* my mom.

I've seen her at work, but only superficially and only in passing. We've got the store put back together now, but she made sure she had things to do on the floor when I've arrived in the afternoons. Most of our communication has been through email and texts, and it's all been about work.

And that makes my heart heavy. I think of Perserverance's last words—*My batteries are low and it's getting dark*—and that's how I feel.

"Hello," a woman says, and I blink my way out of the duplicity of my life. "I'm Lydia. You must be Elliott." She extends her hand toward me, and I latch onto it.

"Yes," I say, a rush of gratitude filling me. After all, guide dogs aren't exactly cheap. "I'm Elliott. Thanks so much for having us."

"Come on it." The dark-haired woman turns and

enters the building, and I finally do the same. "Luna is so excited to meet you."

I'm not sure how Lydia can possibly know that, but whatever. Dogs surely get excited sometimes too, right?

The recruitment center is welcoming and accessible, with great big lettering on all the signs, which I appreciate. It doesn't feel babyish or cartoonish, but professional, with silhouettes of guide dogs and their owners on warning signs and big arrows to help you find where you're going. The walls are painted a soft cream, and I feel like I've come to the right place.

"Before we go meet Luna, I want to go over a few things with you," Lydia says, guiding me toward a conference room. My stomach churns, and I swallow as the three of us take a seat together.

"Luna has been specially trained to help you navigate your world," she explains, placing a thick folder in front of me. "She'll help you understand your surroundings and give you confidence to explore your environment safely. Remember, she's going to be your best friend."

Those words make me think of Ryanne, and I can't open the folder right now. I remind myself that I don't have to have every word of it memorized before they'll let me take Luna, so I just smile at Lydia. "I'm excited to learn what to do before I go fully blind."

She smiles. "We do try to get guide dogs with those

with conditions like yours, so you're more comfortable as your vision continues to worsen." She speaks kindly, and I find myself nodding. "You might not have Luna forever, but she should be a good guide dog for you for oh, at least six or seven years."

Long enough for me to go completely blind.

She puts one hand over the folder. "This is a lot of take-home instructions. Reminders for you, if you will. For the next couple of days, you'll be working with Luna and her trainer, Calvin." She glances over to Momma. "You both will, so you can see what Elliott might need help with, and as the fully sighted person, you'll be able to assist if needed."

Momma nods, then reaches up to wipe her eyes. I reach over and squeeze her hand, and I hate that she has to watch me go through this. At the same time, I'm so glad I'm not here alone, which again makes me think of Ry. There's no way she could've come with me, even if I'd been brave enough to tell her about my eyesight years ago. I can't even imagine both of us being gone from the store again.

"So." Lydia exhales brightly. "Let's go meet Luna and Calvin. We really think she's going to be a great match for you, but we never really know until human and dog are in the same room." She stands, and I jump to go with her.

"I will warn you," Lydia says, her voice cheerful as we walk down the hall toward a big set of double doors that look like an elephant could fit through them. "The first meeting can be overwhelming for both you and Luna. Just take a moment to breathe and you be a human, and let her be a dog." She slows and looks back at me and Momma. "I mean, she *is* a dog, after all."

I nod, trying my best to put a smile on my face at the same time. "Sometimes I feel human."

She grins and then moves to the side of the hall and presses a button. The big doors start to swing in, and I would give up watching the Mars rovers online just to see what's beyond them.

Lydia moves into the room, talking about something again, and I catch a whiff of something utterly dog-like: earthiness, warmth, and a hint of playful mischief. I can't focus on what she's saying, as I've caught sight of a lean figure standing beside a golden-furred Labrador with eager brown eyes that seem to look right into my soul.

"This is Calvin," Lydia introduces, gesturing to the trainer. "And of course, Luna."

The dog sits patiently, her tail thumping the ground over and over—the unmistakable canine sign of excitement. I crouch down, overwhelmed by the rush of emotion that fills me. "Hey, Luna," I whisper, my voice catching as I extend my hand, palm up, toward her.

Calvin grins as Luna takes a step forward, sniffing my fingers cautiously, then immediately leans in, pressing her head against my palm. "That's it," he says, his tone encouraging. "Let her get to know you at your own pace."

Everything else in the room fades as I take in the warmth of Luna's fur and the pull of her energy—it feels like fate, as if the universe conspired to bring us together at just the right moment. I can't help but laugh, a sound filled with relief and happiness. "You're so sweet, aren't you?" I murmur, scratching behind her ears.

I stand, feeling a little stitch of embarrassment. "She's great." I look down at the dog, who seemingly grins up at me.

"She's a pretty special dog," Calvin confirms. "Now, we're going to start going over how we trained her, and the things she knows." He smiles at me, and he too has a good air about him. Very calm. "Don't worry. You've got a cheat sheet of all of this in your binder. We'll start with the easy ones. Sit. Stay. Come. Speak. Leave it. Then we'll move into learning how to guide her where you want her."

I thought that was what she'd do for me, but I don't say anything. I'm here to learn, and that's exactly what I'm going to do.

"Okay, Luna," Calvin says as he moves several steps away. "Come."

She immediately gets up and trots over to him, touching his hand with her nose when she arrives in front of him.

"To my side," he says, and she moves to his right side.

I stand there in awe, wondering how many hours, days, weeks, and months it took for her to learn all of this.

Then Calvin looks at me, and my heart feels like it might explode. "Your turn, Elliott. Command her to come and sit at your side."

"We usually start with the dog's name," Lydia adds, and I nod at her, my throat so tight.

But I say, "Luna," and the canine looks right at me. "Come."

She jogs over to me too, and I hold my hand down, my fingers toward her and lined up with my thigh. She touches her wet nose to my first two fingers, and I laugh. Such a simple action shouldn't fill me with such wonder, but it so does. "To my side," I add, and Luna moves to my right side and looks up at me, clearly expecting something from me.

I hope it's unadulterated love and adoration, because that pours from me.

"You can treat her," Lydia says, passing me a small, hard chunk of something. "That will go a long way toward the two of you bonding."

I feed her the dog treat, and she smiles at me again.

"She can't have a treat for everything," Calvin says as he returns to where we stand. "Sometimes, a kind word or a good rub is just as effective. Luna." He looks at her. "And you don't always have to look at her. You'll be blind, so you might not know where she is, though once she's home with you, she'll find her place." He crouches in front of her and takes Luna's face in both of his hands. "She's very cuddly, so she'll probably want to be right beside you whenever possible."

"I have a cat," I say. "Will that matter?"

"Nope," he says. "Luna likes other dogs and cats and people. She's got a great temperament." He stands up. "Luna, sit."

She sits.

Calvin grins and scrubs under her chin. "Good girl." He looks over to me. "Some of her commands have hand signals too. She can open doors and bring you a phone even if you can't talk. But some of her simple commands come with hand signals too. Sit." He holds up his hand in a fist. "Is this."

Luna's already sitting, so she can't show me how smart she is by reading doggy sign language. But Calvin points his first finger at the ground, and without saying a word, Luna slides her front legs forward so she's laying down.

"Incredible," I say, and I reach down and give her a pat this time. She licks me, and I pull my hand back in surprise. When I chuckle, Calvin does too.

"She shouldn't lick like that," Calvin says. "But Luna is very nosy and very tasty. She's like a toddler. She likes to smell and taste the things she's trying to understand."

I grin at her. I want to learn everything she knows, so we can continue to bond and communicate. Calvin and

Lydia continue to walk me through the basic commands, and then we take a break with the promise of going over the movement commands before the facility closes and Momma and I have to find somewhere for dinner and get to our hotel.

I find a place to sit while Momma runs to the restroom, and because I want to share this amazingness with the person closest to me, I pull out my phone and call Ry. She doesn't answer, and my heart sinks down into the soles of my feet.

You must be noshing on steak and M&Ms, I send to her. *Call me when you get a sec, would you? I want to tell you about Luna.*

She hasn't said anything else about the guide dog, my trip to Michigan to get her, or my eye condition. My chest cavity shrinks, and I think maybe I've just sent a text I shouldn't have.

Or not, I say. *It's fine if you're still thinking. I didn't mean to pressure you.* I sigh and tuck my phone under my leg, so I won't send her yet another text that could confuse her. Then, I lean my head back and close my eyes and let the pure contentment flow through me.

Yes, I'm going blind, but for the first time in my life, it doesn't feel like a total death sentence. My eyes snap open, and I realize that Ryanne *needs* to know that. She won't have to take care of me so much now that I have Luna.

Maybe I can be blind and still be with Ryanne, and

that's something I've literally never been able to envision.

But now, as Momma hands me a bottle of peach iced tea she's bought from the vending machines, a brand new future paints itself across the blank slate in my mind.

RYANNE

"All right." Tahlia holds up the pink sparkly microphone. "We're all here now, and some of us don't have a lot of time." She looks to me where I'm sitting in a recliner at the end of the couch.

She's called a big family meeting, which includes all of my roommates, both of my sisters, and my mom. My legs feel numb as I stand up. Tahlia hands me the mic, and I survey the four squares on the big TV screen, where my family members and best friend wait.

Lizzie hurries into the living room with her giant water bottle and says, "Sorry, sorry."

"Okay," I say. "I just need a little bit of advice." I hold up my phone, where I've made my notes from the past few days of research.

Ever since Elliott dropped the bombshell about his degenerative vision condition, I've been on an emotional rollercoaster. But after countless hours of soul-searching, a little crying, and late-night Google sessions, I now need to confirm my feelings.

So I quickly tell them where Elliott is: Paws For a Cause, in Mayflower, Michigan, a small, rural community a couple of hours outside of Detroit.

I tell them about his degenerative eye condition. I tell them that work has been tense, but he's gone now. I tell them, "And now, I guess I'm not sure what to do."

"What to do?" Hillary asks. "It's obvious what you should do."

"I agree," Anna says.

Others seated in front of me on the couch nod, but my stomach swoops left and right. "It's not that obvious."

"Do you or do you not have the man's phone number?" Claudia asks.

I tilt my head at her. I'm so not answering that.

"And his mom's," Tahlia says, almost under her breath.

"Yeah," Emma says. "You hacked into his computer and got his mother's phone number."

"First," I say. "I did *not* hack into his computer." I duck my head a little and add in a half-whisper, "I know his password."

"But you have her phone number," Emma says. "You could do so much with that."

"Like what?"

My roommates exchange glances with each other,

and it's Cosette who says, "Call or text her and find out how you can surprise Elliott."

I spin toward the TV. "Surprise Elliott?" I say it like I don't understand those two words in that order.

"Yeah," my sister says with a kind smile. "It's pretty obvious you're in love with him, and he's going to need to hear you say it."

"Among other things," Lizzie says.

I volley my gaze back and forth, semi-shocked at what I'm hearing. "He'll be back on Sunday," I say.

"And you won't see him until Wednesday," Claudia says. "That's a whole week from today." She shakes her head like she finds that lacking. Severely lacking.

"So...you think I should...what? Go to Michigan?"

"There it is," Emma says with a grin. "Yes, you call his momma, and you ask her how you can show up at the guide dog facility and surprise your hot boyfriend."

I reject her idea immediately, but as I look at the others in the room and then face my loved ones on the television, it's clear they're all thinking the same thing. "I can't believe this," I say. "I'd have to take work off, and Ell's gone, and who will run the store?"

"We'll go," Lizzie says. "You'll fly out early on Saturday, and we'll go over and help Mindy with whatever she needs."

My eyes widen. "You'll go work at Paper Trail?"

"Why not?" Lizzie asks. "Claude, Tahlia, and I can for sure. Em's pretty busy on the weekends."

"I...I..." I sputter.

"You have no other excuses, dear," Mom says, and I meet her eyes. Everything slows then, and I only feel love and acceptance and kindness from her.

"What questions do you need answered?" Tahlia asks. "To make this easier for you?"

"Well, I—" I cut off as my throat closes on itself.

"Do you love him?" Claudia asks. "I mean, I think that's the biggest one, and she still hasn't said it out loud in those exact words."

The others agree, and I feel like they've gotten together without me to team up on me and make sure I do what they want.

"Don't think so hard," Hillary says into the quiet living room. "You tend to think too hard, Ry."

"Do I love him?" As I stand there in the living room, a culmination of all the things I've been doing since New Year's Eve come together into a cohesive whole.

And I come to one undeniable conclusion: I love Elliott, vision problems, love of savory popcorns, the obsession with Mars rovers, and all of it. Absolutely all of it.

Tears prick my eyes, and I nod. "Yeah, I'm in love with him."

Emma whoops, and Lizzie cheers, and Claudia starts the applause. They all join in, everyone wearing a smile while I quickly sweep the tears away and then survey them all again, the pink mic limp at my side.

"So..."

"The real question," Anna says in her dry, bossy way. "Is why you're still talking to us and not booking airplane tickets to Michigan right now."

———

MY HEART RACES as I pull up to the Paws For a Cause facility, the gravel crunching under my rental car's tires. I really feel moments away from passing out, but I take a big breath as I put the car in park. "He's here, and you're ready."

The quaint barn-style building looms before me, its large, colorful sign a beacon of hope. Ell said he felt like this when he pulled up, and though I've only spoken to him a couple of times while he's been here, that's the underlying message to everything he's said.

Hope.

I glance at my phone, rereading the last text from Elliott's mom. *He'll be working with Luna until four tonight, and then they're coming back to the hotel.*

Apparently, Elliott has had Luna with him twenty-four-seven since his arrival three days ago. He's sent me a couple of pictures, but I know it's not nearly the volume I'd get if we were truly together—and I need him to know that's what I want.

Can't wait to meet you, I send to his momma. Her support has been invaluable in orchestrating this surprise. Without her, I wouldn't have known Elliott's exact schedule or managed to book a seat on their return flight tomorrow.

As I step out of the car, my mind flashes back to the frantic planning of the past few days. The hushed conversations with my roommates, the hurried packing, the last-minute flight booking, the "emergency" I came up with to get work off on a Saturday. It's all led to this moment.

"All right, Ry," I coach myself. "Time to go in." I turn off the car and get out, square my shoulders, and head for the entrance. My hand trembles slightly as I reach for the door handle. "This is going to work."

I step inside, ready to fight for the future I want—a future with Elliott. I remind myself that he told me he loved me four times, and if there's anything I know about Elliott, it's that he doesn't say anything he doesn't mean.

I'm immediately enveloped by the warm atmosphere and the faint smell of dog treats. My eyes dart around, taking in the professional yet welcoming décor with enormous words on every sign. I've entered a sort of waiting room, with a few chairs, a couple of couches, and a long counter with computer stations at even intervals.

A woman at the nearest computer looks up as I approach, a friendly smile on her face. "Hi there," she says. "Welcome to Paws For a Cause. How can I help you?"

I ball my fingers into a fist, steeling my nerves. "I'm

looking for Elliott Huston. I was told he's here training with his new guide dog, Luna."

Her eyebrows raise slightly as her dark eyes search mine. "Yes, Elliott and Luna. They're in one of our training rooms right now. Are you family?"

I hesitate for a split second before gazing back at her with full confidence. "I'm his girlfriend." It feels right to say it, even if Elliott and I are in a weird limbo right now, and I've been praying for the past nine days that this conversation will end with us kissing and vowing to face forever together.

So maybe I'm still living in a slight fantasy-land. I can't help it if I'm a romantic.

The receptionist nods, her smile widening. "It's so great to meet you. I'm sure he'll be thrilled to see you. Let me just get someone to escort you in."

As she picks up the phone, a mix of anticipation and nervousness courses through me. My hands wind around each other, and I have to force them back to my sides as the woman looks at me. "Calvin's on his way out." She smiles and looks back over to her computer.

"Thanks," I say, and I don't know which way to watch for this Calvin. Thankfully, a man comes down the hall only a few moments later, wearing a bright blue polo with a dark gray silhouette of a guide dog on the front of it. "Hey," he says, and he smiles and shakes my hand. "You're here for Elliott?"

I nod and swallow my nerves for the hundredth time that day.

"This way," Calvin says, and he starts back down the hall.

I follow him quickly. "He doesn't know I'm coming," I say. "It's a surprise."

Calvin smiles over to me. "A surprise, huh?"

"Would it possible for me to get a few minutes with him?" I don't have to say *alone* for Calvin to hear it.

"Sure," he says. "He can introduce you to Luna, and you guys can talk." He stops outside a door with a window about two-thirds of the way up. "He's in there, and I'll just let you go in."

"Thanks." As Calvin turns and walks back to the lobby area, I peer through the window. Sure enough, there's Elliott, and he's got a pretty blond dog sitting in front of him. He lifts his hand with his fingers in the shape of an L, and Luna doesn't move a muscle. He seems to like this, and he grins at his dog and gives her a scrub along her ears.

Employing every ounce of bravery I have, I reach for the doorknob and twist it. The door opens, and I walk right in, and then there are no more barriers between me and Elliott. He looks up and sees me, the moment of recognition obvious on his face. "Ry."

He jumps to his feet and rushes toward me like he'll grab me and hold me right against his heart. In the end, he comes to a stop like the thin carpet at his feet has turned to ice and forced him to cease forward movement.

His eyes are wide with disbelief, and his chest heaves slightly. "What—? What are you doing here?"

I indicate the dog who's moved to his side. "I wanted to meet Luna," I say, but that's not the real reason I left Paper Trail and flew to Mayflower, Michigan in the middle of the winter. I reach my hand out toward the dog, but Luna just sits there.

I raise my eyes back to his. "I wanted to meet your momma."

Elliott presses his teeth together, his jaw jutting out.

"And I wanted to tell you...I couldn't wait until you got home to tell you—and I certainly couldn't put any of this in a text, so I had to come."

"Who's at the store?"

"Mindy's handling it. We're closed tomorrow, so I only had to take today off." I take a step toward him, wanting my skin against his as I confess. "We're not in the car, so I guess we'll have to extend our confessionals to guide dog training rooms."

He relaxes a little bit, but he still harbors a hint of wariness in his expression.

I throw my arms up and let them clap back to my sides. "I'm in love with you."

His mouth opens, but he doesn't say anything.

"Yeah, that's it," I say. "I'm in love with you, and I don't care if you go blind tomorrow. I'm a good driver, and we work at the same place, so the commute will be easy. I've already started sketching out a plan for laying out your breakfast items before bed, so you can get up and make your own coffee and put together your toast and jam before you come into the store."

I take a breath, so much more to say. "And I'll make our lunches the night before and take them into work, so yours will be there waiting for you already. And did you know there's software out there that will read everything to you? From your phone or computer, so you can have your emails read to you, and you can dictate the answers, and it'll just type it up for you."

"Ryanne."

"And I always want to hold your hand, so when we have to go grocery shopping or up to see my parents, no one will even know you can't see. You'll just be holding my hand, and I'll get you where you need to go." Tears fill my eyes, but I make no move to wipe them away. I want him to see them, want him to know everything I say is real and true and genuine.

He smiles slightly. "Ry."

"I'll hold up all the bowls during the popcorn creation and name them off. You can smell them and decide what you want to make. I'm sure you'll still win."

"What about the de-skunkifying?"

"Well, first, we'll be relying on the forest fairies to help keep them away from you. But if that doesn't work,

I guess I'd go with vinegar, dish soap, and baking soda." I grin at him. "And dragon scales."

He grins fully back at me finally. "Or peppermint."

My mouth wobbles along with the rest of me. "I love you. I can't imagine walking away because of this one little thing."

I expect him to argue that it's not "one little thing," but I've got a comeback for that too.

Instead, he says, "I love you too," and he closes the distance between us and takes me into his arms. Sinking into his embrace is one of my favorite things in the world, as is the scent of his cologne, which is a little Luna-y right now, and breathing in with him is absolutely life-changing.

"Have you thought—?"

"It's been nine days," I whisper-hiss at him. "I've thought about every single thing in the world. And no matter what, it always comes back to this one thing." I pull away enough to still stand in his arms and see his face. "I love you, and love is a powerful thing that makes a person stronger than they know they can be."

"Every day without you feels like a year in the dark." He closes his eyes and leans his forehead against mine, and everything with him feels so easy, so good, so deep. "But with you, my heart finds its dawn. It's not just that I love you—it's that loving you has transformed my world into something beautiful and extraordinary, and it doesn't matter if I can see it or not. I can *feel it*."

I weep quietly as he touches that glorious mouth to a soft place just below my ear. I only startle away when something cold and wet touches my elbow. "Oh." I pull back and look down at Luna. She's touched her nose to my arm, and I can't help grinning at her through my sniffles.

"She's okay," Elliott tells Luna. He grins at me and wipes my tears. "I know you want to meet her, but do you think I can kiss you first?"

"You better," I whisper, and he matches his mouth to mine in the sweetest kiss of my life, only accelerating it after pouring everything he feels into his lips against mine.

I pull away and take a big breath. "We can get married fast, right?"

"Tomorrow, if you want," he murmurs before he kisses me again.

ELLIOTT

THE FAMILIAR SCENT OF PAPER, INK, AND OFFICE
supplies fills my nostrils as I step into Paper Trail, Luna
padding faithfully by my side. Things have been going
pretty good for the past few weeks, since I returned from
Michigan with my momma, Luna, and Ryanne all on the
same flight. It honestly felt like winning the lottery and
getting told it'll be Christmas every day.

Luna and I have been figuring out how we work
together at Paper Trail, and I put a dog bed at the end of
the couch right behind my desk. But Luna didn't like it
there. She kept coming over and curling up at my feet.
So now the bed is there, because I can't stand her lying
on the cold tile without a pad.

Whenever I have to leave the office, she comes with
me. She wears her white harness with the rigid handle,
indicating she's a guide dog, and everyone who works at

Paper Trail knows about my vision issues. Thankfully, only a couple of people have treated me differently, and I simply remind them that I can still see, despite the degenerative condition. And they've stopped; Luna is a staple now, and everyone we work with loves her.

I love her more than I thought possible. Surprisingly, I put her bed next to Peppermint's, and she squeezed herself on the feline's instead of using her own. So I put Peppermint's bed inside Luna's, and they snooze together all night long.

I approach the office, noting the door is closed, and I say to my guide dog, "Luna, open the door."

Luna doesn't leave my side, because that's not what she does. At home, she does go around and get me what I want her to, but when we're out together, she is glued to my side. So we get to the door together, and Luna jumps up on her back feet and uses her front paws to catch the door handle and push it down.

Doorknobs are tricky, and I'm in the process of replacing all the fixtures in my house so they're the handle-doors Luna can open by herself. This one at work was already the right kind, and Luna settles back to my side in a sit as the door drifts open.

"Hey," Ryanne says from within the office, and I head inside.

"Afternoon," I say. Her presence grounds me, reminding me that I'm not alone in this new chapter of my life. We've been inseparable since she surprised me at Paws For a Cause, and the thought of spending the rest of my life with her fills me with joy.

Once inside, I close the door behind us, my hands shaking slightly as I reach to unleash Luna. "Lay down," I tell her, and she goes under the desk and curls into her bed. "What's the news?" I ask Ry, because I need a minute to gather myself together.

I have a plan for today, and I need Ry to head back out to the retail floor at some point, so I can decorate the office appropriately and go over my recording one more time. Luna and I have been working on this surprise for Ryanne since the first day she came to work with me.

"Well, we got the Valentine's Day decor today, so I called our stocking team in to help you get it all up tonight."

I nod as I pull open the fridge and put my dinner in there. Then I sit down, letting my chair slide across the tile to the whiteboard above the couch. "So Jake, Jimmy, and Riley?" Only Riley was scheduled for tonight, but when we have to change over seasonal decor, Ry calls in more people to knock it out in one night.

Since I'm the evening manager, the job falls to me, and I've decorated for every holiday so many times, I could probably do it in my sleep. Or blind.

"All right," I say. "We can get it done, I'm sure."

"You'll like the endcap displays," she says with a grin. She slides back into her desk, and her desktop has no less than thirty-four windows open, as per her usual. "They put big dogs on them."

"Holding hearts?" I gasp. "Or wait. The hearts will be on greeting cards, and we'll put them on the endcaps of our greeting card section."

"Don't act like you don't love it," she says without even looking at me. In fact, she takes a slurp of her soda, and it's almost gone so it makes a rattling noise as the straw tries to find liquid and can't. "Ugh, I need more Diet Coke."

"Go dirty it up," I say, hoping she'll take her foam cup and walk halfway down the block to the convenience store she likes. They have a whole wall of flavored syrups, and Ry likes to do half Diet Coke and half cherry Slurpee, then two pumps of coconut. Dirty diet cherry-coconut Coke.

"I'm going to." She gets to her feet with her cup, gives me a *so-there* look, and leaves the office without closing the door. My heartbeat throbs against the top of my mouth, and I force myself to wake my computer and put in my password before I get up and close the door.

Then I lock it.

I need maybe ten minutes, and I hurry to get the recording set up and made as big as possible. I position the mouse just-so, then turn and pull down my own decorations for Ry's surprise. It's not hard to slap up a poster on the fridge, and I smile at the green M&M wearing a wedding dress and a sultry expression. I put the plush blue M&M on the couch like a big corner pillow, and I lay out all the flavors of M&Ms I've managed to gather in only twenty-three days.

I got the candy apple ones, which are seasonal, and some of her favorites, including the minis, the coffee nut, red velvet, and the strawberried peanut butter, among others.

My original plan was to hang streamers from the ceiling tiles too, but I nixed them in the name of time. Instead, I bought these sort of firecracker-looking things normally used for a Fourth of July party. They lie flat, but I open them up to three-dimensional, and the silvery "fire" comes spewing out the top.

They make me smile as I clasp the two sides together, and I place one on my computer tower, several on the filing cabinets, a few on top of the fridge, and the rest on Ry's desk.

Then, the only thing I need is the diamond ring. I get it out of my desk drawer, where I've hidden it in the back. Ry only ever grabs paper clips or my stapler from my desk, so I figured it would be safe there.

Now I just need her to come back, and preferably with her favorite drink and happy as a clam. Even if she doesn't, I'm asking her to marry me today. I'm not in a hurry, but Ry's the kind of woman who wants movement once she has a plan. And she wants to start figuring out how we live together, with a guide dog, and without my vision.

She says her plans are never reality, and she wants to know the reality. I hadn't lied to her when I'd said I'd marry her tomorrow, so I'm fine to propose now and get married whenever Ryanne tells me.

I crack the door so I can hear her when she's getting close, and then I start to pace in the office. Luna comes out from under the desk, where she's been watching me, and she cocks her head at me as if to say, *You okay, Ell?*

I am and I'm not.

"...let you know." Ry's voice comes closer, and I spin to face the door. She enters the office as she says, "Okay, Mom, I'm back. I have to go." She lowers the phone immediately, which means the conversation is about something she doesn't want to talk about. "You will not *believe*—"

She cuts off and comes to a complete stop. "What is going on here?"

"Luna," I say. "Close the door."

My yellow lab moves to do exactly what I told her to, and then she trots by all the laid out bags of M&Ms and comes to my side. Ry stares at me, blinking rapidly with those gorgeous eyelashes.

"Luna," I say. "Start the video."

Luna looks up at me, and I look down at her, my pulse pounding against my ribs. "Start." I point to the computer. "*Start. The. Video.*" I speak in crisp, clear commands, and Luna takes one more moment to process the request before she blessedly moves over to my desk chair.

"If you could..." I say to Ry, nodding to my chair. It rolls, and Luna needs help keeping it steady. Ry's hand shoots out to hold the top of the chair only a split second before Luna arrives. She jumps up into the chair, and Ry grunts and scoffs as the chair moves. Luna does weigh almost seventy pounds, so I probably should've given Ryanne a better warning.

Luna looks at me again, and I bark at her, "Start the video."

It's right there, and everything is ready. All she has to do is drop her paw on the mouse. By some miracle, she does it, and I hear the click as it echoes through the office.

I've given myself ten seconds in the beginning of the recording, and I say, "Luna, come."

She jumps down from the chair and comes to my side once again. I bury my hand in her neck fur and use her to steady myself as I get down on both knees and hold up the diamond ring.

Ry pulls in a sharp breath and clasps her hands in front of her. They start to wind around one another just as the recording I've made starts to play. I've got the speakers all the way up, so it's not quiet when the robotic voice begins with, "Every day is a new adventure," in the voice of the Opportunity rover.

"And I'm feeling good. I've discovered something

amazing, because this is a special place, and I'm exploring new horizons," the robotic voices continue. I've spent hours combing through the quotes and transmissions sent back to earth from the Mars rovers, and I grin and grin at my genius.

Ry's eyes fill with glassy tears as my proposal continues with, "My new home…is breathtaking…and I'm not sure if you'll believe me, but…"

I raise my eyebrows at her as she shakes her head, a slow smile of her own coming to her face. Then my voice comes into the recording. "I love you…" I've said it in the most Marsy-robotic voice I can muster. "And I'm having a blast, living the dream… It's a wild ride…but I'm loving every minute of it. We're ready…to explore…"

My knees are starting to ache, and there's just a little bit more to go. My voice comes in again with, "…the rest of our lives together. I think you're…"

The robots come back in, and I've put the words really close together now. "Interesting."

"Amazing!"

"Spectacular…"

"Really interesting."

"A beautiful sight."

"…pretty cool."

Ry starts to laugh-cry at that one, and I'll admit, that was hard to cut out the last word, and the initial sound can be heard, though the recording continues with, "Exciting!"

"In good health."

"Valuable."

"Fascinating."

"A charmer!"

Only a couple more things now, and my voice comes back on. "You're my favorite person in the whole world, my very best friend, and I would love it if you'd agree to be my wife."

Pause. Ry lifts her eyebrows, but I shake my head.

The Opportunity rover has one more thing to say. "No pressure!"

The recording ends, and I look at Luna. "Luna, speak your mind on whether or not you think Ryanne should marry me."

Luna barks, and I say, "Again."

She gets to her feet and *barks, barks, bark-barks,* and then circles around me before sitting down again. We both look at Ryanne, and this time I hold out the diamond ring and say, "That's all I've got, sweetheart. Will you marry me?"

Ry holds my gaze for a moment, then looks at the sparkling firecracker decor, the bags of M&Ms, and the big green bride on the fridge. She starts to laugh and laugh, and then she says, "Yes." She comes toward me and drops to her knees too. "Yes, yes, yes! Of course I'll marry you."

I slide the ring on her finger and take her face in my hands and kiss her.

"That was the best proposal ever," she whispers against my lips.

"Took me forever," I say. "That's why it's been so long since we got back until I proposed."

"I wondered what was taking you so long."

I simply kiss her again, because this is a memory I won't need my sight for. I can play that recording and visualize Ry's every reaction, taste the cherry-vanilla cola on her lips, and hear the way she says, "I love you so much, Elliott," without having to see a single thing.

———

Mm, yes. Elliott's my official favorite. I love how he makes non-sight memories, and I love how he celebrates Christmas—and Ryanne! I hope you do too!

Read on for a couple of sneak peak chapters at the next book in the Cider Cove series - **A VERY DISASTROUS DARE** - and enjoy spring and summer with Emma and Aaron in Cider Cove as they compete for a pretty major prize!

Get new free stuff every month, access to live events, special members-only deals, and more when you join the Feel-Good Fiction newsletter. You'll get instant access to the Member's Only area on my new site, where all the goodies are located, so join by scanning the QR code below.

SNEAK PEEK! A VERY DISASTROUS DARE CHAPTER 1 - EMMA

THE BELL ABOVE THE FRONT DOOR AT PRETTY IN Petals chimes as I'm still fussing with a vase of cheerful daffodils and tulips. I wish I was as happy as their bright faces, but, "There's something just not...right... about this."

I move another pink tulip, but it immediately creates a hole that looks like a semi-truck could drive through it. Nope.

"Hello?" a woman calls, and I know exactly who it is. Regina Thompson. An older woman, probably a generation older than me, who orders fresh flowers for her monthly book club. I shudder just thinking about getting together with other people to discuss books. *Literature*, I'm sure Mrs. Thompson calls it.

My shiver continues, because it's freezing in the back room where I work with the flowers. I yell, "Be right out, Mrs. Thompson!" and pick up one more tulip. It irritates me that I'm going to give her extra flowers, but the centerpiece just isn't right yet, and more flowers is almost always the trick.

Sure enough, everything finally looks balanced between blooms, leaves, and garnishes, and I quickly sweep the bright pink ribbon around the vase and tie an expert bow in only seconds. I grab the beautiful amber vase and bustle out into the shop, where Mrs. Thompson waits at the counter.

"Sorry," I say breathlessly. "I've had a bunch of rush orders this week, and I've been running from dawn to dusk."

She gives me a closed-mouth smile, her credit card already out, ready to pay. I set her flowers on the counter and start to ring her up as she inspects them.

"What's the book tonight?" I ask her.

"*The Meaning of Everything*," she says, brightening like I'll have read that one. I've never dared to tell her that I only read floral magazines and the occasional domestic thriller novel.

"Sounds amazing," I lie right through my teeth, and I maintain my daffodil-bright smile until the chime above the door rings again, signaling her departure. Then my shoulders slump, and I look around the shop at all the carnage this week has brought.

Spring has officially sprung in Cider Cove, and my little flower shop is bursting with colorful blooms, which usually cheer me up. Today, though, it simply reminds me that everyone and their daughter is getting married. Hillary and Liam's nuptials are next week, and Ryanne and Elliott have set a date in May so as to give everyone a month to recover.

Then, Claudia and Beckett will be married in July— and I'm doing the flowers for all three events.

I swear, if I make it through the next three months, I should get a gold star, a tiara with real diamonds, and a special place in heaven.

I start cleaning up the shop, as I don't have any more orders being picked up today, and I should have a presentable retail space for anyone stopping by with the thought that their wife or girlfriend would like some flowers.

The door opens as I'm walking toward it, and Regina has returned in all her dark-haired sophistication. "I forgot to ask you," she says. "If you're coming to the small business meeting at the library tonight."

I'd completely forgotten about it, but I hitch my smile back into place and nod. "Yes, I usually do. What time is it again?"

"Six," she says with an air of importance. "I had them move it so I could still do book club at seven-thirty."

"Mm." I give her the closed-mouth smile now, because I'm open until six, and the small business meetings are usually later in the evening. But apparently not when Regina Thompson has book club. I mean, *book club*, you guys. It's gotta be the key to *the meaning of everything*.

I'm so glad others can't read my sarcastic thoughts, and Regina smiles at me. "I'll see you there." She leaves again, and though it's only four-ten, I want to go lock the door, pull the shades, and put out my "I'm sorry, we had to close early" sign. Who would it harm, really?

My stomach growls, a reminder that I haven't eaten since I grabbed a protein shake from the fridge at the Big House that morning. I keep tidying up, moving the bouquets and arrangements that didn't sell today to the refrigeration unit so I can preserve their freshness as much as possible.

There's nothing I like as much as sweeping up the shop, and I start to do that as I think about the business meeting. I did have it in my calendar, but I've just had such a busy day— "And this whole week," I say—that I'd forgotten. Now, with a little less to get done, my mind has more freedom to wander, and I remember that we're talking about the Summer Faire at the meeting tonight.

The town of Cider Cove is expected to open sign-ups for various things, from the parade entries, to vendors at the fair, to fair and boutique participants, and I've already determined that I'm going to apply for a booth this year. I didn't last year, because I was in the process of buying Pretty in Petals outright, and there was no time for anything else.

But as a local business owner, I want to make sure Pretty in Petals has a prime spot at the boutique and fair this year. Even if all I do is hand out business cards, it'll be a win. Cider Cove doesn't have another dedicated floral shop, but it's also one of several small communities that have glommed onto the bigger city of Charleston—and there are plenty of places to buy flowers in the metropolis that extends past the physical boundaries of the town.

In fact, most people who live in Cider Cove commute to work in the city. That's literally the definition of a suburb.

I mist the potted plants near the window, thinking about how much has changed since I bought this place last fall. It hasn't been easy, but every day I fall more in love with my little shop and the joy it brings to me, and to everyone who comes in to buy flowers for someone else.

That's the best part about flowers—they're usually given to someone else as a loving gesture. I love that about them, and I love providing that for people. No one ever buys me flowers, but I know how to take them home for myself or my roommates. With the thought of having my boyfriend come buy flowers from me, for me, I think of Aaron Stansfield.

We had a few "friend-dates" over Christmas and New Year's, but he started seeing someone else after that. "Avery," I mumble to myself. "Or Adrielle. Amy?" I don't remember her name, but I know it starts with the same letter as his. Aaron owns the hardware store right next door to my flower shop, and we're friends, but we're not like, call-each-other-and-talk-about-our-dates-with-other-people type of friends.

He took over the store from his father in January, and he's been going to the small business meetings for years. In fact, I learned about them from him.

For some reason, my heartbeat does a weird ping-pongy thing through my body, like someone's slamming it up to my skull and it's getting bounced around from left to right in unstructured ways.

I finish with the shop and finally return to the cold room to check my phone. I've missed several texts on my roommates' thread, which isn't all that unusual. I swear, some of them can text by blinking and they have their phones with them and available all the time.

Hillary: *Final dress fitting tomorrow! You better be there, maid of honor!*

She's sent it to everyone, because all five of us in the Big House are her maids of honor. She moved back in about three weeks ago, but she's only got the essentials—clothes and toiletries—as if she's on an extended vacation. Everything else was moved into Liam's house next door, because that's where she'll live once they get married.

A sense of sadness looms over me for a moment, and then I see Aaron has texted. I leave the confirmations of my roommates that they'll be at the dress fitting and go see what he has to say.

Are you going to the meeting at the library tonight?

The message came in twenty minutes ago, probably right when Mrs. Thompson had her toe tapping as she waited to pay for her flowers.

He's messaged again with, *My truck is having issues, and I need a ride if you're going.*

Then: *It's fine if you're not. Just let me know. I'll be at the store and can just walk over.*

He'd been living in Liam's house while Liam and Hillary have been in LA, and in fact, I think Aaron is still there. He's been working on rebuilding and refinishing his grandfather's house closer to the center of town, but he hasn't moved in yet.

I'm going, I say. *In fact, I haven't eaten all day, so I'm going to close early and go grab dinner first. Do you want anything?*

I send the message before I even think or read over it. Only when my phone rings and Aaron's name sits there do I realize I've offered to buy the man dinner.

I'm obviously on my phone, so while I worry over what he might think of my offer, I swipe on the call and say, "Hey." So eloquent. A real masterful conversationalist, I am.

"Hey," he says in his semi-husky, all-sexy tone. He seems happy, and again, I start to stew over literally every single thing I've ever said to the man. "I'd love something to eat." Something scuffs on his end of the line, and his voice is lower and deeper when he adds, "Gill brought in lunch today, and it was disgusting. I don't think I'll ever get the heat out of my mouth."

I laugh, because Aaron does not like spicy food. "Did his wife cook again?"

"I swear, it should be a crime for the woman to be in the kitchen." He sighs like he's really suffering. "Where are you going?"

"I don't know. I haven't decided."

"Maybe I'll just come over." He almost phrases it like a question and almost doesn't.

"Sure," I say airily. Just because I think Aaron is good-looking doesn't mean I have to start dating him. Besides a brief stint over the holidays, I've never thought he's liked me as more than a friend. He's Liam's best friend, so we've been at parties and events together for almost a year now. "We'll decide when you get here."

"On my way."

The call ends, and I hurry to go lock down the shop and put up my We're Closed Early sign. Aaron will come in the back door, and it too has a buzzer, so I'll know when he's there.

In my office, I start gathering my things to leave, and my eyes land on the framed photo of Grams and me from last Christmas. Her proud smile as she stood in my shop for the first time still warms my heart. "I'm doing it, Grams," I whisper. "Just like you always said I could."

I take one last look around the office, breathing in the sweet floral scent that has become my signature. Lilacs, roses, and a hint of eucalyptus – a perfect spring blend scent, if I do say so myself—and turn to leave.

"Emma."

I yelp at the sound of a man's voice coming from the front of the shop, and I spin that way, holding up the only thing I'm carrying—which happens to be a black pen wrapped with floral tape with a fake white lily on top of it. Like that's going to do any damage at all.

Then I think of my spy novels, and the heroines in those books can definitely incapacitate a man with a lily pen.

And the man in front of me is definitely someone I need to incapacitate...because it's my former boyfriend.

"What are you doing here, Tucker?" My back is pressed into the wall behind me, and I don't lower the pen as he smiles. He's the reason I haven't dated in over a year. He's the reason every time I even start to *think* I could maybe go out with someone, I put myself in a boyfriend-free zone.

He shrugs like he just happened to be in the neighborhood, but I know that's so false. My heartbeat thrashes at me as the buzzer for the back door sounds, and I twist that way. "You need to leave," I say. "I know I locked that front door."

"It wasn't closed all the way," he says like it's no big deal that I just told him to leave.

As much as I don't want to put my back to him, I turn and stride down the hall toward the back door, because I know who'll be on the other side of it.

"I was thinking me and you were good together," Tucker says, and my whole world turns upside down.

I open the back door and find Aaron standing there. Well, kind of. It's an elvish version of the hot handyman, and I take a moment to blink at his robes, his pointy ears, and his goofy grin. "You're not dressed up," he says.

"Should I be?" I scan down to his shoes—also pointed—and back to his face. "Why are *you* dressed up?"

Some of his fun, flirty demeanor falls. "The invite for the meeting said to come dressed as your favorite book character."

I can somehow sense Tucker behind me, maybe getting closer, maybe about to say something. I look right into Aaron's eyes and barely move my mouth as I say, "I need you to play along with me, okay?"

His eyes search mine, and at least he realizes how serious this situation is. "Okay?" He looks behind me, and I'm sure Tucker is there based on the way Aaron's expression changes in a split-second. "Oh, I thought you'd closed."

"I did," I say. "Tucker was just leaving too." I nod slightly and then turn to face Tucker, who has advanced down the hallway. He looks at me and Aaron, and oh, how I wish Aaron had on his dark-wash jeans and one of his hardware store tees—the ones with the tight sleeves because his biceps are so impressive.

"Who's this?" Aaron asks, and thank the stars above, he puts his arm around my waist.

"You remember him," I say sweetly. "Don't you, baby? I know I've told you about my exes." I've done no such thing with Aaron, but he doesn't miss a beat.

He kneads me closer as an entire fireworks show explodes through my hip from where he's touching me. "Oh sure," he says almost dismissively. "Tucker." He says his name with pure distaste, and we all hear it. Then Aaron takes a deep breath and looks at me. "We're still going to dinner before the meeting, right, sweetheart?"

"Mm, yes." I tip my head back and stretch up at the same time. Aaron realizes I'm going to kiss him point-five seconds before I do it, and I register the surprise coursing from him the moment my lips touch his.

After that, it's only an inferno of heat, the fizzing bubbling of a violent chemical reaction, and the musky, husky, manly, sexy scent of Aaron Stansfield. Everything else melts away, and he kisses me like I've never been kissed before.

SNEAK PEEK! A VERY DISASTROUS DARE CHAPTER 2 - AARON

I'M NOT SURE HOW LONG WE STAND THERE KISSING, but it's nowhere near long enough. When Emma finally pulls away, I have to force myself not to chase after her lips. My head spins as I go over every touch, every sensation, ever pounding beat of my heart. The softness of her hair and skin—both of which I've obviously touched. At least my fingers have a memory of it, and I look down at my hands dumbly.

I've imagined kissing her so many times over the past few months, but the reality blows every fantasy out of the water.

I take a big breath, barely able to form coherent thoughts, and look up at her. More stupidity chases through me at her lack of costume, because it only reminds me that I'm dressed like Legolas from *Lord of the Rings*. That invite one-hundred-percent said to come dressed as my favorite book character. I will go to my grave believing that.

Emma's cheeks hold a gorgeous flush I haven't seen before, and dare I think she looks just as dazed as I feel? For a moment, I forget why we're even here, standing just outside the back door of her floral shop, until I notice movement behind her.

Right. Tucker. Emma's ex.

I clear my throat and make an attempt to regain my composure. "So, dinner?" I ask, hoping my voice doesn't betray how affected I am.

Emma nods quickly. "Yes, dinner. Let me just get cleaned up." She turns to give Tucker a dirty look. "And we'll go." She presses her purse into my chest. "Do you want to drive tonight? You can pick me up out front. I obviously need to make sure that door gets closed properly."

"Sure," I say, doing my best to sound like I'm not asking her a question. Or to act like I've driven Emma's car many times. I haven't. Or that I'm fine to leave her alone with her ex. I'm not. I give him a dry look. "You come on out this way with me."

"My car is—"

"Get out, Tucker," Emma says as she steps past him. "I'll see you out front, baby."

I love that pet name for me in her voice, even if it is fake. Tucker doesn't know that, and by the time I tear my gaze from Emma's retreating curves to look at him, he's cocked his eyebrows. He does exit the shop through the back door, which I then pull tightly closed and double-check to make sure it locked. It did.

"How long have you two been dating?" he asks.

"A few months," I say causally. My mouth some-times runs away from me, getting me in trouble, and I vow to stitch my lips together before I tell this Tucker character another thing.

Thankfully, I know which SUV is Emma's, and I dig into her purse to find her keys like I've done so a million times before. The truth is, I don't think I've ever rifled through a woman's purse, and it almost feels wrong to be doing it. And with Tucker watching? And my cape billowing in the afternoon spring breeze?

A sweat breaks out across my forehead, and I feel like he might arrest me for A) lying about being Emma Newberry's boyfriend, and B) kissing her like I'm Emma Newberry's boyfriend.

Oh, how I want to be Emma Newberry's boyfriend.

But I clear my head and focus. It can't be that hard to find car keys in a bag. And yet, I've severely underesti-mated every woman who's ever walked the earth with a purse, because I cannot for the life of me find her keys. Frustrated, I look up to find Tucker standing there star-ing, his eyebrows raised.

"They're in here somewhere," I say, now kneading the bottom of the bag just to see if it'll produce a jangling sound. To my great relief, it does, and I dive back into her purse to pull out the keys. I hold them up like they're a Gold Medal I've just won in the Invasion of Privacy event in the Olympics.

"I gotta say," Tucker says. "You don't seem like Emma's type."

"I'll be sure and let her know," I throw back at him. "See you around." I'm not going to tell him it's great to meet him when it's not great to meet him. And Emma obviously doesn't like him, so I'm not sorry to walk away, get behind the wheel of her SUV—which several adjustments, because wow. Who needs to sit so close to the steering wheel?—and leave her back lot in favor of the street.

She's waiting on the sidewalk, her thumbnail against her teeth, and relief washes over her features as I come to a stop and she opens the door. She blows into the car with all the scents of fresh flowers and her fruity perfume, and I'm all smiles again.

I've really got to tone that down, so I'm not so obvious in how I feel about her. *Well, I think that kiss gave you away,* I think, but I say nothing.

Once we're rolling away from the flower shop, Emma lets out a long breath. "Thank you," she says softly. "I'm sorry I sprung that on you."

I want to tell her she can spring kisses on me anytime, but I know this isn't the moment. "Don't worry about it," I say instead. "That's what friends are for, right?"

She gives me a grateful smile, and I simply keep driving toward the town square. It's so not the answer I wanted to give, nor is her silence what I want her to say in response. Somehow, an elephant got in the car with us, and he's making it very hard to breathe or speak.

Finally, when I'm faced with almost-end-of-day-traffic and nowhere to go, I ask, "Where do you want to go to dinner?"

"Bellyache's?" she suggests. "I'm craving a lot of bacon and cheese right now." She won't look at me and instead keeps her focus out the passenger window.

Bellyache's is an old diner that serves American fare, and I can eat a burger for any meal, any day of the week. So no problem for me there, and I make the turn that'll take us a little bit away from downtown—and right past my house.

"So," I say, gesturing to my ridiculous elf costume. "I guess I should explain this."

Emma laughs, the tension from earlier melting away. "Please do. I'm dying to know why you're dressed like you just stepped out of Middle Earth."

"The invite said to do so." I quirk my eyebrows at her, since she clearly knew which book character I'd dressed as. "The real question is why you didn't do it. Or what you would dress as if you had gotten the memo."

"I gotta be honest, Aaron," she says, too much glee in her tone. "You took the memo to a new dimension."

"I've read all of Tolkien's books," I say. "Four or five

times. Love the movies. Play the video games. It's something I can do with my brother, and well, I don't have a lot in common with him."

And just like that, I've killed the fun, flirty, *I'll-kiss-you-again-later* vibe between us. I've done so at least fifty times in the past several months, because just when I think I'm getting close to blurting out my feelings for the gorgeous blonde in the passenger seat, I chicken out.

Or she says something that puts me in my place, that lets me know we're just friends.

I scoff right out loud. *Just friends.* Two of the worst words on the whole planet, in my opinion.

"You okay?" she asks.

"I'd love to hear all the stories of your exes," I say instead. Maybe wearing this elfin garb, I can say things the normal Aaron Stansfield wouldn't say. I can be someone else. Someone brave and ferocious and very, very good at what he does.

I drive by the huge corner lot that's been sitting dormant for the better part of three years now. Cider Cove's been in a legal battle with the construction firm, and the huge hole they built before a judge executed a stay order has been a stain on the town since. But Belly-ache's is just around the bend, and I swing the SUV that way while doing the same with my attention as it moves over to Emma.

"And you know what?"

"What?" she asks, her eyes finally coming to meet mine.

I want to talk about that kiss, I think inside my head. I can even hear myself saying it in a movie-type setting. And Emma will confess her undying love for me, and I'll somehow rope a horse the way Legolas would, and we'll ride off into the Middle Earth sunset.

But in real life Cider Cove, I say, "Maybe I could stop by my house and change before we go to the meeting. It's just around the corner from Bellyache's."

And just like that, I'm back to being the cowardly Aaron Stansfield, the upstanding oldest son who runs his daddy's and granddaddy's hardware store, and who can't keep a girlfriend for longer than three months.

All women say they want a guy like me. A man with a good job. Nice house. A *nice* guy.

All women are lying.

———

I MANAGE NOT to make a fool of myself during our burger binge, and I leave Emma standing in the fully remodeled living room at my house while I hurry into my not-fully-remodeled bedroom to change out of the elf costume. I pull on jeans and a tee, grab my sneakers, and hurry back out to her.

"We're not going to be late," I promise her, though we probably are. I swear, every restaurant, cafe, and bistro in town has some Thursday night special, as if people will only come out to get food if it's on sale, and traffic around the library is pretty insane this time of night.

They have a big parking garage that's used for a lot of the downtown business district, and I fear having our small business meeting so early will make it hard to find a place to park. So I pull my shoes on as fast as possible and jump back to my feet. "Ready."

Emma giggles and shakes her head. "No, you've got an extra ear still, Mister Stansfield."

I love it when she calls me by my last name in that flirty tone. I find it hard to believe she likes me as only a friend, though she's never, ever, *ever* given me an indication that I'm wrong about that.

Now, she steps over to me and lifts her hand to my right ear. "This one looks a little otherworldly still." Her fingers gently brush up my neck, along the bottom of my beard, to my ear, and my word, I feel like a star that has exploded. I'm in a hundred million tiny pieces, everything shooting out at the speed of light and sound.

Our eyes meet, and Emma's smile slowly drifts off her face. Her touch is light, careful almost, and oh-so-sexy as she sweeps her fingers around to the back of my ear and releases the costume piece. "There," she whispers. "I got it."

Her hand drops, and I immediately cover the ear in her palm with mine. Maybe if I want to get the girl, I have to act more like Tucker. *At least in the beginning,* I tell myself, because I'm not sure I can be a jerk long-term. My momma will cuff me upside the head and demand, "What are you thinking, Aaron?"

Right now, I'm really thinking I'd like to kiss Emma again, but I know Mister Nice Guy isn't going to get the job done. So I step back and toss the ear to the end table beside my couch. "Now I'm ready." Then I lead the way out of the house, not even bothering to hold the creaky front screen door for Emma.

In fact, it slams in her face, and I hear her grunt behind me as I go down the front steps. The man I really am wants to run back and make sure she avoids the rotting parts of the porch, since I replaced it and it immediately rained before I could preserve and protect the wood. The whole thing needs to be redone, but I'd already moved on to the interior of the house.

My best friend, whose house I've been living in, is back in town and has been for the past few weeks. He's marrying the love of his life—and one of Emma's best friends—next week, and I'll move out while they're on their honeymoon. It's another ten days, and I can do a lot in ten days' time.

Not when pining after Emma, I tell myself sternly, because I'm not going to do that anymore.

I drive her car and her over to the library, where sure enough, it seems the whole population of Cider Cove has converged. We're only ten minutes late to the small business meeting, and they haven't started yet, thankfully.

I act like I don't care as I take a seat in the back row. Emma pauses at the end of it and looks up front, then back to me. I pretend to be engrossed in something super amazing on my phone, and I even smile like a really beautiful woman has texted me back that she can't wait to see me for dinner later.

Emma walks away, and a tiny piece of my heart turns black and falls to the soles of my feet. Is this how the bad boys feel all the time? Because I feel like I'm going to throw up, and I think I'd have rather walked into this meeting wearing my elfin gear than sit on the back row alone while Emma finds a seat closer to the front next to a woman who owns a dog treat bakery.

The meeting starts, and I pay attention the way I normally do. I take the information packets for the upcoming Summer Faire, as it's something my family always participates in. We do simple household task demos, like fixing doorknobs and painting a sunroom, and sealing a deck.

Then, the woman who's been running our meetings this year, Margaret Pajonas, who owns a daycare and preschool on the opposite side of town from where Emma and I work, holds up a yellow folder. "And we just got something exciting from the City Council." Her eyes hold hope and excitement, and I sit up a little.

This meeting has gotten a little stale, but maybe just

for people like me who've participated in the Summer Faire before. But this is something new.

"The City Council and the city of Cider Cove have finally resolved the issue on the corner of Sweetbriar and Salty Dog."

A murmur moves through the crowd, because this is big news. The hole I'd driven by earlier? That's the lot on the corner of Sweetbriar and Salty Dog, and it could be such a beautiful place for apartments, a hotel, or even just a park. Everything just got abandoned, and it's become a wasteland.

"And they're hosting a city-wide event specifically for small businesses to get involved in the community. We don't have a bunch of information yet, but the bottom line is, every small business has a chance to help beautify that twenty-four acre lot, and..." She holds out the word and surveys the whole room.

I'm holding my breath, because this feels important, and a few people a couple of rows ahead of me actually lean forward.

Margaret really has us all on the edge of our seats. She grins and flips open the folder. "And I quote, 'More information and rules and regulations will be coming within the next two weeks, emailed to all small business owners on record within the city boundaries of Cider Cove.'"

She looks up, just to make sure we're all still with her. And I am. I'm *so* with her, and I glance up to where Emma's sitting. She's practically on the edge of her seat.

Margaret returns to her folder. "And we'll be revealing an event where small businesses can show off what they provide to the community by participating in a contest that will have winners chosen based on voting from the general population of Cider Cove, government officials, and City Council members, with a proposed grant provided to the winning small business in the amount of twenty-five thousand dollars."

I suck in a breath, and it's like that action has vacuumed out all the oxygen in the room, because I'm not the only one who's just gasped like they've just met the most popular member of their favorite boy band. Everyone has. People are murmuring the same thing running through my mind.

"Twenty-five thousand dollars?"

"Twenty-five thousand dollars!"

Emma turns around, and I stand up and look at her, completely forgetting that I'm going to play the bad boy and ignore her, act like I don't like her at all, and that that kiss didn't rock my world.

"Twenty-five *thousand* dollars," we say together, and I can't *wait* to get the email about this community service project that could change my life.

She hurries toward me, the meeting obviously over, and I turn and leave the room ahead of her. "Can you believe that?" she asks. "That's so much money."

"Yeah," I say in a short, clipped word, my stride long so Emma has to jog to catch up to me.

"Can you slow down?" she grumps at me, and that only makes me want to go faster. Or slow down? I honestly don't know.

I slow down slightly, and I glance over to her.

"Why are you mad at me?" she asks.

"I'm not," I lie. Fine, it's only half a lie, because I am sort of mad at her, but I'm totally not at the same time.

"It's because I kissed you, isn't it?" She makes a sharp detour and pushes open the door to go into the stairwell instead of joining the throng of people queueing up at the elevator.

I follow her, annoyance singing through my veins. "You know what? Yeah, I'm mad about that. We agreed a few months ago that kissing was a very *unfriendly* thing to do."

"But helping a friend is a very *friendly* thing to do," she throws over her shoulder at me, then turns and practically flies down another flight of stairs.

We burst out into the parking garage on level two, where I'd managed to find a space, both of us huffing and puffing. I glance over to her, and oh, I am so losing this battle against her. In the end, I will lose. I know that in this moment.

But right now, I mentally dig my heels in and vow to myself to hold on for a little longer.

Her car is locked, and I have the keys, so when we

get there, she stands outside the passenger door, waiting. I stand at the back bumper and glare at her. "You know what, Emma?" I have so many things I want to tell her, and none of them would come out of a nice guy's mouth.

I have to get out of here. Just leave.

"I'll find my own way home."

Her breath catches, and for a split second, our eyes lock, the air between us crackling with something electric. Something dangerous. Something half-alive and real, but also abstract at the same time. I'm pretty sure it's attraction, because that's all I can feel for her right now. But she might just be experiencing an extreme case of fury.

Without another word, I toss her the keys—which causes her to yelp, throw her hands up, and miss the keys. They jingle-jangle as they bounce on the concrete.

But I'm already walking away.

A point goes to Mister-Not-Nice-Aaron, and I do my best to hold my head up high as my heart wails at me like I've just done the worst thing possible.

————

OH, Aaron has a plan...and it really seems like it might backfire on him. LOL. **Preorder A VERY DISAS-TROUS DARE by scanning the QR code below!**

BOOKS IN THE SOUTHERN ROOTS SWEET ROMCOM SERIES

 **Just His Secretary, Book 1:** She's just his secretary...until he needs someone on his arm to convince his mother that he can take over the family business. Then Callie becomes Dawson's girlfriend —but just in his text messages...but maybe she'll start to worm her way into his shriveled heart too.

Just His Boss, Book 2: She's just his boss, especially since Tara just barely hired Alec. But when things heat up in the kitchen, Tara will have to decide where Alec is needed more—on her arm or behind the stove.

Just His Assistant, Book 3: She's just his assistant, which is exactly how this Southern belle wants it. No spotlight. Not anymore. But as she struggles to learn her new role in his office—especially because Lance is the surliest boss imaginable—Jessie might just have to open her heart to show him everyone has a past they're running from.

Just His Partner, Book 4: She's just his partner, because she's seen the number of women he parades through his life. No amount of charm and good looks is worth being played...until Sabra witnesses Jason take the blame for someone else at the law office where they both work.

Just His Barista, Book 5: She's just his barista...until she buys into Legacy Brew as a co-owner. Then she's Coy's business partner *and* the source of his five-year-long crush. But after they share a kiss one night, Macie's seriously considering mixing business and pleasure.

―――――――

Bonus for newsletter subscribers! Just His Neighbor, Prequel: She's just his neighbor...until his dog—oops, his brother's dog—adopts her.

Get this book by joining my newsletter here: https://readerlinks. com/l/3887964 **or scan the QR code below.**

**A Very Terrible Text, Book 1:
Sometimes the thumbs slip...**

She's finally joined the dating app everyone in Cider Cove is raving about...when she accidentally sends a message about wanting to meet up for a first date to her enemy.

A Very Bad Bet, Book 2:
Sometimes a wager only makes things more fun...

She's got seniority over the obnoxious grump next door, and she's determined to beat him out for the top job in their charming home-town. But a bold bet spins their rivalry into a flirty attraction that could change everything.

———

A Very Merry Mess, Book 3: *Sometimes the holidays are messy...*

Christmas is the season of joy, mistletoe, and, unfortunately for Ryanne, the pressure of bringing home a date. When she vents to Elliott, her best friend and co-manager at the small-town office supply store, he impulsively grabs her phone and texts her mother that they're dating.

Date. Ing.

A Very Disastrous Dare, Book 4: *Sometimes a person speaks before thinking...*

She's just bought the flower shop and he's taken over the hardware store for his dad. Sounds peachy, right? Sure, until they both want an assistance grant from the city...and now Emma and Aaron are rivals *and* neighbors.

ABOUT ELANA

Elana Johnson is a USA Today bestselling and Kindle All-Star author of dozens of clean and wholesome contemporary romance novels. She lives in Utah, where she mothers two fur babies, works with her husband full-time, and eats a lot of veggies while writing. Find her on her website at feelgoodfictionbooks.com.